LOVEWRECKED

A ROMANTIC COMEDY

KARINA HALLE

SUMMARY

LOVEWRECKED

Daisy Lewis is experiencing a relentless string of bad luck.

Fortunately, Daisy has her sister's destination wedding coming up. A week of sand, sea, and sun in the South Pacific as the maid-of-honor is exactly what Daisy needs to forget her upturned life and focus on the positive.

That is until Daisy meets the best man.

If you take tall, dark, and handsome, and add a dash of rugged, a pinch of brooding, and a whole lot of sexy, you've got Tai Wakefield. Unfortunately he's also a major grump, total alpha, and seemingly out to antagonize Daisy at every turn.

As if being part of the wedding party with Tai wasn't bad enough, Daisy's bad luck soon resurfaces when she ends up on a cramped sailboat with Tai and the newlyweds.

Which then shipwrecks on a deserted island near Fiji.

Okay, so they aren't completely alone. There's an oddball research scientist who has been isolated for far too long, they have rundown bungalows as shelter, stores of water and canned food, plus a feral goat named Wilson.

It's *Lost*...without the smoke monster.

But with rescue weeks away, Tai and Daisy realize the only way they're going to get through this mess is to stop fighting and start working together.

And with their guards down, they get closer.

A lot closer.

Soon, Daisy realizes that the only thing worse than being stuck on a deserted island, is being stuck on a deserted island with a man she hates to love and loves to hate.

A man that can break her heart.

For anyone and everyone who needs an escape right now—I've
got you.
And for my wonderful parents, Tuuli & Sven, who allowed me to
pursue my own escapes for so many years.

1

———

DAISY

Have you ever tried to stab someone with a butter knife?

Because that's exactly what I'm about to do.

Granted, my hand is shaking as I hold it, and I could barely cut the tomato for my sandwich moments before, which makes me think that the most damage this piece of cutlery will do is some light bruising, maybe a scratch.

But even so, it's worth an attempt.

The possible victim?

My boyfriend, Chris, who is standing in front of me totally naked, a pillow jammed in front of his crotch, pure panic on his face.

Behind him, in the recesses of our bedroom, is my friend Michelle.

Wearing a lace peekaboo bra and G-string.

The kind of lingerie set you wouldn't wear every day, unless you knew you were going to get naked with someone.

In this case, someone's else's boyfriend.

Mine.

I should have known something was wrong the moment I came home to make myself some lunch. I had told Chris I was going for a long walk at Golden Gate Park. Usually we would both run it together, but he'd been weird and moody lately, and so I thought I'd go alone. Of course, being me, I got distracted and decided to do some window shopping on Haight, and then I got hungry. I hate eating in restaurants alone, so I came back to fix myself a quick sandwich before heading out again.

I didn't notice her shoes at the front door, though now I can see them out of my peripheral.

I didn't think it was odd that the bedroom door had been shut, though now I know why.

I assumed Chris had gone out.

That was until I had just finished making my sandwich and heard a muffled sneeze.

High-pitched and stunted, like someone was trying to hide it.

I grabbed the butter knife and flung open the bedroom door, backing up in horror to the kitchen counter, as I stared at the two of them together.

Oh, they were trying to hide it, hoping that if they didn't make a noise, I wouldn't notice.

Jokes on them.

"I can explain," Chris cries out, stepping closer.

I thrust the butter knife out into the space between us, shaking it violently.

"Stay back, asshole!" My voice is caught between rage-induced hysteria and choking back tears. For the sake of my pride, I hope the tears never fall.

Both of his hands go up like I'm holding him at gunpoint, and the pillow drops to the floor.

I almost laugh. His penis is naturally deflated, and he

looks like a sad sack of a human being. Funny how someone can go from being the love of your life to a repulsive enemy in a matter of seconds.

Okay, so maybe Chris wasn't the *love* of my life. But he was still the first boyfriend I ever truly loved, the first one that I finally let my guard down for, the first one I potentially, one day, possibly, maybe saw myself marrying.

And this is how all that worked out for me.

With him sleeping with my friend.

Oh, I'm mad at her, too.

Furious.

But the betrayal is different. I can't say I ever got too close to Michelle. I never let my guard down with her the way I did with Chris. Still, I considered her a good friend since I had worked with her and we often spent lunch hours scarfing oysters on the embarcadero. We used to do hot yoga together on Thursday mornings before work, and we had margaritas on Mondays at this dive bar in the Mission district with the rest of the old work crew. Our conversations were usually superficial, but occasionally I'd complain about Chris (as couples do), and she'd complain about San Francisco's lackluster dating scene.

Never in a million years did I think she'd try and fix that by turning her sights on him.

"How did this even happen?" I cry out, shaking the knife again.

"Just put the knife down and we'll talk," Chris says. He takes a step forward, and as my gaze drops again, he pauses and hastily picks up the pillow. "Look, it was a mistake."

"A mistake?" I say at the same time Michelle makes a scoffing noise. I point the knife at her. "Something funny, bitch?"

"Yes, a mistake," Chris says imploringly. I stare into his

baby blue eyes, but they're no longer the eyes of the guy I loved. They're the eyes of a stranger. One I want to murder with a butter knife.

"Uh huh. A mistake. I see. So she slipped and fell on your dick?" I ask. "Or you slipped and landed in her vagina?"

"It didn't mean anything!"

Somehow that makes everything worse.

My blood begins to boil.

"You threw away our relationship for some screw that didn't even mean anything!?"

I make a half-hearted attempt to calm myself but it doesn't work.

I turn around and pick up the cut tomato I used for my sandwich, holding it in my palm like a baseball, seeds slipping through my fingers.

"He's lying," Michelle speaks up, eyes flashing. "He told me he loved me."

I don't even think. I launch the tomato and get Chris right between the eyes with a messy *plop*, the tomato splattering everywhere. The pillow drops to the floor again.

"You asshole!" I yelp.

I whirl around and pick up the top slice of toasted bread and wing at him like a frisbee. It hits him squarely on his junk and he goes down to his knees on the linoleum with an *oof*. I used to play disc golf on my parents' apple orchard growing up, and apparently my aim is as good as ever.

"Daisy!" Michelle cries out, as if I'm the one with the problem, and then I'm reaching for the remainder of the sandwich.

I pelt it at her. The slice of turkey flies ahead of the sandwich layers with swift velocity and slaps her on the cheek with a satisfying *thwack*, while the other pieces of mayo-soaked bread and juicy tomato slices explode over the bedroom.

"Get out!" I scream at the both of them. "Now!" I threaten with the butter knife again. "I'm not done throwing things."

Michelle swipes at the cold cut that just bitch-slapped her, and runs to the opposite side of the bed where she yanks on her jeans and sweater. She quickly sidles past me, avoiding eye contact. I'm not a violent person, but it really takes everything in me to not open the fridge and find what other food I can whip at her.

While she's shoving on her boots at the front door, I turn to Chris who is getting back to his feet, wincing.

"There's a lot more where that came from," I warn him as she slams the front door.

He groans, reaching for the pillow again, as if he's suddenly bashful. "Please, just...hear me out."

My eyes widen. "What the hell could you possibly say? Chris, I just caught you screwing my friend!"

"It's not what she said. I don't love her. I love you...I just got...I got confused."

"Confused?" I repeat, my voice beyond shrill. "*Confused?*"

He winces dramatically again, putting his hand to his ear. "Can you stop being so hysterical? You're hurting my ears."

"Maybe I'll slice your ear off like in *Reservoir Dogs*. That should fix the problem," I sneer at him, waving the knife again. "It won't be easy with this thing, but *believe me*, I could make it work. Would leave some pretty nasty scars."

He glares at me. "You know, you haven't been easy to be around since you lost your job."

Oh my god.

He isn't...

He isn't suggesting this is *my* fault??

He must read the look on my face because a rush of fear goes across his brow, and he quickly says, "It isn't your fault. I'm not saying that. I know you've never been laid off before, I know you've worked for that company forever, I know it's hit you hard. You're just...not your sunny self."

I can only stare at him, mouth agape. My emotions are zipping from outrage to frustration, and when I get frustrated I tend to cry.

"Excuse me for not always being my sunny self," I tell him. "And, by the way, I think I've handled the layoff extremely well. You don't see me moping about and focusing on the negative, *and* you don't see me sleeping with other people's boyfriends."

He stares blankly at me.

"Michelle was laid off, too!" I yell at him. "And screw you for even bringing any of that shit up. That makes you an even worse person for cheating on me when I'm already down on the ground."

He laughs dryly and I want to deck him right in the nose. "Down on the ground? In the two years we've been together, you've never been down on the ground. You've never even faltered. Everything just seems to fall in your lap."

I bristle. He's not the first person to say that. "Well things are falling out of my lap now, aren't they? First I lose my job, next I lose my boyfriend."

Oh, now he's looking *sad*. "Daisy...this isn't over..."

"That's bullshit and you know it. It's over. And it's probably been over for a long time, hasn't it? Even before I lost my job. You've been pulling away. I didn't want to see it, didn't want to admit that was happening, but it's true, isn't it? It's like you *wanted* to get caught."

Chris looks away and absently wipes a tomato seed off his face. I'd laugh if I didn't feel so broken inside. "Maybe I was pulling away to see if you'd pull me back in. Maybe I wanted to see just how much you cared about me." He looks at me, and now he looks more like the man I fell in love with, even though I know he'll never be that person to me again. "I stepped back but you never came forward."

I don't have time for this. He wants to play the blame game, as if somehow this is all my fault.

"There's something called communication," I tell him. I'm still seething but it's starting to meld into something else, something sadder, something I don't like. "You could have talked to me instead of playing a stupid game. Instead of *cheating* on me. And if you wanted to end it, you could have just done so, like the man I thought I knew. This is all on you, Chris. I'm not going to be the bad guy here." I pause, summoning up my courage. "I'm going to go back out for my walk. And when I get back, I want you and all of your stuff gone."

"Daisy," he cries out pathetically, gesturing. "I live here! Where am I supposed to go?"

I cross my arms. "No idea. Maybe Michelle's? And you should have thought about that before bringing her over here to screw her. In *our* bed."

"You're being unreasonable."

"You're an asshole! And don't you even think about squatters rights, because Big Jim is just a text away."

Yeah, I have a friend called Big Jim, who is...wait for it...a bouncer. The two of us have been tight since I used to sneak into clubs with my fake ID, and he's never liked Chris much anyway.

His eyes narrow. "So that's it, huh? I'm just written out of your life? Just like that?"

"Just like that," I tell him. I pick up my purse from the chair and sling it over my shoulder.

I start down the hall toward the front door.

He calls after me.

"Daisy."

I pause, but I don't turn around.

"We're supposed to fly to New Zealand next week," he reminds me. "Your sister will be so disappointed if you show up without a date, and I know you can't do anything social alone. Let's just go together and see what happens. If you want it to end after that, then we can end it. Let's not waste those plane tickets."

My chest feels iced over. Part of me wants to take him up on it. I hate the idea of flying there alone, I hate the idea of going to my sister's wedding without him there. Hell, the idea of going to any wedding alone.

But as much as I need him as a crutch, I know it would be a mistake.

I'll have to go on my own.

I glance at him over my shoulder and give him a small smile, maybe because I know this is probably (hopefully) the last time I'll see him.

"I'll be back at ten tonight. That should give you enough time to get your life sorted. Take care, Chris." I pause. "And eat shit."

And with that, I step out of the door and away from the man I thought I loved.

One week later

. . .

"WELCOME ABOARD," the tanned flight attendant with a stunning shade of red lipstick says to me as I step off the jetway and onto the plane, a huge Air New Zealand 747. "What row are you?"

I wave the ticket at her. "I'm one of the Skycouches," I tell her gleefully.

She nods and gracefully points down the body of the never-ending plane. "Excellent. They're at the rear of the craft."

I thank her and cart my rose gold carry-on luggage behind me down the length of the plane to the very back. Normally, I avoid the back of airplanes if I can help it (I have a somewhat irrational fear of the plane breaking apart during flight and the bottom half landing on some island somewhere, but that's what I get for being obsessed with *Lost* back in the day). But for this flight from SFO to Auckland, New Zealand, I opted for the Skycouch, which is when you have a whole row to yourself, and each seat extends so it turns into a bed of sorts.

These days it's the little things that excite me.

Last week I was living my normal life, this week everything has changed.

Okay, so maybe I should go back in time a bit.

Four weeks ago I was living the good life. I had my boyfriend, I had my friends, I had my job. I was happy...I think. At any rate, I was looking forward to flying to NZ for my sister Lacey's wedding, with Chris in tow.

Then I lost my job. None of us at Deschutes even saw it coming.

One gloomy morning where the fog was cold and dense, Harold the CEO, announced there was to be a merger with Yogalita, another even more successful athleisure wear company, and that massive layoffs would be imminent.

Everyone in the office was panicking. Everyone except me, that is. You see, I sort of lucked into that job, working for the company straight out of high school. Within a few short years I was moving up and up and up, until I accepted the position as head of marketing. When Deschutes became too big for the office in Beaverton, the company relocated to San Francisco, and I went along with them. I was somewhat vital to the company's overall branding, and without tooting my own horn too much, helped push them to new levels of success.

So you can see why I assumed they wouldn't let me go. How could they when I've been working for them for ten years? I was as hardworking and loyal as they come.

Apparently though, that wasn't enough.

I was deemed easily replaceable by the head of marketing for Yogalita—after all, they were more successful than we were and they were the ones that bought us out— and that was the end of that.

I was out of a job.

A job that had become my identity.

For the first time in my life, I didn't know what to do with myself. It was like I didn't even know who I was.

Yes, I had money saved up over the years, and I knew the right thing to do was start applying for other jobs. But I couldn't bring myself to do that yet. It's like I've been in mourning, even though I've tried desperately to not dwell on it, to try and use this as a good opportunity for change, to look at it as a blessing in disguise. I've always tried to see the sunny side of life.

But that sunny side is hidden by a layer of clouds I can't

seem to see through. As much as I try, I'm not seeing the light.

Adding insult to injury, I obviously then caught Chris cheating on me with my friend. Both of those relationships dissolved so fast, it made me realize how precarious and empty they were to begin with.

"Excuse me," I say to the couple that is blocking the aisle and taking way too long to put their stuff away and get in their seats.

The guy turns to me and gives me an apologetic smile. He's cute and he knows it, and that smile is way too friendly for someone who looks like he's in a serious relationship with the girl currently trying to sit down.

He apologizes and steps out of the way, and I swear to god he winks at me as he does so.

Ew. Even on my best days I have disdain for guys like that, but ever since the breakup, my tolerance is at an all-time low.

I bend down and grab my suitcase, hoisting it up over my head to put it in the bin.

"Let me help you with that," he says, moving closer, even though it's obvious I don't need any help at all. Working in athleisure wear has ensured I work out a lot and I'm a lot stronger than I look.

Meanwhile, I can't help but glance at his girlfriend who is sitting down in her seat and glaring at me, as if I'm not to be trusted. I'm distracted enough that the suitcase slips out of my hands and before I can stop it, it falls and *bonks* the guy right in the head.

Ow.

That's gotta hurt.

"I'm so sorry!" I cry out, awkwardly trying to regain control of the suitcase.

The guy holds onto his head where the wheel hit him, wincing in pain, trying to smile like he's fine.

I quickly manage to shove the suitcase into the bin and apologize again, just as his girlfriend says, "That's what you get," to him in a smug voice.

"That's what I get for trying to help?" he asks her, voice raised, as if that hit a nerve more than my falling suitcase did.

Oh boy.

I swiftly get in my seat by the window, shove my purse beside me, and bring out my noise-cancelling headphones. I can tell the couple is about to get into a fight and I don't want any part of it. My own wounds are too fresh.

It's a thirteen-hour flight across the Pacific, the longest flight I've ever been on. After dinner is served, and I've had some complimentary red wine, I've watched every move I want to watch, and it's time for the Skycouch.

I take off my headphones, the cabin lights already dim, and bring out the information card that tells you how to create your bed.

I've only read the first sentence when I notice the row in front of me is starting to shake.

Repeatedly.

The dregs of wine in the bottom of my glass start to slosh back and forth on the tray table.

There is some turbulence, so I don't think much of it.

But the seats don't seem to be moving with the turbulence.

Wait...

Are they...?

And then I hear it.

A low moan.

Oh my god.

They can't be…

"Oh god, yes," the girl's breathless voice comes from the seat, and through the tiny gap between the seats I can see bodies moving.

Oh my god.

They *are*.

They're having sex right in front of me!

Even though I know they can't see me, I can feel my cheeks immediately go to Tomato Zone One. I'm notorious for blushing easily, and if it gets really bad my whole face will match my dark strawberry blonde hair and all my freckles will meld together.

What do I do?

I look around, trying to see if anyone else is seeing (or hearing) this, but everyone is lying down, sound asleep. I crane my head around, hoping to spot a flight attendant, but I don't see any. Besides, what am I going to do, rat on them?

I mean, I probably should…

"Lower, lower," the girl says. "Yes!"

Oh hell no.

I put my headphones back on and sit back, trying to watch another movie on the seatback. But of course that keeps shaking and shaking. The turbulence has nothing on those two.

How long is this going to go on for?

I'm getting over a breakup, I'm heading across an ocean to go to a wedding all alone, can't I catch a break?

But no, the seats continue to shake, and I swear I can hear the moans through my headphones, and they aren't showing any signs of stopping.

This is hell.

There's only one thing for me to do.

I undo my belt and raise the arm rests, slowly sidling out of my row.

I know I shouldn't look at them, I know I need to just ignore them.

But either watching strangers do it on a plane is some new kink of mine, or curiosity killed the cat.

I stand at the end of their row and look down.

I can't see anything, blankets are covering them as they go at it from the side.

And at it, and at it.

Way to rub it in.

Oh, he's rubbing something alright.

I'm in the middle of turning around when suddenly the plane hits an air pocket, the turbulence causing the plane to drop some feet.

I lose my footing, thrown forward.

I fall right over on the couple, face down where you don't want to be face down.

Oh. My. God.

"Hey!" the girl cries out.

"Sorry!" I say, placing my hands on their hips and other body parts, trying to push myself back up. "So sorry!"

I can't even look at them.

"As you were," I say.

I straighten up somehow and then, feeling panicked, head right to the galley at the back of the plane.

There are two flight attendants back there sitting down and chatting. They both look at me with weary smiles, the kind that says they'd rather not be dealing with passengers right now, especially not someone like me who must look all flushed and wild-eyed.

I'm tempted to tell them about the sexcapades in row 50, but decide they probably don't need the extra stress.

So instead I ask for a glass of wine and if I can just hang out in the galley with them, because I am *not* going back to my seat.

I think they can tell I'm desperate for company or something, because they say yes.

I go through another glass of wine.

And then I start talking about my old job, and then Chris.

And they start feeling sorry for me.

The wine keeps coming.

2

DAISY

When I was a little girl, one of my favorite things was to go on family trips to Portland, something we did just a handful of times a year. But it wasn't the supposed glitz and glamor of the big city that made it so special (*everything* was glitzy and glamorous when you lived on a farm, in Oregon, in the middle of nowhere).

What I remember most fondly is the car ride back home.

We'd leave at dusk, the city lights twinkling behind us, and then we'd be on the I-5 for hours heading south. My sister and I would bicker in the backseat for a while but it wasn't long before I'd fall asleep. I was such a sound sleeper those days, that I wouldn't wake up until we were in the driveway. My parents thought I looked peaceful, so they let me sleep back there until my father either carried me to my bed, or when I was older, gently shook me awake.

I'd wake up with this sense of wonderment, how it was possible for me to fall asleep somewhere and wake up somewhere else, like I was time traveling.

Well, I'm having that exact same feeling again.

Except I really have time traveled (to the future), and instead of waking up all blissful, I've got a raging headache and queasy stomach, and instead of my father shaking me awake, it's a flight attendant.

"Miss?" she says gently in her strong accent, her hand on my shoulder. "We're landing soon."

I open my mouth to try and say thank you, but it's so parched my words come out in this creaky groan. I open my eyes, blinking hard at the bright light coming in through the windows.

Dear god, I feel *awful*.

Slowly, and rather awkwardly, I sit up on the Skycouch, the fleece airplane blanket sticking to me in an aura of static cling. The world seems to swirl and my stomach flips on itself.

I can't remember the last time I've been this hungover.

Though I can't say it's undeserved.

I remember one of the flight attendants giving me two mini bottles of wine and ushering me back to my seat, but only after I must have spent at least two hours talking their ears off and drinking most of their cart. Thankfully, the boinking couple were asleep by then, though it wouldn't have mattered because I was drunk as a skunk, and must have passed out soon after that.

Speaking of, the couple are now sitting up in their seats and sipping coffee and giggling intimately, so obviously their bout of makeup sex made everything right again in their world.

Maybe it would have worked with Chris.

The thought flits through my mind as it has a million times this last week.

Had I been too hasty to break-up with Chris? I mean, I

would imagine most people in my shoes would kick them to the curb and never look back. But was there something between us that would have been worth saving, something worth the sacrifice of looking the other way, of having all trust burnt to the ground?

Truth is, no. I know I did the right thing. But it's been weighing on me anyway, like my life split into two on that day, and I had a choice to either continue on with Chris in my life, or cut him out and go out on my own.

And so here I am, out on my own.

I sigh but even that makes the knives in my head dig deeper.

Not the best way to arrive in a new country.

I slowly put the bed away and head to the lavatory to wash my face, brush my teeth, then go back to my seat and spend a good twenty-minutes doing my makeup, hoping to hide all traces of my hangover. The last thing I want is to see my family while looking like an ogre.

It's not long before the wheels are bouncing on the tarmac, which causes my own stomach to do the same.

Oh...*no*.

Please, no, no, no, no.

I *hate* throwing up. If I had ever gotten sick or hungover in the past, I would do everything possible to keep the contents of my stomach firmly inside me where they belong.

I'm trying desperately to do that now, but as the plane bounces again, going for the worst landing ever, I know there's no stopping it. I'm reaching for the barf bag in the seat pocket just as it's all coming up, making a very vain attempt to hurl inside of it as quietly as possible.

No such luck.

As the noise from the plane's brakes dim, I'm yakking so

loudly I sound like a bear trying repeatedly to cough up a honking goose.

"Oh my god, gross," the girl in front of me says, while a few other people on the plane make sounds of disgust.

I can't even care. It just keeps coming, louder and louder. I'd laugh at how ridiculous I sound, if only this wasn't so horrible.

Finally, the plane comes almost to a stop and the barf bag is full and I've never felt so gross and embarrassed in all my life. It's one thing to throw up on a plane, it's another to do so sounding like a bleating goat on helium. My face is so hot, I'm at Tomato Zone 2 (when my skin on my forehead matches my hair).

I just sit there, gingerly holding onto the edge of the bag, wanting so desperately to head to the lavatory and throw it out, but the minute the seatbelt sign comes on, everyone is an asshole and stands up, blocking my way to the back. I have no choice but to sit in my seat and wait until everyone passes me by.

So I sit there for literally ever, brushing my hair over the side of my face so I don't have to make eye contact with anyone, and wait until the plane has pretty much unloaded.

Then I rush to the lavatory and dispose of it.

When I come out, the flight attendant who got me drinks all night is looking at me with an overly sympathetic look on her face.

"I guess I should have cut you off a little earlier last night," she says to me softly. "You're not having the best of luck."

That's the understatement of the year.

I give her a meek smile and then hurry over to my seat to gather my stuff and get my suitcase, so damn grateful to get off this plane.

I've never been to New Zealand before. Hell, I haven't traveled anywhere outside of North America, except to Chile once for an athletic wear convention, and most of my trips have been for work. I should be more excited than I am, but it's kind of hard when this vacation is getting off on the wrong foot.

Somehow though, I make it through customs without any problems, though the official did seem to study me carefully, probably because I still look a little green and antsy.

I'm here for only one week, which was the most vacation days I was willing to take for this trip, you know, when I had a job. I rarely took days off at all, deciding work was more important than a jaunt to Hawaii or something. Now, with the visitor's visa in my passport, I'm permitted to stay for up to three months. I won't, but there's something so strange about my newfound freedom. It doesn't feel real yet. I still keep thinking that I have a job and a boyfriend to return to.

I'd never given New Zealand that much thought, other than it's the place where my sister went to do her doctorate in botany. When she said she was getting married here to Richard, her long-term boyfriend she met in college, I figured I'd finally get a chance to come and see her. It's been nearly five years since I saw her last, and my parents, who arrived here a week ago, have only been out to see her once.

It does make me wonder if perhaps all this time apart has led my sister to forget about me, because she never answered the text I sent her when I got off the plane and I've been standing here in the arrivals area for a good thirty minutes, scanning the crowd for her familiar face.

A feeling of dread sinks inside me and I text her again, wondering where she is. I could text my parents since they are in the country, but I don't want to bug them.

The shitty thing is, I don't even know where I'm

supposed to go. Usually I'm so on top of things, planning it all to the finest detail, but I really dropped the ball this time. I know I'm not supposed to go to a hotel. Or wait, maybe I am supposed to go to a hotel? Or was it Richard's cousin's house? And what was the place called? Something with a P? It feels like every town in New Zealand starts with a P.

With my sister still not texting me back, I open up my emails and try to get some sense of a plan. I must be flipping through them for a long time, trying to get a handle of things, hoping my sister gets back to me before I really start panicking, when I hear a throat clear from behind me.

I whirl around and, *hello*, standing before me is probably the most ruggedly handsome man I've ever seen.

He's tall, at least six foot two, which makes him look like a giant compared to my 5'1" frame. Factor in broad, rounded shoulders, and a chest like a wall of bricks and strongman arms, plus deeply browned skin, all shown off perfectly by a navy blue T-shirt that says Deep Blue Yacht Charters, and he seems larger than life.

And then there's his face.

Which, as gorgeous as it is—dark mahogany eyes, furrowed brows, thick black hair and a strong jaw—looks a little ticked off. It takes me a moment to register that his eyes aren't narrowed seductively, they're narrowed in annoyance.

"Are you Daisy Lewis?" the man asks me with a thick New Zealand accent. Husky and rough, the kind of voice that would normally make me flush internally (voices and hands are *so* my thing), but I'm able to ignore it because I have no idea who this guy is, or how he knows me and why he seems mad.

"That's me," I tell him cautiously. "And you are?"

"Your ride," he grumbles.

My brows raise. "My *ride*? Where's Lacey?"

He stares at me for a moment, as if he's expecting more from me, but in my hungover, queasy state I don't have the energy to think.

"Your sister," he says carefully, "is busy. I was busy too, but when she called, begging and pleading for me to head back down to Auckland to pick you up, it didn't feel right saying no to the bride-to-be."

"I don't understand." I balk, shaking my head. "The last email she sent she said she was happy to pick me up."

"You're a day early."

I blink at him for a few moments. That doesn't make sense. "I don't..." I press my hands to my temples, trying to think. It's like trying to push over a concrete wall. "I said I was arriving on the 22nd."

When I open my eyes, he's staring at me like I'm a complete idiot. Can't say I like that look. Makes me want to take back all the nice things I've thought about him, even though all those nice things pertained to his body, which unfortunately still looks hot. Especially as he folds his arms across his chest, and mama mia, those are some delicious forearms.

"Have you taken note of the date today?" he asks. "Either on your phone, or the form you filled out at customs? Taken a look at the stamp in your passport?"

Holy condescending tone.

I can't help but glare back at him for a moment before I whip my phone out, fully expecting to see the 22 on the lockscreen.

But it doesn't. Of course it doesn't. Not with my luck these days.

It says it's February 21st.

"How did this happen?" I ask, more to myself than anything else.

"Your sister didn't seem surprised," he says with a weary tone.

My gaze snaps up to his. "What's that supposed to mean?"

His darkly handsome face gives me nothing but disdain.

"Look," I say, feeling flustered, hoping my face doesn't start going red. I feel like he'd thrive on my discomfort. "How on earth am I missing a day? I accounted for the fact that this place is in the future. You know, that New Zealand is a day ahead."

"However you counted it, you overshot the landing," he says, his eyes flitting over my body, as if searching for some kind of sign on how I could be so stupid. They seem to pause on my pink metallic luggage set. Then they focus on the Tory Burch flats on my feet, my yoga pants, my giant fluffy cardigan, my Louis Vuitton Speedy in the crook of my arm.

I know I must look like some rich bitch compared to his worn jeans and tee.

"Well, shit," I say. I hate that this must have added so much extra stress to Lacey.

For some reason I don't hate that this has added extra stress to this guy.

Whoever he is.

"What's your name, anyway?" I ask. "Or should I just refer to you as my driver?"

Wow. His dark eyes are practically simmering, his full lips pressed together into a white, thin line, the muscles along his jaw are tense.

"It's Tai," he says, practically spitting out the words. "And I'm not your driver. I'm doing your sister a favor. I was at Whangaparaoa by the time she called me."

Fangawhat? "I don't even know what you just said."

"It's a…" He stops himself and narrows his eyes. "It doesn't matter. Point was, I had to turn around and come all the way back here. Now I have to bring you all the way up to Russell."

"Who is Russell?"

He stares. "Russell isn't a *he*. It's a town. Where the hotel is?"

You idiot, he seems to silently fill in.

"I thought it started with a P."

He rolls his eyes. "That's Pahia, where you can catch a ferry to Russell." He pauses. "Do you have any idea where you're going?"

I did. I swear I did when my sister first invited me. It's just life was so busy and Chris said he'd handle it and…

Tai cocks a brow and I'm aware that he's studying me, my slumped shoulders, the confusion and sadness that must be etched on my face. For a second, it looks like he's feeling sorry for me.

I straighten my shoulders and paste my happy-go-lucky smile on my face. "Sorry if I don't seem one hundred per cent with it. It was a rough flight. Thanks for asking."

A lightbulb seems to turn on in his head as he gives me a sympathetic look. "Your sister warned me that you may or may not have a bloke in tow." He glances over my shoulder, searching. "Guess he didn't make it."

"You mean my ex-boyfriend?" I repeat, stiffening. "No, he didn't make it. Hence the term ex. And that's not why my flight was rough."

It was all the alcohol I drank because of said ex.

"Lacey wasn't sure," he says. "But it's all the better if you ask me. I've only got a two-seater truck. One of you would have had to sit in the back."

And from the look on his face, I can tell that I'd have been the one banished there.

"Well, it's just me."

Alone.

"And your entire closet, it seems," he observes, eyeing my suitcases.

"Hey, not only will I be here a week, but it's for a wedding. Do you know how many accessories and extra clothes you need for that?"

He shrugs. "Wouldn't know. I've got a tux waiting for me and that's it. Come on."

He reaches down and grabs both suitcase handles from my hands, our skin brushing against each other for an electrifying moment.

Then he turns and starts walking off, hauling the suitcases after him.

Okay, it was pretty gentlemanly of him to do that, but he also seems like he's stealing them.

I jog after him— slowly, so to not jostle my brain. "I can handle them," I say as I catch up alongside him, my little legs moving fast as we step through the airport's automatic doors and out onto the curb.

"And yet I'm sure you're used to this kind of thing," he says to me idly. "Having someone to handle things for you."

"What's that supposed to mean?"

He pauses at the crosswalk, looking to the right.

"It means if you wanted to refer to me as your driver, I might as well play the role."

Oh, brother.

I make a scoffing sound and look to the left.

No cars.

I step out onto the road and in a blinding rush he quickly reaches out and puts his body in front of mine just as wheels screech and a car honks, the suitcase handles clattering to the ground.

My heart thuds against my chest.

"You fucking donkey!!" Tai bellows, shaking his fist at the taxi that nearly ran me over. "Pedestrian crossing means pedestrians are crossing, you chucklefuck!"

For a moment it looks like Tai is going to smash through the taxi's window and pull the driver out by his collar, but the driver hits the gas and speeds through the crosswalk, thankfully not hitting anyone.

Tai's dark complexion has turned deep red as he looks back to me. I'm about to thank him for saving my life but his eyes are fiery. "Why don't watch where you're fucking going? Look right, not left."

I'm speechless, and I think I'm approaching Tomato Zone One because once again, I'm totally embarrassed. Not only that I forgot they drive on the other side of the road here, but that Tai is reprimanding me for it.

But I refuse to cower before him. "Give me a break, I just got here," I tell him, hoping he can't pick up on the warble in my voice.

He glares at me and snatches up the suitcase handles, looking both ways again before he starts crossing.

My pulse is racing in my neck as I follow behind him. He's really getting all worked up about this and I don't know why. He must think I'm the biggest idiot.

Probably because he's used to dealing with Lacey, I think to myself. *And you're her airhead sister.*

Yeah, the words are harsh. I know I'm not an airhead in the slightest, I just come across that way sometimes. Usually because I try to look on the positive (at least that's what pre-job loss and pre-break-up Daisy used to do), and I guess if you're always smiling you're seen as dumb. Whereas someone like my sister, who rarely smiles and is always serious, seems smart by comparison.

Okay, she *is* smart. Like, brilliant. She's got her damn PhD in botany. She's a doctor and she's marrying her equally as smart fiancé. And me, well I was the head of marketing for yoga pants and white-washed self-care. A job I couldn't even hold on to.

I take in a few deep breaths through my nose as I follow Tai into the short-term parking area. I'm getting all worked up and I only just got here.

We don't talk, I stay right behind the suitcases. He doesn't even glance over his shoulder to see if I'm following him.

Finally, we stop at a shiny red pick-up truck, an old model that looks straight out of the 50's. He throws my luggage in the back of it without a care.

"Hey, I have breakables in there," I tell him, but he doesn't seem to hear me. I suppose he's not doing any different than the baggage handlers.

Then he gets in his side, which for a moment I mistake for the passenger side before I remember, again, how everything is switched around.

My poor hungover brain doesn't like this one bit.

At least by the time I get in the passenger side, my face has calmed and he seems to have simmered down.

It's a nice truck, shiny tan leather seats, but it's awfully cramped. He wasn't joking about someone else having to sit in the back, because my thighs are pretty much touching his and I am not ready for this amount of intimacy with this man.

I need to ignore it, even though at this proximity I can pick up on the scent of his cologne, or maybe his body wash. Something salty and bracing, like ocean air. It's definitely not aftershave since he has a respectable five o' clock shadow, the kind that would tickle the soft skin between your legs.

Oh my god, stop it.

I blink and buckle up, trying to shift my weight to the outer corner. These thoughts are entertaining but they're bad news, especially since this guy seems to hate me for no real reason.

Maybe I won't have to deal with him much at the wedding.

"So, how do you know the bride and groom?" I ask as he pays for the parking.

"Grew up with Richard," he says out of the corner of his mouth as the parking attendant hands him his credit card back.

"Oh," I say. "You know, I haven't even met him."

"I did know that," Tai says as we exit the lot. "Lacey's mentioned how you've never come to visit."

"Well, you know…I've been busy. *She's* been busy."

He doesn't say anything to that, still the set of his brow implies that this seems to be an issue to my sister. I guess five years is a long time…

I clear my throat. "So I take it you're close with Lacey, too."

He nods.

"I'm the maid of honor," I tell him, as if I'm trying to prove how close me and Lacey are.

"I know," he says grimly. "I'm the best man."

The best man?

So he's part of the wedding party?

Well, that's just *great.*

I gulp and eye the clock on the dashboard. It's almost noon.

"How long is the drive to…Robert?"

He just shakes his head. "Russell," he corrects me, eking out the word.

"Sorry! *Russell.*"

"Four hours."

Four. Hours?

In this truck? With this man?

My stomach does an unsettling little skip at that.

This is going to be hell.

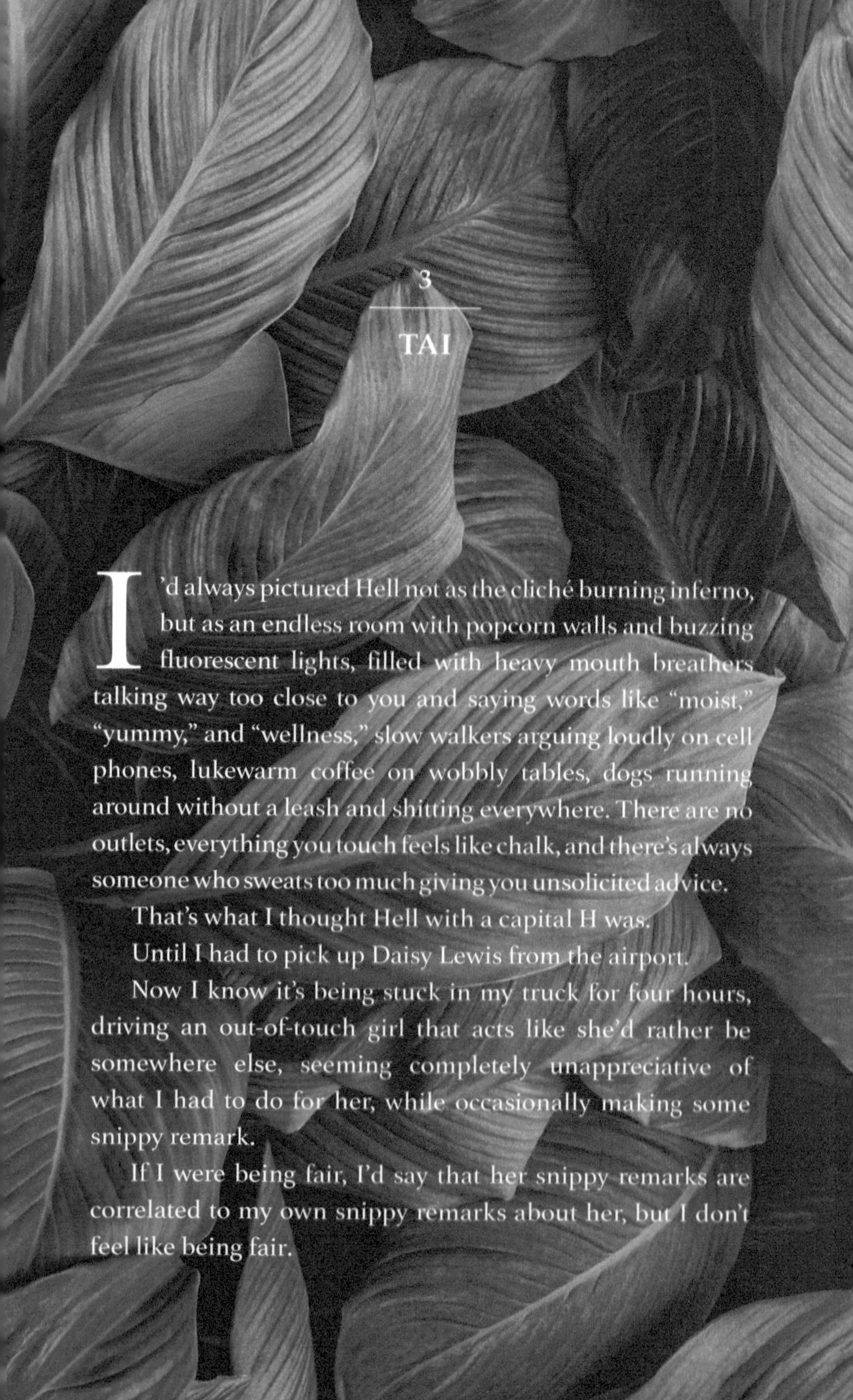

3

TAI

I'd always pictured Hell not as the cliché burning inferno, but as an endless room with popcorn walls and buzzing fluorescent lights, filled with heavy mouth breathers talking way too close to you and saying words like "moist," "yummy," and "wellness," slow walkers arguing loudly on cell phones, lukewarm coffee on wobbly tables, dogs running around without a leash and shitting everywhere. There are no outlets, everything you touch feels like chalk, and there's always someone who sweats too much giving you unsolicited advice.

That's what I thought Hell with a capital H was.

Until I had to pick up Daisy Lewis from the airport.

Now I know it's being stuck in my truck for four hours, driving an out-of-touch girl that acts like she'd rather be somewhere else, seeming completely unappreciative of what I had to do for her, while occasionally making some snippy remark.

If I were being fair, I'd say that her snippy remarks are correlated to my own snippy remarks about her, but I don't feel like being fair.

Besides, she seems like the type of girl that needs to be put in her place. I mean, she's fucking *humming*, for god's sake. The worst part is, I can't figure out what tune it is. I want to ask her, but at the same time I don't dare get into another conversation.

We're just past Whangerei, about another hour and a bit to go, when I finally snap.

"What song is that?" I ask, unable to keep the edge out of my voice.

"I don't know," she says, and she says it in such a way that I can't tell if she's fucking with me or not. "Why, do you like it?" She adds a sweet smile.

She's been giving me that smile a lot. And I don't like it, *or* that smile.

At all.

It makes her look ridiculously pretty. Which is unwarranted.

Not that she's hard on the eyes—she's the opposite.

Daisy Lewis is hobbit-sized with a narrow waist and curves that give you whiplash if you look at her too quickly. Her hair is long, this dark golden-red color that reminds me of autumn fields at sunset, her nose is delicately upturned, her skin is pale and dotted with freckles, a look that reminds me of the crushes of my youth.

Then there are her eyes.

Dangerous eyes.

Impossibly big and icy blue.

The kind of eyes that are used to holding men hostage, I'm sure.

She's not perfect of course. Her ears stick out and her front teeth are big. I've been trying to focus on that, along with her annoying personality.

"I love it," I tell her, knowing if I told her the truth she would keep doing it. "Please keep going."

She narrows her eyes and studies me for a moment before she looks out the window.

"What are these trees called?" she asks.

I sigh. She's been awfully curious this entire ride, asking question after question about New Zealand, which I guess isn't a bad thing. I'm just not used to speaking so much, and I hate that she's bringing this out of me.

"Kauri," I tell her. I hesitate. "There are a lot of them in the Northland."

She makes a thoughtful "huh" remark, and then I feel her gaze back on me.

Don't look at her eyes, you'll drive off the road.

I can practically *feel* her knowing smirk. "You didn't want to tell me that last part, did you? You know, talking to you is like pulling teeth. Anyone ever told you that?"

I tighten my grip on the steering wheel in annoyance, wishing she wasn't so close to me. Occasionally I get a whiff of vanilla and roses, which must be her perfume. I have to say, even though she looks a little uneasy at times, she looks pretty damn good for having been on an airplane for thirteen hours.

"I'm used to keeping to myself," I tell her, and immediately regret even giving her a snippet of information. She's going to use this as a jumping off point, isn't she?

She twists toward me slightly, her thigh pressing against mine. "So, tell me how you know Richard. I know you said you were neighbors."

"Yes. We were neighbors."

"Uh huh. And where did you grow up? Auckland?"

I clench my jaw, wondering how short my answers can be.

"Russell."

"Oh. Robert," she jokes, and it makes me growl a little in response. "Just kidding."

She jabs her elbow into my side.

I try to move my torso out of the way. I'm ticklish there. "Please don't do that while I'm driving."

"Jeez," she says slowly. "Has anyone also told you that you're a grump?"

I don't need to answer that.

"So, in Russell," she goes on after a moment, dashing any hopes I had of her shutting up, "have you lived there your whole life?"

"Yes."

"And Richard was your neighbor?"

I exhale as loudly as possible. "Yes. Yes. We've been over this."

"I'm just making conversation. I'm trying to get to know you."

"Well, *please don't*."

"About the conversation or about getting to know you?"

"Both."

She crosses her arms, her tits pushed up.

I will not look at her cleavage, I will not look at her cleavage.

"You're a grump," she says after a moment.

"Fuck yeah I'm a grump. You would be a grump too, if you were in my shoes."

"I wouldn't know what it's like to be in your shoes since you don't talk about yourself."

"I meant I'm grumpy today, because I had to backtrack and pick your unappreciative ass up."

"I appreciate it," she protests, but it sounds rather weak.

"Do you really?"

She waves at that dismissively. "Fine. Be grumpy. Doesn't

mean I can't get to know you. You're the best man, I'd like to find out why. How do you tie into all of this?"

I shoot her a loaded glance, eyes resting ever so briefly on her tits, and then look back to the road. "I was born in Russell. Richard moved next door when he was six. We went to school together. All the kids picked on Richard because he was a skinny nerd who was always falling down and always crying and couldn't swim. But because I was Richard's neighbor, I started to feel sorry for him. I started standing up for him. With my fists. We've been friends ever since." I pause, briefly raising my fingers off the steering wheel. "Happy now?"

She nods thoughtfully. "Figures Richard was a nerd from the start. I mean, you'd have to be to be marrying my sister. Plus his last name looks like *boner*."

I almost laugh. "It *is* Boner."

"Yeah but it's pronounced Bon-air," she says.

I rub my lips together before I look at her. She's serious.

"You think his last name is Bon-air? It's not. It's Boner. It's Richard Boner, AKA Dick Boner, reason one million why he's been made fun of his whole life."

She shakes her head, her eyes wide. "It can't be. When he added me on Facebook, I immediately started making fun of his last name and Lacey insisted it's pronounced Bon-Air."

"Lacey is lying," I tell her. "Haven't you figured that's why she's hesitant on taking his last name."

"I thought it was because of our Lewis legacy."

"Legacy? Aren't your parents apple farmers?"

"So...she might become Lacey Boner." She giggles for a moment, and then sobers up. "If she's lying about Dick Boner, what else could she be lying about?"

"I don't know, and I don't care. You've got your issues."

"What does that mean?"

Why did I open my mouth? I should have stopped talking hours ago.

"What does that mean, *Tai?* If that is your real name."

I give her a look. "Why wouldn't it be my name?"

"It sounds made up."

"It's not. It's Maori."

She's silent for a moment. "Oh. Are you Maori?"

I nod. My skin gets pretty dark in the sun, and it's the end of summer now so I'm pretty brown, but perhaps it isn't obvious to her.

"Yeah. Maori on my mother's side."

"So what does Tai mean?"

"It means 'Great Extreme'."

She rubs her lips together as if she's trying not to laugh.

"What?" I ask testily.

"Great Extreme what? Great Extreme Grump?"

My eyes roll back. "Whatever you want to call me, it makes zero difference to me. Anyway, you're named after a weed."

"I don't know what you call them here, but at home a daisy is a flower. A pretty one." She's so indignant, I'm almost smiling.

"Yeah, they're weeds."

She practically jumps in her seat. "Daisies aren't weeds! They're flowers!"

"They're weeds and I mow them down every spring." I give her a smirk. "Pretty fitting name if you ask me."

The glare returns to her eyes. "Forget grump, you're a full-on dick."

I shrug. "As I said, whatever you want to call me makes no difference to me."

And at that, she seems to shut up.

I glance down at the dashboard clock and sigh internally at how slow this has been going. It's been a hell of a day so far.

I woke up early having spent the night on one of the boats I had to sail from the Bay of Islands last week, down to Auckland Harbor for a client. I met the client, handed off the boat, and then started up on the motorway back up to Russell.

That's when Lacey called me in hysterics, saying her sister Daisy had arrived a day early and she hadn't arranged any pickup for her. I guess tomorrow Daisy was supposed to arrive at the same time as another guest was passing through and they were going to give her a ride or something. At any rate, I thought it was odd that Daisy was arriving on the day of the wedding rehearsal, as if she was trying to cut the trip as short as possible. But from the way that Lacey sometimes refers to Daisy as being flakey and pampered and distant, I figured it was normal.

Naturally, Lacey was busy doing last minute wedding things with her parents and Richard, so I was her only hope. It was this, or stick Daisy on a bus, which would have been the preferable option for me, and probably for Daisy as well. But I like Lacey a lot, even though she can be hard on you, and so I did her a favor.

I suppose it's not the worst thing in the world, at least it isn't now since Daisy has finally grown quiet and I've had time to think.

That is until we drive through the town of Opua where I have my boats. As we head over the bridge that crosses the bay, I crane my neck to try and see the marina.

"What are you looking at?" she asks.

"Boats."

"I don't think I've ever seen so many," she says,

seeming to admire them dotted on the emerald green water, the sun glinting off the masts. Then she glances at my shirt. "I'm going to guess you have something to do with them?"

I nod. "I own a chartering company. Deep Blue. Have twelve yachts in total, based out of here and Auckland."

"Wow," she says. "Impressive." And she actually sounds impressed for once. "I guess you do look like you'd be pretty good with your hands."

Now she's looking at my hands, my knuckles all scarred up from my boxing days.

"Ever been sailing?" I ask her against my better judgement.

"Ha," she says. "Yes, once. With an ex. I was rather useless, I have to admit. I think I like the whole drinking cocktails at the dock type of sailing."

"Uh huh. And this ex, was it the one that was supposed to be in the back of the truck?"

She gives me one of her sweet smiles again and it nearly knocks the wind out of me. I force myself to focus on the road. "I thought *I* was going to be the one in the back! Have you changed your mind about me?"

Never.

But she looks out the window, her shoulders sinking. "No," she says wearily. "That was some other ex. My latest ex was Chris."

I should drop it. Take the opportunity for more blessed silence. But if she got to poke and prod at me, I get to poke and prod at her.

"So what happened?"

"That's very direct."

"I'm a direct guy. So what happened? Why isn't he here? Did you talk him to death?"

"You know what, I only talk like this when I'm nervous, it's not all the time."

I grin at her. "So I make you nervous?"

"No," she says hesitantly and then shields her eyes. "I think this is the first time I've seen you smile. Has anyone ever told you that your teeth are blinding?"

"Has anyone ever told you that you say *has anyone ever told you* a lot?"

She exhales slowly through her lips. "Chris told me that. He told me lots of things, before I came home one day to make lunch and caught him having sex with an ex-coworker."

Fuck.

I let out a low whistle. "That is rough."

"Yeah. And, like, a few weeks before that I was let go of my job of ten years."

"Shit."

"Mmmhmmm." She starts tapping her fingers along her thighs.

"What did you do? I mean, what was your role?"

Another sigh. "I was the head of marketing for an athleisure company. You know, clothes for yoga, products for wellness, that sort of thing."

I shudder inside at the word "wellness," one of my pet peeves. Figures.

"And so what did you do?" I repeat. "Meaning, why were you fired?"

"I wasn't fired," she snaps at me, her face starting to flush. "I was laid off."

"Okay, take it easy, Gingersnap."

"Gingersnap?"

I shrug. It's fitting and I'll use it again. "So company layoffs. That's got to suck."

"What I probably should have done is just not come here at all. Stayed at home and focused on getting another job, focused on getting over Chris."

"You would have done that to your sister? Skipped out on her wedding?"

Her shoulders lift. "I don't know. I don't know if Lacey would care, to be honest. I haven't seen her in five years, we don't talk all that often anymore. Not like we ever did."

She catches me looking at her and puts a big smile on her face, a practiced, easy smile, a smile that most people wouldn't notice is fake.

But I do.

"Anyway, I'm here." She sits up straighter, a forced chipper tone to her voice. "And I'm going to enjoy the hell out of this trip. Maybe all this shit that happened to me is a chance to start over, really find myself. You know, maybe I'll take the advice that my old job was spewing all those years. Go on a spiritual journey and all that horseshit."

I laugh. "Sounds like you're heading in the right direction."

She nods, returning the smile.

But I don't think she believes it.

$$4$$

DAISY

This has been, no doubt, the longest drive of my life.

I mean, four hours is pretty long no matter how you spin it, but four hours stuck in a cramped space with the grumpiest guy alive with his fresh ocean scent and big hands and growly voice, a guy that couldn't hide his disdain for me even if he tried (and he wasn't trying), pushed my sanity to the limit.

Not to mention a lot of the road was winding and my nausea reared its ugly head once again. Tai was probably grateful that I shut up for once, but the truth was I was trying to keep from being sick. The last thing I needed was to further embarrass myself. Can you imagine if I hurled all over his vintage truck? He'd probably have kicked me out and made me hitchhike without even a second glance.

Truth be told, I was almost tempted to do it. Just to piss him off.

Finally, we reach the cute town of Russell, with its quaint shops and people milling along the sparkling harbor with dripping ice cream cones in their hands. But we keep going and the road twists and turns again though forest until it opens on a narrow peninsula full of houses. We pull into a driveway and park.

I can't get out of the truck fast enough, I practically fall out of it. Wedding party be damned, I hope that was the last and only time I'll be stuck in such close proximity with Tai.

I take a moment and lean against the passenger door, immediately taking in a deep, calming breath. We're at the end of a long gravel driveway, rolling green hills on either side that slip down to a wide, pale beach and the turquoise of the water beyond. If I had to describe New Zealand in one word so far it would be *saturated*. Every color, from the green of the land to the blue of the sky is vibrant and electric, almost like it's been digitally altered.

And the air here! It's so fresh that I think it's curing my hangover.

I turn my attention to the big white house in front of us, and the bunch of cars parked on the grass around it. Tai gets out, reaches into the bed of the truck and pulls out the heavy suitcases effortlessly. His tanned muscles pop and flex and I have to look away before he realizes I'm ogling him.

"Where are we?" I ask, peering around the neighborhood of what looks like small summer houses. "I thought we were going to a hotel."

"This is my parent's house," Tai says begrudgingly as he hauls my luggage through the gravel to the paved stone path to the front door.

"Your parent's house?" I run after him. "Is this where you grew up? It's gorgeous."

And it truly is. The house is two-stories with a porch, boxes of flowers beneath each window. It reminds me of my own parents' house in Oregon, except the white paint on this one is clean and shiny, and I think my parents painted their house once in in the '90s and left it to the elements ever since. My mom insists that it's shabby chic, but I know that they're just too busy with the farm to pay attention to anything else, like the house, or their children, for example.

Speaking of, while I'm gawking at the cuteness of Tai's parent's house, the front door opens and *my* parents step out onto the porch, my father leading the way.

"Well, well, well," my dad bellows as he comes down the path toward us. "If it isn't the early bird." He gives Tai a nod. "Thank you for bringing her here. Wouldn't have blamed you if you left her at the airport. I know what it's like to have been Driving Miss Daisy."

"Thanks dad," I say with a roll of my eyes as Tai gives my father a disapproving grunt and disappears inside.

I haven't seen my parents since Easter last year. My parents have always been religious, so skipping Easter with them at the local community church is akin to disowning them, though this winter I spent Christmas with Chris, which, in hindsight, was the wrong move.

My dad looks good. Relaxed for once. He's always had a tan because he works outside so much, but the dark circles under his eyes have disappeared and his face looks rounder, happier.

"You look great," I tell him as he pulls me into a hug. He smells familiar and comforting, and I hadn't really realized how badly I needed affection from someone I love. "New Zealand looks good on you."

"It's the wine that's agreeing with him," my mother says from behind him, while Tai takes the suitcases into the house.

My mother looks the same as always, just as short as I am, but delicate-boned, like a bird, instead of athletic and curvy. She's wearing khaki shorts and a plaid shirt, the same damn thing she wears at home all year long, though here she has Reef sandals velcroed to her feet instead of rainboots.

We couldn't be more different. I don't think she's ever worn makeup, her hair is a long and frizzy grey, always held back in a ponytail. She has an ever-present ball cap on her head and glasses. She must look at me sometimes and wonder where the hell I came from.

She's giving me that look right now, as she eyes me up and down. She's not the type of mom to give some snotty or passive aggressive remark, instead she keeps things to herself and looks at me as if I'm an alien.

Right now I feel like one. It's weird to see my parents here, in a foreign land, not surrounded by mounds of work and apples.

I go to hug my mom, and she pats me lightly on the shoulder. She's never been very good with hugs or physical affection, which has probably rubbed off on me in some way. Still, I'll take what I can get.

"I'm glad you're here," she says, then pulls back. "Are you okay? Jet-lagged? Did you sleep on the plane?"

"Kind of," I tell her. "I'm just tired from the drive. And a bit confused as to why we're all here. I thought I was staying at a hotel."

"That was the original plan," my dad says. "But everybody has been so easy-going, they decided that since the wedding is being held on the beach out back, might just be easier for everyone to stay here."

"Easy going?" I repeat. "I'm guessing you're *not* talking about Lacey."

"My ears are burning," Lacey's quiet voice sounds from behind my mom and we turn to see her stepping out of the house.

Wow. It's weird to see her after so long, even though I see her on social media all the time.

Lacey is five inches taller than me, getting the "height" from dad, though she got the skinny physique from my mother. Her style hasn't changed much either, sensible sandals, jeans even though it's fairly hot out, a black blouse that looks a little too stuffy on her. Her bright blonde hair is in a long bob and to my surprise she's wearing magenta lip gloss, perhaps her attempt at dressing up. She's always worn glasses but these new ones are a little more cat-eyed, like a sexy secretary.

Lacey is beautiful. She would fit every guy's fantasy of a blonde bombshell, except her resting bitch face is some pretty powerful stuff and I was witness to a lot of guys in high school being scared of her. They'd confide in me that they thought she was hot but too smart for them, too intimidating, too serious. Add in the fact that my parents were super strict with her, and she grew up never really knowing how pretty she was.

That, or she didn't care. All she cared about was school.

It's worked out well for her.

"Hey," I say to her brightly. "I made it!"

She scurries over to me—that's Lacey's thing, always spry, never has time to lose—and brings me into a quick hug. She smells like Pantene Pro-V, and I'm immediately transported back in time to when I used to share a bathroom with her. Feels like another life.

"You made it," she says. Her voice is still quiet, controlled, but there's a hint of accent now. "I was worried, but now I can see I had no reason to. You always land on your feet, don't you Daisy? Like a cat."

I give her a stiff smile. There is a hint of resentment in her words. I glance at my parents to see if they've noticed, but they both look happy (or maybe just in shock) to have us here all together.

"So, I met Tai," I tell her, skirting over her tone. "Did you purposefully send me the grumpiest man in New Zealand?"

Her lips pinch together and I notice her lip gloss is feathering a little. She should have worn lipliner. Beginners makeup 101.

"It was Tai or the bus."

"I would have rather taken the bus," I tell her.

She folds her arms, the ring on her finger flashing. "Well had you told me the right date, I would have arranged for someone more suitable to pick you up."

"Holy crap, is that your engagement ring?" I ask, reaching down and picking up her hand.

She stiffens. The ring is much bigger and more sparkly in person.

"Richard did well," I tell her. She blushes and looks away, taking her hand out of mine.

"He's been great," my father says. "When Lacey has her little meltdowns, Richard is there to rein her in."

"I don't have meltdowns," Lacey snaps, and my father and I chuckle in unison, because Lacey always has to be in control, and if she's not, a meltdown ensues. "Weddings are stressful for anyone. I would have rather eloped."

"Don't say that," my mother scolds her. "This was a great excuse for all of us to get together."

"Yeah, because you all need an excuse to come visit me, not because you want to," Lacey says.

"Hey, this is a two-way street, you haven't come to visit us," I tell her. "It's been five years and you could have come back to the States at any time."

"Whoa, whoa, whoa," a voice says cutting through what

was sure to be an epic argument. "Let's not start off on the wrong foot here, folks."

Richard appears behind Lacey.

Dr. Dick Boner.

I have to chew on my lip to keep from laughing.

I've obviously seen Richard's face all over Lacey's social media, and I even spoke to him on the phone after he proposed to Lacey, but I have to say he looks as dorky in person as he does in photos. I thought perhaps the man just wasn't photogenic, but that's not the case.

He's sort of cute, in like a Jon Cryer kind of way. Someone you'd put in a headlock and ruffle up his hair. He's got thick glasses and is wearing a polo shirt, tan slacks, and brown loafers, like he took a page from Bill Gates's style book.

That said, he also strikes me as someone who has money. Like Bill Gates. That ring didn't come from teaching about plants, that's for sure.

"So glad you decided to pop by, Daisy," Richard says to me, extending his hand. His Kiwi accent is very strong and very high-pitched. "I know time zones can be flabbergasting to the novice traveler, but I think you might need to take a refresher in maths." He starts laughing.

Dear lord, don't make me hate him. He used the term "maths."

"I know, I know, silly me," I say with a forced laugh, smacking the side of my head to indicate that I'm an idiot. "But I'm here now."

He doesn't seem like he's going to drop it. He puts his arm around Lacey and gives her a squeeze. "You made my little lingerie here all worried. I had to remind her that things always seem to work out for you."

"I'm sorry, lingerie?"

He kisses her on the top of the head, and her cheeks grow redder while avoiding our eyes. "It's my nickname for her. Lacey...lingerie. Lacey lingerie." He laughs again, slapping his thigh as if it's the funniest thing.

Okay, I can't handle this.

"And what's your nickname?" my dad asks him. "Little Dicky?"

I burst out laughing, wanting to high five my dad, especially as Richard stares at us in confusion.

"I'm not sure I understand the context, Mr. Lewis," he says.

My father sighs. "Never mind."

"We should probably go back," Lacey says. "Daisy, you can put your stuff away upstairs if you like and then please join us in the backyard for a cocktail."

Please join us in the backyard for a cocktail? I feel like I'm at a timeshare presentation or something.

I watch as Lacey and Richard walk back inside the house, arm-in-arm.

What a bunch of dorks.

My dad claps his hand on my shoulder. "Come on, better do as your sister says or she'll have another meltdown. I'll make sure to get you a glass of sauvignon blanc when you're done."

Once inside my father tells me to go upstairs. It's a nice house and it feels really weird that I haven't met the owners yet, and that the owners are Tai's parents. It's like I shouldn't be here.

But when I get to the second floor, most of the doors are open and people's suitcases are piled in. My parents' suitcases are in what looks like a study, I see the shape of Lacey's wedding gown hanging in a guest bedroom, and then I spot my suitcases in the room right across.

This has to be Tai's old room because it's as if I've walked into a museum exhibit devoted to showcasing the inner workings of a teenage boy.

The walls are covered from top to bottom with posters, I can't even find an inch of drywall. It's all surfing shots, big waves, or boxers in a ring, or the All Blacks rugby team, or sailboats, and the occasional pin-up girl is thrown in for good measure, often posing beside said surfboards. This room tells me everything I need to know about teenage Tai. Hell, it might tell me a lot about grumpy adult Tai.

I do have to admit I'm disappointed that the pinup girls he chose all seem to be the same type, tall, skinny and blonde with rich tans and big boobs. I've got the boobs but that's about it.

Then, of course, I'm disappointed in myself for being disappointed.

The presence of someone behind me immediately makes me whirl around.

Tai is standing in the doorway. Or rather, he's leaning against the doorway and observing me, an apple in his hand that he's munching on.

"Hope you don't mind your digs for the night," he says, taking a rather loud crunch of his apple. I don't know if this is a new kink or what, but there's something very sexy about watching a man eat an apple with such gusto. Or maybe it's just that it's Tai doing it.

"Are you sure you don't mind me sleeping in your room?" I ask him.

He shrugs. "Not really my room anymore."

I look around at the walls. "Are you sure? It's so perfectly preserved."

He's silent. I look back at him and somehow his eyes seem even darker than normal.

Then it passes. He shrugs again. "My parents like to pretend I still live here."

"So where do you live?" I know I'm pressing my luck by asking him even more questions but hey, he's the one who decided to stop by and seductively eat an apple.

"Not too far from here."

That's as good as I'll get.

"How old are you?"

He narrows his eyes. "Thirty-four." Pause. "Why?"

"Because I'd like to know how many years have passed between this version of Tai," I gesture to the room before gesturing to him, "and this version of Tai."

He bites the apple again. Munch, munch, munch.

I stare at his throat as he swallows and why, oh why, do I find that so hot?

"Who is to say they aren't the same person?"

"Uh huh," I tell him, pointing at one of the pinups. "So you're telling me that these cheesy artificial babes are still your top choice for a wankfest?"

He coughs, nearly spitting out the apple, his temples darkening. Then he smiles. "Wouldn't they be your first choice for a wankfest?"

I look back at them and their vacantly cheery eyes. I mean, they *are* pretty. "I suppose..."

"So maybe my tastes have changed," he goes on, adjusting his casual pose against the door. His eyes rake over my body in such a dark, heated way that I get goosebumps. "My top choice for your so-called wankfest happens to be petite and spicy redheads with big tits." He grins. "But they have to know when to shut up. Luckily for you, you don't."

And with that he leaves the room.

Wow.

He went there.

My cheeks feel hot and I immediately press my hands there, hoping to calm the flush. The last thing he needs to know is how that look of his made me feel.

It made me realize how desperately I need to get laid.

And desperate is something I've never been.

I straighten up, ignoring my body that seeks to betray me every time I'm around him, and then I head downstairs.

I take a quick look around the kitchen and living room, just being nosy, and then head through the screen door at the back that leads into a sprawling green yard.

There's about a dozen people here that I don't know, all holding glasses of white wine or beer in dark amber bottles, a BBQ along the white fence is smoking and smelling like grilled meats and tangy sauce. In the distance, a group of guys, including Tai, are tossing around a rugby ball on the beach.

Shit. I didn't realize it was a party. I look like ass, probably smell like ass. I'm about to head back inside to get changed and redo my makeup when Richard, of all people, waves me over.

"Oy, Miss Daisy Lewis," he says, wiggling his fingers at me.

Ugh, please don't do that. It's creepy.

He's with Lacey, and another young couple. My father heads over to join them, double-fisting white wine. He raises one of the glasses to me when he sees me.

Sigh.

There's no escape.

But at least there is wine.

I head across the grass, giving everyone a big smile, the one that I'm used to, the one that tells everyone that I'm fine and always will be fine. That's the Daisy they expect.

"So nice of you to join us," Lacey says, as if I wasn't in Tai's room for a maximum of five minutes.

"Here you go sweetie," my dad says as he hands me the wine.

I take it and thank him, waiting to see if the sharp mineral smell of the sauvignon blanc will either worsen my hangover or better it.

"Daisy, this is Eaton and Jana," Richard says. "They're both part of the wedding party."

I politely say hello to them both, though I can tell right away that they aren't my type of people. They seem to be in their late thirties and, judging by their boring outfits, they're probably professors like my sister and Richard, or at least scientists. And though their smiles are innocent enough, I get the feeling they're looking down at me.

But I fake that it doesn't bother me. I'm good at that. All throughout high school, whatever few friends Lacey did have, they all treated me like I was some dummy. I liked makeup and I talked too much and smiled too much. It didn't matter that at the time my whole goal in life was to be a marine biologist, *and* I was just as studious as my sister was. I swear Lacey tells people lies about me and I have no idea what they are or why she would do that. I guess it says a lot about me that I would even think that about my own sister.

And now you're here for her wedding, so how about you focus on the positive? I tell myself.

"Did you make the journey by yourself?" Eaton asks me, swirling the wine in his glass.

"I did," I tell him, mimicking him by swirling my own glass.

"She was going to bring her boyfriend but..." Lacey says, trailing off.

"We broke up," I say to her, flashing her a smile that says *shut up* in sister-language.

"Oooh, that's tough," Jana says, wincing in an exaggerated way. "Weddings are awful to attend alone."

Rubbing salt in the wound, are we?

I shrug, still swirling the glass. "I guess. I mean, I am the maid-of-honor so I wouldn't even have had any time for him anyway."

"You need to stop swirling the glass," Eaton says, nodding at me while he sips his wine. "You're bruising the flavor."

Bruising the flavor? Give me a break.

I look at dad who is grinning ear-to-ear. "Well, shucks, Eaton. Who knew there was a wrong way to drink wine?"

"Oh, Eaton is an expert on wine," Richard says proudly. "He did his dissertation on the hybridization of New Zealand's pinot noir in Blenheim."

"That's great," I say. Fascinating stuff.

"So, your sister tells me that you're the head of marketing for some big company in the US," Jana says.

Oh goody, a subject change from the fact that I'm here alone to the fact that I no longer have a job.

"Was," Lacey speaks up. "She *was* the head of marketing. She was laid off."

"Wow," Jana says to me, her expression full of pity. "You're having a hell of a time."

"But she'll be fine," Lacey interjects, giving me a look I can't read. "She's always fine."

I want to ask her what the hell she means by *that*, but my father says, "Of course she'll be fine. She's my daughter."

Lacey rolls her eyes.

"So how long are you in the country for?" Jana asks. "Got any fun plans?"

"Aside from this?" I ask cheerily. They probably don't pick up on sarcasm very well. "No plans. Just here for the wedding. Going back home in a week."

But what are you going home to?

"That's a shame," Eaton says. "New Zealand has so much to offer."

"You should do what your sister is doing and charter a boat," Jana says.

I frown. This is the first I'm hearing of this.

I look at Lacey and Richard. "You're chartering a boat?"

"For our honeymoon," Richard says. He jerks his chin to Tai playing rugby in the background. "Tai gave us a fantastic deal."

I have so many questions. "What happened to Fiji?"

"We're sailing *to* Fiji," Lacey says, annoyed. "Don't you read any of my emails?"

"And don't worry, I'm an excellent sailor," Richard says, as if I was worried. "Tai has taught me a lot over the years. It's been a pleasure to be in the student role instead of the teacher. Besides, the yacht is practically push button. Top of the line."

"How long is that trip?" I ask.

"About ten days, sometimes more," he says. He looks to my father. "I invited your parents along with us, but I think your father has cold feet."

It's my father's turn to look annoyed. "It's not cold feet, little Dicky. It's called work."

"Why on earth would you want them on your honey-moon?" I ask, then give my father an apologetic smile. "No offense, dad."

He shrugs and sips his wine, a much heartier gulp than the one before.

"Here's the thing, Daisy," Richard leans in and says in a

conspiratorial tone. "A honeymoon is just a vacation for us. Your sister and I have been having sexual relations for many years already."

"Ew," I say, scrunching up my nose.

"It's not ew," he says haughtily. "It's a very natural expression of the human body."

"And here we thought Lacey would remain a good girl until her wedding," my father says in such a way that I can't tell if he's joking or not.

All I know is that I am out of here.

"I'm going to go talk to mom," I tell them and quickly hurry across the lawn to the BBQ where my mother is standing with a couple her age. Couples, couples, everywhere.

My mother introduces me to Tai's parents, Sebastian and Keri Wakefield. His father is just as tall and tanned and handsome as his son, his hair grey at the temples with a peppering of a mustache. It's like looking into Tai's future, and I like what I see.

His mother is a lot shorter, brown skin, black hair, very pretty in an old-fashioned way, like nobility. The way she carries herself reminds me of a queen. And while his father is more quiet and stoic, a lot like his son, his mother is talkative and warm. I like her immediately.

"So you're the one that Tai went to pick up," his mother says to me.

"Guilty as charged," I tell her.

"I bet he was about as agreeable as a bag of cats," she says with a cheeky smile.

I can't help laugh. "That's a rather fitting analogy. But seriously, I'm so grateful he was able to give me the ride. I've been having a bit of bad luck lately, so it helped."

I don't mention that the ride itself felt like a continuation of that bad luck, at least it did at the time.

The funny thing is, even though that drive was hell of sorts, I felt way more comfortable with Tai in that truck than I do talking to most of the people here, and that includes my own sister. Tai's a grump but there's at least something real about him. He judges me, but he at least tells me he's judging me.

Don't get carried away now, I remind myself. *He's a dick and he'll make this trip miserable if you let him.*

Lord knows why there's a part of me that wants to let him.

DAISY

As far as weddings go, I have to say my sister's was pretty much perfect.

Granted, we've only just made it through the ceremony, but I wasn't sure what to expect. Weddings are always slightly chaotic, a drunken mix of bad blood and buried feelings, different friends and families mixing together, creating this soup of heightened emotions.

I thought my own emotions were going to run away on me, especially when my father walked Lacey down the sandy aisle, the music swelling to a crescendo.

She looked gorgeous, in a simple white strapless gown, no frills or gimmicks, but her glasses were off and her hair was pulled back into a chignon. She was smiling so broadly at Richard that I really felt the love between them. Obviously they do love each other, but they're such odd personalities, and Lacey is so rarely affectionate, that seeing them practically gush at each other was affirming.

And then of course there was my father, who looked so proud that my own heart sank a little. As completely and utterly selfish as it sounds, *I* wanted to be the one that made him look so happy. That look of pride doesn't come easily from him.

It's not like I never thought about getting married. As I said, with Chris it did cross my mind a few times. I wasn't exactly excited about the idea, but I figured if I had to settle down, then I guess it was best I do it with him.

But that's all over now, so there's no use entertaining it.

The last few days leading up to the wedding have actually been pretty good, as if making up for the rough start. I spent most of my time on the beach, sipping wine and slathering on SPF 50. Sometimes Lacey would ask me for some wedding advice, usually with regards to aesthetics, which I appreciated, other times I would be just hanging out with my parents and the Wakefields, which was time well spent.

I also met some of Tai's friends, who were a hell of a lot more down to earth than Lacey and Richard's friends. Tai has been behaving, too. Maybe a little too well.

In fact, I don't think I even saw him up close until it was time for us to walk down the aisle together as best man and maid-of-honor. His gaze rested on my breasts for just a moment (it's a low-cut halter, Lacey said I could choose whatever dress I wanted so as long as it was lilac, and I chose the one that played up my assets), then gave me the kind of smirk I wanted to wipe off his face. I hate guys that smirk. I hate the word *smirk*.

"Trying to steal the attention from your sister?" he had asked glibly as he took my arm, and before I had a chance to even reply to that, we were going down the aisle.

"Not my fault I like to look my best," I told him out of the side of my mouth, smiling broadly for all the guests who were craning their necks in their seats, impatiently waiting for the bride. The wedding was set-up on the beach with seashells and vases of ferns lining the aisle, white chairs sinking into the sand.

"I'm not complaining," he said. "If you're always the bridesmaid and never the bride, you might as well live that up."

It took everything in me not to jab him with my pointy gel nails. It would have been worth losing one of them. I don't care that he was kind of right.

Anyway, once we were up at the altar, everything went smoothly. The vows, as dorky as they were, were touching, and everyone hollered and cheered when Richard went to kiss the bride.

I might have even shed a tear.

"Daisy," the wedding photographer, Mara, says to me. "We need you."

I'm currently sitting on a piece of driftwood on the beach, drinking a glass of rose champagne, feeling a buzz and gathering my thoughts. Down by the water, Mara was shooting endless pictures of Richard and Lacey, though I knew I'd be called in for some shots soon, so I didn't stray too far.

"We need the best man too," Mara says, scanning the guests who have filled the beach and the Wakefield's yard, standing around in their evening best and drinking.

And there is Tai, talking to one of his friends, oblivious.

"I'll go get him," I tell her, and head across the beach.

When I get to Tai, both he and his friend—I think his name is Cam—stop talking and look me over. Tai's expression doesn't change and he manages to keep his eyes off my chest, staring at a point just past me, while Cam full-on ogles.

Lord, I hope I don't look like that when I'm looking at Tai.

"So this must be the babe," Cam says, elbowing Tai in the side.

Tai grunts, avoids my eyes.

"Babe?" I repeat.

"Don't think I haven't been asking about you," Cam goes on, clearly drunk. "I said, oy, mate, who is the American ranga? Introduce me to her. And you know what? This fucker wouldn't do it."

"What's a ranga?"

"It means redhead here," Tai says warily. "Though I prefer Gingersnap."

"And so the real question on all our minds," Cam says, leering at me, "is..."

Oh boy.

Here it comes.

"...does the carpet match the drapes?"

I roll my eyes just as Tai winds up and smacks Cam across the back of his head, so hard that Cam's drink flies out of his hands, narrowly missing me.

"Get some fucking manners, you cockweasel," Tai roars at him.

"For fuck's sake, Tai," Cam says, holding the back of his head. "I'm not a punching bag."

"You are when you start talking like a prick. Now fuck off and think about what you've done."

Cam stares at him, bewildered, as Tai makes the motion for Cam to run along.

To my surprise, Cam does so, with his tail between his legs.

Then Tai makes a huffing sound and starts marching off toward the beach.

As usual, I run after him.

"You didn't have to hit him so hard," I tell him. "I can handle myself. I'm used to it."

"I didn't hit him that hard," he says, glancing at me quickly. "Believe me, I was holding back. And that's pretty fucking sad that you're used to that."

"It's just a stupid question," I tell him. I'm playing it off like it's no big deal, when actually the question always made my skin crawl. It's pretty disgusting, if I'm being honest with myself.

And if I'm being honest with myself, there was something very thrilling in a primal way to see Tai react like that. It was like he was in full-on protective caveman mode, and I didn't mind one bit.

Tai growls in disapproval. "Well then, perhaps I should have introduced the two of you when he asked."

Hmmm. I see. Back to acting like he doesn't give a shit. Or maybe the protective part was the acting.

"No, thank you," I tell him.

"How are you holding up, anyway?"

"How am I holding up? Why? I'm fine."

He shrugs but there's more to it.

"There you are," Mara says as she walks over to us. "I thought maybe I would take a couple of pics of the two of you together before we do the entire wedding party. You're such an attractive couple."

Both Tai and I laugh in unison.

Awkward.

She gets us to stand where we are and link our arms together, posing with the reception in the background, our drinks raised. We do a few of these types of photos before she calls over the bride and groom and the rest of the wedding party.

Tai and I unlink arms and I turn to him. We're still in

such close proximity that I'm practically right up against him and he's not moving back. He's built like a cedar, roots in deep.

I glance up at him, brushing a loose strand of hair out of my face. "What did you mean, how am I holding up?"

A dark brow raises. "Does it matter? You said you were fine." His voice is low, in a murmur, and we're so close I can smell his breath. Whisky and mint.

"And why wouldn't I be fine?"

"You're awfully defensive, Gingersnap," he says, eyeing me for a moment before looking away.

"Don't call me that. And I'm not defensive."

His lips twitch. "I just know you've been having a go lately, with your ex-boyfriend and all. Thought maybe you weren't handling the wedding very well. The celebration of love, everyone coupled up, etcetera, etcetera."

Don't act defensive, don't act defensive.

I have to repeat this in my head because the first thing I want to do is lash out.

I paste a smile on my face and look at him calmly. "Who said I don't love being single? After all, I'm the one who broke up with him. And you're single too, aren't you? How come weddings are only supposed to be hell for single girls and not for single guys?"

Something dark comes over his gaze, and for a moment there I'm afraid that he actually isn't single. I mean, he could totally have a girlfriend...one that's away and couldn't be here.

"You have a fair point," he says after a moment.

Then he walks off toward Richard and Lacey.

Meanwhile, I try to brush off what he said, but I can't.

I need a drink.

FOR THE SECOND time in a handful of days, I've woken up massively hungover.

Thankfully, it's not as bad as the other time.

Least I don't think.

Let's see.

I slowly sit up in bed—Tai's bed—and try to assess the damage.

My head aches.

My mouth tastes sour.

There's a mysterious bruise on my arm.

I'm wearing my nightshirt backwards.

The light coming in through the windows tells me I've slept in, which I must have needed.

I close my eyes, and try to remember the last thing that happened. I don't even think I remember going to bed.

Oh.

Oh wait.

There's a fragment of a memory, grainy, like an old photograph.

Someone carried me up the stairs.

And gently placed me in bed.

I remember the gentle part the most, just the feeling of it, because it reminded me of my father when he'd pick me up from when I fell asleep in the car and take me to my bedroom. I was always in a half-awake, half-asleep state. Comforted and cradled.

Ugh. Did my dad have to do that last night because I was so drunk?

I can feel my cheeks flushing with embarrassment. Shit.

So much for trying to make my dad proud of me. Hi, I'm Daisy, I'm twenty-eight years old and my dad has to put me to bed.

I exhale slowly and pick up my phone from the bedside table. It's noon and there's a text from Laura, one of my friends back home, wondering how the wedding was. But other than that, no one has asked if I'm okay or has tried to wake me up, which makes me feel even more uneasy.

How much of a wreck was I?

I open my phone and go straight to the photos because I'm the type of girl who brings her phone out when she's drunk and tries to take selfies with everyone.

And there I am, in drunken Daisy mode, just as I thought.

I'm in a selfie with Lacey, whose one eye is half-closed, a sign that she's drunk too. We look happy though, which is nice. Like real sisters should.

Then I'm posing with Richard, who has somehow slicked his hair off his forehead and is wrinkling his brow like a wannabe De Niro. It's creepy.

I'm also in a photo with my parents, with Eaton, with Jana, with Eaton and Jana together, all of us drinking wine at once, then I'm with Tai's parents, then I'm with some of Tai's friends, then I'm with someone's grandmother doing a funky dance, then I'm back with Richard and Lacey yelling happily about something. I'm getting progressively drunker and sloppier in each photo, but then again, so is everyone else.

Then I come across a photo I hoped I wouldn't see.

A photo of Tai.

I've taken a picture of him from the side. He's got a drink in hand, the bow tie on his tux has been loosened and the collar unbuttoned, showing a nice slice of dark skin. He's laughing at something someone has said off-camera and his expression takes my breath away. There's something so loose and freeing and...happy about him here. For a moment I wonder what it would be like to be the one that makes him laugh like that.

I pause on that picture for a long time, studying it.

Then I flip to the next one.

In this picture Tai is looking at me and, naturally, his expression has totally changed. He's frowning, lips pressed together as if he must not ever smile. The Great Extreme Grump. Guess I really must do that to him.

I sigh and scroll to the next one on the roll.

It's a blurry selfie of the two of us.

My arm is around his neck, holding him down to my height.

He's looking deep into the camera, frowning to the extreme.

My mouth is open, smiling, all teeth, loving this.

The next photo my arm around his neck is even tighter and I'm pressing my thumb between his brow as if to stop him from frowning. In this photo, his eyes are dancing and it looks like he's trying not to smile.

Then there's the next photo, where I've pulled him right to me, like literally right on top of my boobs, and he's laughing and I'm kissing the top of his head.

Oh my god.

This photo.

Not only did I get him to laugh, I'm actually kissing him, with his head on my boobs. Granted it looked to be in a non-intimate kind of way considering there are people in the background of this photo. But *still*.

Then there's the next photo, which is a selfie of just me,

making a dramatic sad face, my hair all messy, my lipstick smeared.

Oh wait, I can see Tai in the background, walking away.

That was the last photo.

Thank god.

I put the phone back down, feeling that guilty, shameful and anxious mix of feelings that you get the day after you've had too much to drink and have made a fool of yourself, but can't quite remember. I just hope that the photos were the worst of it and I didn't do anything stupid.

I sigh loudly and decide I can't hide in my room any longer.

I get dressed into a simple white sundress and then head over to the bathroom across the hall to do my business and apply a little bit of makeup. I don't hear anything in the house, which is strange. Perhaps they all went somewhere and left me here.

Oh, I know what it is. They probably took Lacey and Richard to the marina to see them off. Shit, I would have liked to have at least said goodbye.

After I've done my best to cover up the hangover on my face, I step back into the hall. I poke my head into my parent's room and see all their luggage. The door to the Wakefield's bedroom is open and when I call out, no one answers. There's one more room that has always been shut and I'm tempted to open it, but instead I look inside Lacey and Richard's.

To my puzzlement, all their luggage is still here. In fact, one duffel bag is on the bed, half-packed.

That's weird.

I head downstairs, still finding no one, and then finally head out the back.

Sitting at the patio table in the backyard are Lacey and

Richard, with Tai leaning against the house, a beer in hand. There's a laptop open in front of them, and everyone's phones are out.

"Hey," I say to them. "I thought you left without saying goodbye."

Lacey looks up at me, tears running down her face.

Oh shit.

"Oh my god, what happened?" I ask her, quickly coming over. My heart jolts in my chest, thinking the worst. "Are mom and dad okay?"

"Your parents are in town getting provisions," Richard says calmly. "We've had some unexpected bad news."

Then both Richard and Lacey look at Tai.

He gives them a chagrined smile. "I'm telling you, we can work this out."

"So, what happened?" I ask, pulling out a chair and sitting down. I have to remember that Lacey does cry over the slightest thing. She has two moods: resting bitch face, and crying.

"Intrepid, the boat that they were supposed to charter," Tai explains with a long sigh, "has a problem. A big problem. The last people who chartered the boat put in bad fuel. Meaning, water got in the tank. And I wasn't here to check on them, so now the boat is fucked and draining the tanks is going to take a few days, at the least. Might even need to bring it out of the water."

"My honeymoon is ruined," Lacey wails, throwing her head back and sniffling into a tissue.

"It's not ruined, angel boo," Richard says, and I cringe inwardly at the nickname. "We're still going to go sailing."

"Isn't there, like, a shitload of other boats you can charter?" I ask. "I mean, what about all these boats." With a bold sweep of my arm I gesture to the bay, which has at least a dozen of them at anchor. "They're everywhere. And they aren't being used."

"Those are private boats and they're out of the question," Tai says. "Unless you feel like being arrested for theft. As for chartering, it's peak season right now, all over the country. Everyone is trying to get their last trip in before autumn comes. Some are available later in the week but…"

"But we need to leave today or tomorrow in order to make it to Fiji, and then fly back to Dunedin in time for work," Richard explains. "It's just not feasible otherwise."

"Well, shit," I say, crossing my arms.

"But there's a solution," Richard adds, eyeing his new bride. "Lacey isn't too sold on this particular proposition."

"What is it?"

"*I* still have a boat," Tai informs me. "My boat. I'm talking my pride and joy. I don't charter her out. She's just for me."

Richard nods solemnly, then gives me a smile. "Tai has graciously offered to captain the ship to Fiji for us."

"Oh," I say. "Well, that's great."

"He doesn't trust me with it," Richard adds under his breath.

"You're right, I don't," Tai says.

I give Tai an impressed look. "Well, that's awfully generous of you to do that for them. I can't imagine this will be easy."

"You're right. It won't be easy," he says. "But it's something I've always wanted to do, and they can consider this an extra wedding present."

"You mean you haven't sailed to Fiji before?" Richard asks, his voice going to a higher frequency.

Tai has an easy sip of his beer and gives him a dismissive wave. "Relax. It's a piece of cake."

"Fine," Lacey suddenly says, tossing a rumpled Kleenex into the middle of the table. "Fine, we'll go on Tai's boat." Then her eyes meet mine and there's some sort of look in them that I don't like. "But only if Daisy comes with us."

I blink at her. "Sorry, what?"

Meanwhile Tai and Richard both break out into laughter, Richard doing that annoying slapping his knee thing. Who does that?

"Your sister? On a boat?" Richard can hardly breathe.

"Yeah, so what?" Lacey asks.

I mean, Richard has a point, but even so.

"Lacey," I say carefully. "I don't think that's a good idea."

And I'm absolutely shocked that she'd actually invite me. Since when has she wanted to do any kind of bonding? Maybe getting married is making her turn a new leaf, maybe...

Then I recognize that look in her eyes.

This isn't about bonding.

This is a challenge.

"Oh, please," Lacey says, reaching across the table and putting her hand on mine. "It would be so good for us to finally get to spend some quality time together. You and me, sister to sister."

She's really laying it on thick.

"Besides," she adds. "With Tai, that's an uneven number. I hate uneven numbers. With you it would be four."

"I don't know..." I say. There's a part of me that is actually considering the idea, just because I'm secretly afraid to go back home to my life of nothing.

There's another part of me that feels like I'm stepping into a trap.

And there's another part that wants to prove that I can do this.

"She won't last a day," Tai says with a dry chuckle.

I glare at him, hackles rising. "Excuse me?"

Tai gives me a wicked grin. Stupid sexy smile.

"You yourself admitted to me that drinking cocktails at the dock is your kind of sailing. You won't last a day."

"I suppose you're right," Lacey says with a sigh.

"Wait, what?" I protest. "Just because I like some cocktails—"

"Last night you definitely proved that," Tai mutters.

I feel my cheeks flame as I try to ignore that. "It doesn't mean that I'm not up for a little adventure. Don't you remember me as a kid, Lacey? I wanted to be a marine biologist. I wanted to be one so badly that I used to steal rides on the fishing boats out of Newport. I volunteered at the Newport Aquarium every summer. I was obsessed. The ocean never scared me, it fascinated me."

"Every girl wants to be a marine biologist as a child," Richard comments.

Lacey nods. "And one day you just decided to give up on that idea and move onto something less hard."

"Okay, whoa. Things are getting a little personal now," I tell her.

"Look," Tai says, coming over to us, raising his hands for a moment. "If Daisy really thinks she can handle it, I say the more the merrier."

I give him a look. *Oh do you now?*

"Where are you going to sleep?" Richard asks him. "There are only two cabins."

"Two cabins?" I repeat. "How small is this boat?"

Tai glowers at me. "It's not small. It's a forty-two-foot Tayana." He looks to Richard. "And I'll sleep on the couch. I've had naps on it before, it's comfortable enough."

"Enough for a ten day voyage?" Lacey asks. "Maybe

Daisy should have the couch since we're going to need the captain operating at his best."

Everyone is looking at me.

I shrug. "Fine, I'll take the couch. Whatever."

"You will not take the couch," Tai tells me.

"So does this actually mean you're coming?" Lacey asks.

"What about your flight home?" questions Richard.

"I guess I'll look into changing it."

"Air New Zealand does flights out of Fiji," says Tai. "You'll probably be able to fly straight home from there."

"Good," I say. "Then it's settled." I look at everyone. "Isn't it?"

They all exchange glances, brows raised, and at that moment I can tell that I was never meant to come, that I wasn't part of the plan.

But none of this was part of the plan, was it?

And I'm up for the challenge.

I'm not backing down.

"It's settled then," Lacey says, exhaling loudly. "The honeymoon is still on. Four's company."

Tai puts his beer down on the table. "Well if that's that, I'm going to head down to the boat and start prepping it. If we leave tomorrow, there's a bloody lot of things I need to get done."

He goes back into the house and I get out of my chair, following him inside.

"Hey," I call out as I walk over and see him grabbing a glass of water in the kitchen. "Is this going to be okay?"

He frowns at me. "What do you mean?"

"I mean…a last-minute voyage across the Pacific," I say. "Don't you have to spend months planning this?"

He shrugs. "As long as you have all the best equipment and the right food and a steadfast boat in capable hands, no.

Not for a ten-day passage." He gulps down the glass of water, then studies me. "I wouldn't go if I couldn't handle it. And to be honest, in a way I'm glad this happened. I'm sure Richard and Lacey would have been fine on their own on the other boat but...sometimes that passage can get pretty gnarly. Would hate for a storm to have caught them when Richard doesn't have the experience."

"What do you mean it gets gnarly? A storm?"

"It's just an infamous passage," he says, as if infamous is a good thing. "But this is a fair time of year to go. We'll be fine."

He puts the glass down and takes a few sauntering steps over to me. "At least, *we'll* be fine. I'm not too sure about you."

"What does that mean?"

"Right now you look a little ill."

"I'm hungover."

"Oh. *I know.*"

"I'm sure we're all hungover."

"It was a good party. I just hope you won't be falling overboard any time soon. I don't want to be the person to fish you out of the ocean and put you to bed, like a repeat of last night."

"I fell in the ocean?" I ask, horrified.

You put me to bed?

The corner of his mouth ticks up. "No, but you did want to go skinny dipping really badly. I had to fight to keep my clothes on."

"*What?*"

Suddenly a few images filter through my brain like dust.

Oh my god. I don't think he's joking. I remember my hands on his shirt, trying to undo his buttons, him laughing and prying my hands off of him.

"Shit," I swear, pressing my hand into my forehead.

I'm blushing. Tomato Zone Three, all hands on deck.

"Hey, nothing to be embarrassed about," he says, but there's a mocking tone to his voice.

Oh, lord.

"I know you've been having a rough time," he goes on. "That Chris guy sounded like a real wanker."

"Oh my god, I was talking about Chris?"

"More like you were crying about Chris. Then you did some shots and passed out and I carried you to bed."

I feel like I'm going to faint.

"Don't worry, I was the perfect gentleman."

"My shirt was on backwards!"

"I handed you the shirt and left the room. I don't know what you did with it." He walks past me to the front door, nodding his chin at the couch. "I slept there last night, and don't worry, I'll sleep on the couch on the boat, too. I have my manners."

He opens the door and steps out. "You better go and start packing," he calls out as he walks to his truck. I'm trying not to stare at his ass. "The south seas await."

Fuck.

What the hell have I got myself into?

6

———

DAISY

This was a big mistake.

I'm standing on Tai's private dock, surrounded by Lacey, Richard, and mounds of bags, luggage, supplies and food, staring at the boat we're supposed to do an ocean passage in, the Atarangi.

It's *small.*

I know Tai said it was forty-two feet or something but for some reason it looks a lot smaller *and* older than I had imagined. My ex-boyfriend's yacht had to have been at least twice the size, and new. Then again, it belonged to his money-bags father who made a fortune in Apple stock.

"How quaint," my mother comments from behind me. "It's...vintage."

We have a small crowd sending us off this early morning. There're my parents, Richard's mom Edith (a carbon copy of him down to the glasses), and the Wakefields are here too, which surprises me considering this is something that Tai must do quite often.

"Don't be fooled by her age," Tai shouts at my mother

from the cockpit. "She's perfect for blue water sailing. You don't get many ocean-worthy boats like this these days."

Well, that's a little reassuring.

And at least it's a calm, clear morning, no red sky in sight (or however that sailor's proverb goes). It's just after dawn and the sun is slowly rising up over Tai's place behind us, a small three-room house that he's referred to a few times as a *bach* from the 50's, whatever that means. All I know is that it's just as retro chic as the boat, and has a stunning location on a private bay, surrounded by deep brush.

We woke up this morning when it was still dark out and I got a ride in the Wakefield's car with Edith, while my parents took the newlyweds. I managed to get my new flight sorted out last night, with only a minor change fee.

Of course, my travel gear was never meant to go anywhere other than the trunk of a car or the belly of an airplane.

And Tai has decided this morning's scorn isn't devoted to the fact that there are four people's worth of supplies to haul aboard, but is instead focused on my two shiny suitcases.

"Well, shit," he grumbles, giving me a dirty look. "You couldn't have given one of those suitcases to your parents to bring back for you?"

"I need my stuff!" I protest, already feeling vulnerable.

"We offered," my father says, hands raised in a mea culpa.

It's true. My parents offered to take the big suitcase back to the US, and I'm sure it would have been smart of me to send it off with them. But there's stuff in there I need, like snacks I brought from home, bottles of wine, New Zealand kiwi chocolate (*so* good), and clothes of all sorts. I mean, who knows what kind of weather we'll have out there.

Lacey does one of her patented eye rolls. "Great. Now the boat will probably sink from the extra weight."

I glare back at her. "Doesn't matter. The suitcases are waterproof. My stuff will stay dry even if we do sink."

"Ah, perhaps this isn't the best talk before we say goodbye," Mrs. Wakefield says nervously.

I turn and give her a quick smile. "Sorry. I'm sure we'll be fine. We're in your son's capable hands."

The last part wasn't sarcastic, but even so, I can hear Tai scoff.

And so the goodbyes commence.

I have to admit, I'm tearing up as I say goodbye to my parents. It's not that I don't think I'll see them again, of course I will, but I haven't had this much quality time with them since...well, ever. Even when I've come home for Christmas and Easter, it feels like a formality. Like something I'm supposed to do, and I've always gotten the impression that they've felt the same way. Like God is ordering them to have me over, rather than me being someone they want to see.

And these last few days have been about getting to know these new versions of my parents, as an adult, the versions that they become when they aren't at home, surrounded by a million damn apples.

Then it's time for us to set sail.

The cockpit is rather small but there's enough space for all of us, with Tai behind the wheel. The lines are tossed, Richard running around and putting them all in their proper places, and the motor is turned on to a hearty purr, and then we're pulling away from the dock.

The small crowd of our loved ones on the dock wave at us and we wave back as the boat makes its way out of the small bay and into the harbor.

It's bittersweet and exciting all at the same time. There's something so invigorating about being on the water in the early morning hours, the breeze in your hair, setting sail for a far-off land.

"Should I do anything?" I ask no one in particular as the boat sloshes through the water.

"Stay out of the way," Tai says.

I put my hand on my hip and give him a look.

Okay, so there's no denying that this view of him is making my ovaries explode. I never knew I could be attracted to sailors, especially since they tend to be preppy types.

But Tai is the opposite of preppy. He's more pirate than anything.

Sure, he's in worn jeans and a grey t-shirt with a grease stain on it, what seems to be his standard uniform, and he's got a ball cap on and a pair of aviator sunglasses hooked on the collar of his shirt. But it's the way his big, roughed-up hands handle the steering wheel, the commanding stance he's taking, the way his eyes are raking over the water in front of us, all of it equals some new level of kink I never knew was in me. First it was him eating an apple, now it's him being a big boss pirate daddy commandeering a ship.

Then his eyes meet mine and I expect to see a hint of a smile in them.

I smile, anyway.

He doesn't smile back.

"I meant what I said," he says, his voice on edge. "Just stay out of the way."

I blink. Wow.

He's a mean pirate.

I narrow my eyes at him for a moment before tossing my hair over my shoulder and turning around.

I'm immediately reminded of how small this boat is and that Lacey and Richard both heard what he just told me.

"Why don't you go downstairs and try to put your suitcases out of the way?" Lacey suggests, another attempt to get me pushed aside.

"But don't put them in either fore or aft cabin," Tai says, then pauses. "That means front and back."

"I know what they mean," I snipe at him. "I'm not an idiot."

I'm just waiting for one of them to laugh at that, but to their credit, they don't. It's way too early to be starting off on the wrong foot.

And to think, you have ten more days of this.

Shit.

"Come on," Lacey says. She goes to the hatch and pushes it back, walking backward down the stairs and into the belly of the beast.

I follow.

And I'm impressed.

Somehow the boat doesn't seem as small down below. While up top felt a little cramped, I guess how the cockpit is set up a little forward on the boat, down here it feels more open, and everything is made of this gorgeous teak wood. This boat should be in a museum.

"Wow, this is nice," I say. Maybe this won't be so bad after all.

There's a kitchen, or galley as they say, to the right of me, a navigation table and seat to the left. In front of me there's the lounge area with two small couches and a table, and beyond that there's a glimpse of the cabin at the front. There are Maori masks with *pāua* shell eyes on the walls, along with a few of Tai's personal touches that give it this lived-in feel.

It's very Instagrammable.

So, of course I pull out my phone and start taking pictures. Maybe if I don't get back into the athleisure line life, I can start marketing boats.

"There's a cabin back there," Lacey says, gesturing behind us. "The owner's suite, as they call it. But it's ours for the journey."

"Fine with me, I get my own cabin," I say, walking to the one at the very front and poking my head in. It has its own door, a small closet, *and* own washroom. Score!

"Did Tai explain the shifts to you?" Lacey asks, watching as I haul my suitcases up onto the couch and start unzipping them.

"The shifts?" I ask as I rummage through my stuff. There's not enough room in the closet for everything, so what I'll do is put all the stuff I don't need in the small carry-on, empty the bigger suitcase, and then put the carry-on inside it. I'm already proud of myself for the space-saving idea.

"I take it he didn't," Lacey says begrudgingly. "So for an ocean crossing, there must be at least one person on deck the entire time to make sure everything is fine and that we aren't going to collide with any shipping containers that might not show up on the radar."

I stop what I'm doing and look at her with wide eyes. "That happens?"

"Haven't you seen that movie with Robert Redford? Yes, it happens. Hence why we all must take shifts. And since there are four of us, we'll do it two people at a time. Which means Richard and I will be on our own shift during the night and then you and Tai will be on another."

"Wait a minute. Why do I have to be with Tai?"

"Well, each shift has to have someone that knows what they're doing."

"I think I'd rather be with Richard."

She adjusts her glasses. "Uh huh. Remember, this is our honeymoon."

"I haven't forgotten."

"Listen, Tai is fine...just...don't annoy him."

I laugh. "You think I annoy him on purpose?"

"Maybe," she says thoughtfully. "I think your personality in general is an anathema to him."

I flinch. "What's wrong with my personality?"

Now it's time for Lacey to laugh, albeit dryly. "If you haven't noticed, Tai is one of those people who takes things seriously. As he should. He's been through a lot in his life, he doesn't have time for people who seem to coast by."

There are two things there catching my attention.

"He's been through a lot? What happened?"

"It doesn't matter and it's none of your business," she says.

Okay...

"And also, I don't coast by," I tell her.

She stares at me for a loaded moment, as if weighing what to say. "Yes, you do. You always have. You're doing it right now."

I throw my arms out. "How is this coasting by?"

"Well, you're on a free trip to Fiji, for one, jumping aboard your own sister's honeymoon."

"You invited me!"

"And I didn't think you'd come!"

Oh my god. So the truth is out.

"Well fucking hell!" I swear. "Let's turn this damn boat around and take me back then!"

I don't care that I sound like a petulant child, I march right up the stairs to the cockpit.

"Turn this boat around, I'm going back!" I yell at Tai.

He barely acknowledges me.

"Did you hear me? I'm not wanted, and I'm not spending the next ten days on this boat, ruining someone's honeymoon."

"I heard you," Tai says calmly, his eyes on the horizon.

"I also heard you," Richard says, walking down the length of the boat. "I regret to inform you that there's no privacy on this vessel."

Agh, he pronounces it *priv*-acy.

"And we're not turning around," Tai says. "You committed to this trip, now you're in it. There's no going back."

"She doesn't know the meaning of the word commit," Lacey speaks up.

I'm having a hard time forming words against her relentless attack, she's like a piranha with glasses. "What on earth are you talking about? I was committed to Chris!"

"Like you were to every other boyfriend you had before that you so easily discarded?"

Whoa, whoa, whoa. Why is she even going there?

"I'm allowed to break up with people, you know," I say. I almost tell her that it's better than settling for the first guy that ever paid her any attention, AKA Little Dicky, but I know that would open a portal to Hell that I am not prepared to deal with.

"Because you can't commit. And had Chris not cheated on you, I'm sure you would have kicked him to the curb eventually. It's just that for once in your blessed life you have a little bit of bad luck."

I am seething. I angrily gesture to the boat. "And you're happy about that, aren't you? The fact that I lost my boyfriend and my job. Well guess what, my bad luck streak isn't over. I'm on this boat with all of you guys and apparently I'm not going anywhere."

"And the irony is that we're all stuck with each other for the foreseeable future," Richard says, laughing his stupid dorky laugh.

That's not irony, that's the damn point, I think.

Richard clears his throat and looks to his angry new wife. "But I think if we're all going to survive this, Lacey, you'll need to start being more courteous to your sister. She means well, despite the way she comes off."

"Thanks," I tell him dryly. Real compliment there.

Lacey just huffs, arms crossed. She can barely look at me. Finally she says, "Sorry."

"There we go," Richard says. "All is well."

Yeah right. We haven't even made it out of the Bay of Islands and we're all ready to kill each other.

Or at least, everyone is ready to kill me and vice versa. This trip is going to turn into an unfair battle of three against one, three fucking serious grumps, versus me, the only normal person.

Thankfully, the early morning argument didn't set the tone for the rest of the day. It actually passed by in a fairly peaceful way, probably because I put in some extra effort to keep my mouth shut and stay out of everyone's way. Believe it or not, conflict isn't my forte and the boat isn't big enough to handle all my anxiety over it either.

We also come up with a routine of sorts for the next ten days, something that Tai says is extremely important when you're trapped on a boat and time seems to work differently.

At night, Lacey and Richard will take the ten to three a.m. shift, then Tai and I will wake up and take the three a.m. to eight a.m. shift.

At 10 a.m., I will make breakfast (the only meal I'm good at).

At 1 p.m., Richard is in charge of lunch

At 6 p.m., Tai will make dinner.

At any time during the day Lacey will make bread or cookies, since she's got the same level of cooking skills as I do and can only bake stuff. But Tai does say making bread on a boat is a popular thing to do during a long voyage, and that it's something we'll all look forward to.

Then, at sunset, we'll all sit up top and have a couple of cocktails (heavy drinking is banned since we're all on watch and I guess falling overboard is a real thing...Tai looked at me when he said that).

Meanwhile I've started a tradition of my own. After I put all my stuff away (well, almost, the big suitcase does take up a whole loveseat), I took out one of my blank notebooks I bought in the San Francisco airport. It has this really gorgeous cover, textured floral patterns over metallic pink. I decided to turn it into a log of sorts.

Currently, I'm sitting in the cockpit, facing away from Richard who is at the wheel, while Tai is making dinner downstairs. The journal is in my hand, as is a new pen that has the Golden Gate Bridge, a little reminder of home. Land disappeared from sight a few hours ago and Richard says we've traveled about a hundred nautical miles. The sun is low in the sky and bright gold and there's nothing but ocean around us.

I begin to write.

· · ·

Daisy's Log: Day 1

I AM WRITING this journal in hopes of having some sort of respite from what is sure to be a tumultuous voyage across the sea.

Okay, I don't know why I'm writing this like it's 1881 and is actually going to be read by someone, lol.

Anyway, I've never been good at keeping a diary but I hope I do this time since I'll probably need someone to talk to that isn't one of the three grumps on board.

I suppose Richard, AKA Little Dicky, isn't a grump like Tai, nor is he super serious like Lacey. But he is a dork and he's in cahoots with the two of them, so he's not to be trusted.

He's watching me right now as I write this, staring down at me through thick glasses. He's a hybrid of Bill Gates, Milhouse VanHouten, with a bit of Ross Gellar thrown in. Don't believe me? I asked a question about kiwi fruit and I got an hour-long lecture about pollinating, bees, and manuka honey.

Richard aside, everyone else seems to have calmed down from this morning. That was pretty intense. I really hoped that Tai would have sailed me back to the dock and dropped me off, but no such luck. We're all in this together, which I guess is another term for making each other miserable.

But yes, Lacey has been nicer and even Tai has loosened a little. I can hear music playing down below, some reggae group, and Lacey and Tai are talking animatedly about something interesting. I have to say, I'm looking forward to dinner, just to see what kind of meal Tai can prepare. And then of course there's cocktail hour, which we all desperately need. At least I do. I've needed a drink since I stepped on this boat.

Well, I guess that's it for now. I am a little curious (okay, a lot curious) about what Lacey said about Tai's past...how he's been through a lot. It could explain why he's such a prickly person....or *maybe that's just his personality. Either way, I would like to know more about him. I suppose with our shifts coming up, maybe I'll get that opportunity.*

Of course that doesn't mean I'll get any answers.

Over and out.

7

———

TAI

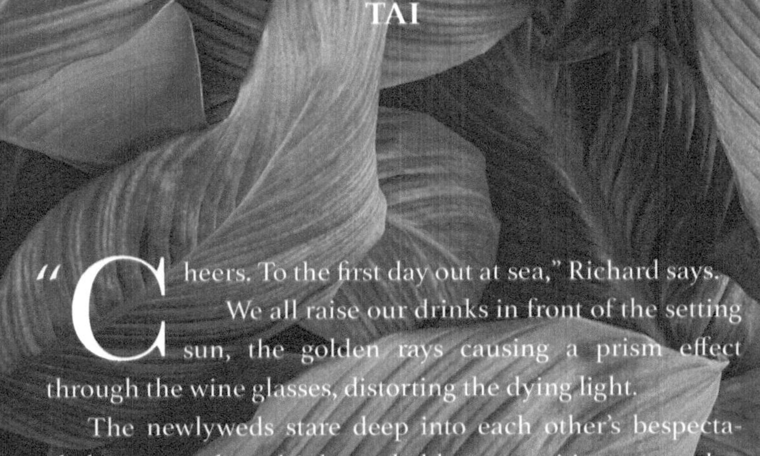

"Cheers. To the first day out at sea," Richard says. We all raise our drinks in front of the setting sun, the golden rays causing a prism effect through the wine glasses, distorting the dying light.

The newlyweds stare deep into each other's bespectacled eyes as they drink, probably superstitious over that whole seven years bad luck (or bad sex) thing.

I figure Daisy must be wanting to avoid that also, since she's had so much bad luck these days (not too sure about the bad sex, and I don't want to know), but she's avoiding my eyes, looking off into the sunset instead.

She looks astoundingly pretty, the red in her hair looking like fire in this light, dancing around her face in the ocean breeze.

There's a pinch in my chest as I drink my wine, watching her. I've been a little harsh on her. I guess we all have been, though Lacey's reasons I'm sure are different from mine.

Mine are pretty simple.

Daisy is a distraction.

She's not sailing material, she's drawn the ire of

everyone on the boat, she tends to get in the way no matter what she does, and she rarely shuts up. This ocean passage isn't as easy as I've made it out to seem, and I need to stay focused on getting us all to Fiji in one piece, if we all don't kill each other first.

Plus...look at her.

Right now I should be scanning the horizon for freighters, but instead I'm watching her. I'm always watching her when she's not looking. I like studying the real her, the one behind the bright smile, the one that pretends everything is fine.

Although, I have to say that's been hard for her to do lately. Lacey has been going after her whenever she can, and even though their sibling rivalry is none of my business, and I'm staying out of it, I do think she's being a little unfair to her.

Which, of course, makes me feel like a dick for being a dick.

Hey, I'm not heartless. Daisy may be a distraction, and she may live to annoy me, but I feel for her.

I just can't let myself feel for her too much. Been down that road before.

At least everyone seems to have calmed down. The drinks help, of course. Though I don't want to be a part of the whole social aspect of it, it's good for the rest of them to loosen up a little.

That's a tall order with Richard and Lacey though, and Daisy can take the loosening up thing a little too far.

Judge her all you want, but you loved the way she was falling all over you at the wedding.

I elbow that voice in my head to shut up.

For clarity's sake, there's truth in that.

When the wedding reception really got going, Daisy got

going as well. As in drunk. At least she was a happy drunk and was running around taking photos of everyone. I kept watching her, wondering if she'd eventually get around to taking a photo with me.

Had to say, I think I might have been jealous of the attention she was giving everyone else.

It was almost as if she smelled those jealousy fumes coming from my direction, because then she turned her attention to me and would not let up.

I pretended it bugged me. I'm good at that.

In reality, I liked it.

She wanted photo after photo and I obliged her. I liked the feeling of her arm around my neck, I liked watching her smile and laugh and blush, I *especially* liked the feel of my cheek against her breasts, as playful as it was. Her skin is on a whole other level—warm, silky and sinfully soft.

Then she asked me to dance.

It was a slow song, some sappy Ed Sheeran, and I said no.

I guess I could see where she was going with all of this and I got cold feet.

Can't really say why, just that it's been happening to me a lot lately when an opportunity with a woman comes up. Those roads I don't want to go down. Even when it's just for a night, they never end up being what I want them to be, they're always far more complicated than that.

She looked so sad and heartbroken for a moment, but she laughed it off.

I went back to the bar and watched her, thinking she'd turn her sights on someone else.

Instead she went to the dance floor and closed her eyes, swaying to the music by herself, lonesome among a sea of couples.

Don't know why that sight affected me so much, but it did.

I went back out there and took her into my arms before she could say anything.

I'm glad I did too, because she was toasted and leaning into me like deadweight.

So I held onto her, both because I needed to keep her up, and because I liked holding her. She was so soft and warm and tender that it moved something deep inside of me, and no, it wasn't my dick. Although I can't say I wasn't hard as hell. Thankfully, she was too drunk to notice. I don't even think she remembers any of this.

After the dance, I knew the right thing to do would be to get her to bed.

Daisy had other ideas though.

She had bolted from the dance floor in the backyard and run all the way down the beach to the water.

"Come skinny-dipping with me!" she cried out, trying to undo the tie at the back of her neck. I hate to admit that I was a complete pig and just stood there, watching her struggle, hoping that the top would fall loose and those gorgeous tits of hers would be on display.

But her breasts stayed covered and she gave up. Probably for the best. Not sure what I would have done if I was presented with them. I'm getting hard just thinking about them right now.

"Tai?" Richard asks, making me jump in my seat.

"What?" I say, clearing my throat, instinctively about to get to my feet and look at the bow, but my hard-on makes me stay put.

Richard watches me carefully, then glances over at Daisy who is sipping her wine and still staring at the waves, the sky a splash of purples and pinks. Gorgeous sunset, infuriatingly gorgeous girl.

He looks back to me, brow raised. "I was saying, I wonder about our VMG."

Right.

VMG is Velocity Made Good, a nautical measure of how fast you're going in the actual direction of your waypoint based on speed, distance to target, and a little trigonometry. Richard loves the trigonometry part.

"It's about 0.5 at the moment," I tell him, which isn't great. It doesn't particularly matter if you're rocketing at eight knots heading west if your destination is east. At the moment, the wind is trying to push us away from Fiji, which means just after dinner we had to do some course correcting. Hopefully the winds will switch when a new front comes in. And hopefully that front isn't too bad.

I limit myself to one glass of wine, even though what I really want is a highball of whisky, maybe with a squeeze of lime. I need to stay sharp, especially if I'm going to be waking up at 3 a.m.

With Daisy.

Yes, I'll need to be especially sharp for that.

THE ALARM GOES off at 2:45 a.m.

I can't remember the last time I had to get up at this hour, maybe when Holly and I sailed to Marlborough Sound.

The thought of my ex-wife makes my brain stutter. I'm relieved that I don't seem to have any complicated feelings along with that thought, after all it's been a few years since our divorce. It's just an odd feeling sometimes to have so many memories wrapped up with one person, a person that's no longer part of your life. It's unfair. If they don't exist in your life, they shouldn't exist in your memories.

But life isn't like that, is it?

I get out of bed before my thoughts get any darker. It doesn't help that I had the world's most uncomfortable sleep. Even with earplugs in, which I hate, it was hard not to listen to Lacey and Richard talking as they did their night shift. Plus the couch is awful to sleep on, too short for me, and my lower back is already sore.

No wonder I'm a fucking grump, I think as I head over to the stove to boil water for the coffee. *Complain, complain, complain.*

While the water is boiling, I stick my head up top.

"Good morning," I say to Richard and Lacey, who are in each other's arms. Lacey is asleep, snoring, Richard has one hand on the steering wheel, barely holding on.

"Oh thank god," Richard says softly. "I was afraid I couldn't hold out any longer. I never even stayed up this late at university."

That doesn't surprise me in the least.

"Go to sleep," I tell him. "You're officially being relieved."

I head back down while he wakes up Lacey, and go straight to Daisy's cabin.

I knock, but there's no answer.

I swear I saw her set an alarm on her phone. She probably should have used an actual alarm clock like the one I have. You can't trust phones in a dire situation.

"Daisy?" I call out.

I open the door and peer in at her.

The sidelight is on.

She's sleeping on her back, mouth open, drooling.

I have to stifle a laugh.

On her chest is her phone, rising and falling with each breath.

She's so not made for this.

"Daisy," I say louder, reaching over and shaking her shoulder until her phone slides off her.

"Huh, what?" she mumbles, rolling over until she sees me.

Then wipes the drool from her face.

"Shit. Sorry. What time is it?"

"Time to get up."

"I must have turned off my alarm," she says, looking embarrassed. She's cute when she goes red.

"It happens. Come on."

I wait until I see her reaching for a hoodie, making sure she doesn't fall back asleep. I could let her keep sleeping. I'm totally fine up there alone for the rest of the night.

But I want to put her through her paces. Just in case Lacey is right and Daisy is used to coasting by, I figure it can't hurt to put her to work.

While she's getting ready, I stop by the kitchen, fill up a thermos of coffee and grab some insulated mugs, then head up top. Lacey and Richard are no doubt fast asleep below in their cabin.

I get behind the wheel and put my head back, taking in the night sky.

Being on a boat at night is a view that will never fail to take your breath away. A velvet black sky so dense that you swear you can see just how deep the universe goes. The stars are embedded like white diamonds, some of them fully formed prisms, others just speckles and stardust, like someone threw a bunch of sparkling sugar up into the night sky and it stuck, swirling around in multicolored galaxies.

"Holy bejesus," Daisy says as she appears on deck, looking extra small in her hoodie. She's staring open-mouthed at the sky above. "Is this for real?"

I nod. "This is dark sky territory," I tell her. "No night pollution from anywhere. You'll never find as many stars anywhere as you do right here."

"Wow," she says, breathlessly. There's something about her wonder I find so refreshing, like she's looking at the stars for the first time.

"Guess you have a lot of fog in San Francisco," I comment.

"Yeah, but even on my parent's farm, the sky never looked anything like this."

I hold out the cup of coffee for her. "Here. This will help wake you up."

"I'm already wide awake," she says and then fixes her big blue eyes at me. Even in the dark they seem to glow. "But thank you."

She reaches for the mug and our fingers brush against each other.

It shouldn't mean anything. And it doesn't.

But it shouldn't be something that stands out either.

And it does.

The feel of her finger as it brushes against mine shouldn't take me back to being a child and holding hands with a crush for the first time. But it's more than that. There's a buzz, an electricity between our contact that can't be imaginary.

Get a grip, I tell myself. *Eyes on the horizon.*

"So this is the night watch," she says as she sits down to the left of the wheel, cradling the mug between her hands.

"Generally unexciting."

She gives me a look. "I should hope so. Dare I ask what an exciting episode would be like?"

"I guess it's something only I'd find interesting. If the winds were in our favor, we could really be skipping along here. Have you ever been on a boat like this, when you're going downwind, constant breeze, doing five knots at ease so you can just sit back and let it go?"

"Obviously not," she says, placing her mug between her knees and tucking her hair beneath the back of her hoodie. "But it sounds nice. This is nice."

"This is a challenge," I tell her. "The winds keep pushing us in the wrong direction. But in time, it should work out. Maybe add a day to our journey."

She stiffens at that.

"Don't worry," I tell her. "Not all days will be like today."

I'm kind of lying because it'll probably just get worse.

"I'm hoping for the best and expecting the worst," she says wryly, then sighs. "Which is kind of sad, because once upon a time I hoped for the best and expected the best."

I watch her carefully, the way she is worrying her lip between her teeth. "You know, I think that's how we all want to operate. You're lucky to have done so for so long."

She tilts her head back to look at the stars. "I've heard that all my life. That I was lucky. Now I'm not so sure I was."

"What makes you say that?"

She shrugs. "I don't know. It's not that things haven't been easy for me...I've worked hard, contrary to anything Lacey might say."

"Lacey can say all she wants, but she wasn't there and has never been in your shoes."

Her eyes focus on mine and an impish smile plays across her lips. "Are you sticking up for me?"

"I wouldn't go that far."

"So diplomatic," she muses. Then her expression darkens as she stares into her coffee. "Lacey thinks everything has been handed to me because she got the shit end of the stick when it came to my parents."

"What do you mean?"

"She's only three years older, but it feels more like ten years when you look at how my parents raised her versus how they raised me. They're religious, right? Not in a bad, cult-ish way. They've always been very supportive of us. But...with Lacey, they were very strict. I guess my mother struggled a bit before she finally got pregnant, and they were so fearful of losing her that they never let Lacey out of their sight. They didn't let her have many friends, never bought her new clothes, never let her eat junk food, never let her go to sleepovers. In high school they monitored what music she listened to, she wasn't allowed to date. They knew she had no interest in the family farm, so they pushed her into studies."

"I have a hard time believing Lacey would be pushed into that."

"You're right. But they put a lot of pressure on her to be the best and maybe that made Lacey worse, I don't know. Because she puts a lot of pressure on herself in order to please my parents and she's still acting that way, to this day."

"And what about you?"

"Me? I was given nothing but freedom. I got away with murder. I had boyfriends galore, I stayed out late, I drank and smoked weed, I did whatever I wanted. I'm lucky that I loved school because I don't think they would have even pushed me to do well."

"So Lacey resents you because you got all the freedom and she didn't."

"Yeah, resent is the right word. But...the thing is, I'm no

better off than she is. Because she's the one who got all the attention. My parents cared enough about her to be that strict. They didn't care about me. They let me do whatever because I was barely a thought in their minds."

"That's not true," I tell her. "I spent a lot of time with your parents, they're very proud of you."

"Maybe...maybe now we're closer. But it wasn't like that before. So while Lacey resents me for my freedom, I resent Lacey for the love and attention she got."

The words seem to hang in the air between us until they're blown away by the wind and I get the feeling that Daisy has never said those words out loud, has never articulated that to someone else.

Why that makes me feel special, I don't know.

"So..." she goes on, her voice lower. "It's complicated." She glances at me. "You're lucky you don't have any siblings."

I freeze and I can feel my skin pale.

Because she doesn't know.

And it's not a secret at all, it's something I should be able to talk about.

But I can't. Not here, on the water. Not when there is so much at stake.

It's not healthy, that voice speaks up, the voice that roars the loudest on the sea. *You named the boat after her and thought that was enough, you thought that was how you dealt with her death. But you haven't dealt with it at all. None of you have.*

I close my eyes, fighting the feeling.

Not here. Not now.

"I don't know what I'm supposed to do with my life now," Daisy says.

I blink, pushing the grief deeper into my heart.

Focus on her. Focus on Daisy.

I clear my throat. "In what way?"

"In every way, man. In every single way."

"I have no doubt you can get another marketing job. Perhaps one even better."

"I know," she says. "I don't doubt that. But...I'm not sure I want that. I took that job because I lucked into it right out of high school. My boyfriend at the time, his father worked there and got me an internship and that was it. I never went to college. I wanted to, but I never went because I didn't have to. I stayed with that job because it made my life easy and I went with it. But...I'm starting to think that it didn't fulfill anything except a paycheck."

"But there's nothing wrong with that," I point out, remembering many times in my life where I did whatever jobs I could in order to make money. Then again, I had a goal in mind and it was always to buy boats and to do what I'm doing right now.

"There isn't," she admits. Her brows knit together delicately. "Do you think there's something wrong with wanting more, though?"

I shake my head. "There's nothing wrong with that either. We should always want more. More for ourselves. To be greater versions of ourselves. It's better to be in a state of becoming than to be in a state of being. I believe that."

"My whole life I've just been in a state of being," she says. "I haven't become anything."

"But you will."

She gives me a small smile. "I hope so." She pauses. "I just have to figure out what."

"I have no doubt you'll get there," I tell her.

She grins. "I have to say, I might like supportive Tai better than grumpy Tai."

I roll my eyes and adjust my hands on the wheel. "Still the same Tai."

She nods and sips her coffee, staring at the stars.

Hours pass by in small talk, though now that Daisy has calmed down and is less nervous around me, our conversations have become more thoughtful. I actually enjoy them, her views on society, the world, even politics.

Finally, the night sky begins to fade into a dark orange, the colors threading the horizon line, mixing together like a watercolor palette. Pinks and reds and purples form and change and blend, the clouds soaking in the saturation as the sun slowly rises.

"We have no idea how important this is," I find myself whispering, my voice feeling rough and raw.

"The sunrise?" Daisy asks. She's in awe as the colors change before our eyes.

I swallow the lump in my throat. "To see the dawn of the new days. Sometimes it feels like the world around us is collapsing. Sometimes it's the world inside us. But the sun always rises. It always promises that we can start again. It's the one thing we can count on when we can't count on anything else."

She sniffs. I realize I'm being a sap and it's not like me.

But at this moment I don't care.

"Atarangi," I find myself saying, the word holding so much reverence.

"That's the name of the boat," she comments, looking back at me.

I nod.

It was my sister's name, too.

"It means morning sky," I tell her.

8

———

DAISY

Daisy's Log: Day 2

I'M WRITING this from up-top, at the bow of the ship, the only place where I can find some privacy. It's mid-day and though the breeze is fresh, the sun is soooo strong that I'm swaddled in a long-sleeve shirt, plus that Deschutes ball cap that I stole from the swag room back at work, trying to protect my skin.

I was hoping to find the space here to do some yoga, or my daily meditations at the very least, but the up and down of the boat through the water has been challenging for my positions. Twice I attempted a simple half-moon pose and was nearly pitched overboard.

I'm sure the boat wouldn't stop to pick me up.

I thought we were making good progress last night.

Tai had cooked up this Korean stir-fry with loads of kimchi and it was freakin' delicious. Everyone seemed in good spirits by the time cocktail hour came and we all sipped wine and watched the sunset on the horizon.

It was really nice! For a moment, I got so wrapped up in the excitement of what I'm doing—on a boat, traveling across the South Pacific to the tropical bliss of Fiji—that I forgot all the tension of earlier that day.

Then came bedtime. Lacey and Richard had first shift, so I went to bed at ten to try and get five hours of sleep before I had to get up. I felt bad that Tai had to sleep on the couch so I offered the bed to him, but naturally he refused.

Let me tell you, I could have slept forever. When that alarm went off in the middle of the night, it felt like pure torture getting up. So I didn't. I turned off snooze and fell asleep for probably five minutes before Tai was shaking me awake.

Did I mention I was DROOLING?! Yes, Mr. Sexy Pants Pirate probably got a great view of that. Ugh. Anyway, I pulled on my joggers and a hoodie and joined him. I could already hear Richard snoring loudly from the rear cabin.

Tai had a Thermos full of hot coffee for us, so at least that was good, and the stars made up for it. I've never seen so many stars before. It was like looking at the universe for the first time and seeing ALL of it. It was pretty intense. It woke me up.

And you know what? We actually TALKED. Or I did. About Lacey, about life...about things I've never voiced to anyone, things I never voice to myself.

It felt so damn good, even though I was telling it to Tai of all people.

I guess I just trust him with my thoughts.

He at least was being supportive. Made me feel a little less alone, which is something I'm realizing I've felt my whole life. All the boyfriends and friends I surrounded myself with did nothing to stop me from feeling alone.

But hey, at least I'm recognizing that now.

Better late than never.

Or as Tai said, better to become than just be.

Then the sun came up. Just a hint of red at the horizon before it slowly rose and the new day began.

It was probably the prettiest sunrise I've ever seen.

Daisy's Log: Day 3

It's past bedtime but I'm awake. The ocean was rougher today and the boat is still doing this back-and-forth up-and-down thing, and it turns out that doesn't rock you to sleep like a baby, instead it's like someone attached said cradle to a rollercoaster.

I don't like it.

It scares me. It makes me realize how far from anything we are.

I kept on looking at the GPS chart today and it's just...there's nothing out there.

NOTHING!

Just endless sea.

And there's nothing going on in here. None of our phones work, we don't have any internet, there's the satellite phone but that's only for emergencies.

Thank god I brought my Kindle and a few paperbacks, otherwise I would be bored as hell.

I think the others are starting to feel the pinch too.

Lacey is baking bread all the time.

Richard is fishing off the boat (and not catching a thing).

Tai is being Tai. We talk to each other, of course, and occasionally he'll say something charming, and then I'll admire the way his lips move when he's talking, and then he'll put up some wall again to keep me in my place.

But the food has been good and cocktail hour, albeit bumpy as hell, is a nice way for everyone to come together.

Hopefully that was the last of the waves.

Daisy's Log: Day 4

Today Richard defied *the odds of his dorkiness and caught a Mahi-mahi!*

Tai cooked it for dinner. Highlight of the day, hands down.

(Have I mentioned there's nothing sexier than a man that can cook?)

Oh, Lacey ran out of yeast and had a meltdown.

I read two books back to back.

The seas are calmer today. Last night wasn't as bad as I thought it would be though, since I actually felt better being on deck in the fresh night air.

I'm starting to look forward to Tai's extra strong coffee and our middle of the night rendezvous.

I'm starting to appreciate the silence.

Daisy's Log: Day 5

. . .

I'VE DISCOVERED *that there are fifteen steps from the cockpit to the front of the boat. I walked those fifteen steps for an hour, just to try and get my steps up. I miss working out. I miss going for runs. I miss going for a walk ANYWHERE.*

Instead all I see is water. All I see is this boat.

All I see are Lacey and Richard and Tai.

Richard is growing a mustache and it looks awful, like someone glued pubes to his face.

Lacey is making flatbread now since she ran out of yeast. We pretend it tastes good.

And Tai has a sore back from sleeping on the couch. I only know this because I noticed him wincing when he was going up the stairs and I had to literally bug him forever until he finally admitted it.

The couch is way too small for his frame at any rate.

So I gave him my room.

He wouldn't take it.

Then I lay down on the couch, so that if he really wanted me to move, he'd have to carry me (again...ugh...nice reminder there).

He tried. Oh, he tried to pick me up.

But then his back went out.

So I won.

He's asleep in the cabin now. Richard and Lacey are up top, quietly arguing about something. This forced proximity is even starting to get to them.

And I'm scribbling into my journal, wishing I had something more important to talk about.

Oh yeah...five more days of this hell left! First thing I'm doing when I get off this damn boat is heading straight to a bar. I'm going to get drunk, I'm going to hook up with some hot tourist and let loose what will be ten days worth of sexual frustration of being so close to Tai (I mean, my dreams have been filthy).

Then I'm going to say adios to these three amigos for a very long time.

Maybe forever.

Daisy's Log: Day 6

Guess what?

There's no news at all, and there never is and never will be, because this sailing trip is like Groundhog Day, with every day exactly the same. There's no relief, there's no escape.

We are in a timeless loop.

WELL, except it turns out I'm an excellent poker player. I guess there's something vacant about my face that makes it hard to tell if I'm bluffing or not. If I have bad cards, I'm smiling, if I have good cards, I'm smiling.

Seems like that's been how I've operated most of my life, or at least Lacey made that comment slip once I beat her ass for the millionth time. Hey, got to work that shit to my advantage—plus I made fifty dollars and I won the last bottle of vodka. Not like I'm going to drink it all in the next four days but...actually, yeah I might.

Tensions on the ship are high.

What else is new?

All the good food ran out a few days ago and we've eaten all of our snacks, so we're just down to canned food now. Gross. I feel the sodium swelling through my veins, along with the fact that I haven't been able to exercise in nearly a week.

Honestly, Tai said something today that I never thought I'd hear him say.

He said, "I want this to be over now."

And hell if he didn't sum it up for all of us.

We are ALL dying to get off this boat. Lacey is having some weird panic attacks, Richard shaved his mustache off while the boat was rocking and cut himself up really bad, Tai has had a little too much wine at dinner, probably so he can pass out earlier (and cocktail hour is canceled since we can't stand the sight of each other).

Fingers crossed the wind that's been picking up lately will help push us there faster.

Daisy's Log: Day 7

Here's what I've been dreaming of lately.

I'm warning you...it's pretty detailed.

I'm back in San Francisco. It's a Saturday night and I'm in my apartment. I have my own space, I have my own room. I have privacy again.

I sit at home, in my own bed, enjoying a glass of Paso Robles Cab Sav, admiring my nails. Earlier I had gone to the salon to get them done and talked the technician's ear off.

Then I get ready for the evening. I take a long shower—so much space! It's not some cold hand-held thing in the tiny bath-room, it's a real shower that I can turn around in and everything. I even have my wine in the shower!

I take a ridiculously long time washing my hair, getting it really clean, because there's no one yelling at me to stop wasting water. I shave my legs, exfoliate, and use a hair mask. I step out into my huge bathroom and slather on body butter and let it dry and then I blow-dry my hair (I miss my blow-dryer! Why did I think Tai would have one?). Once dry and shiny (no more of these salt-soaked tangles from the wind), I curl my hair in long waves like I used to, then I spend extra time on my makeup. Not the two palettes I'm stuck with here, but the collection I have at home that is overflowing with choices.

Then it's time to get dressed. I open my closet and ta-da! I have scores of clothes to choose from. They're all freshly laundered, none of them are wrinkled and smell like diesel after being on this godforsaken boat.

I get ready. Choose a purse and then head out.

Where do I go?

I can go anywhere!

I can walk down the street to Hayes St, stand in a ridiculously long line for Salt & Straw and be around people, people who aren't these three idiots. Or I could go to Blue Bottle for a coffee, perhaps catch the eye of a cute guy working in the shop. I could get a spicy mango margarita at the Sugar Bar, or head up the street to A Mano, my favorite Italian restaurant and eat my heart out. I would order every single dish, drink every wine, so grateful to not be slurping on cans of soup and watching the alcohol slowly run out.

Then, THEN, when I was good and ready, I would find myself a guy.

Not just any guy.

A guy that looks exactly like Tai, down to his battered knuckles and the scar at the bottom of his lip, and the flecks of gold in his mahogany eyes. I would find his exact replica, bring him home, and bring his head between my legs until I had a million orgasms.

And this version of him would be so much less complicated than the version that's staring at me while I write this.

It's five in the morning, by the way. The sun will come up in *an hour or so. I'm holding a flashlight in between my teeth, trying not to drool. Not that it's something Tai hasn't seen before.*

I have to admit, as much as I'm dreaming about being back home, being off this ship, about to bang a guy that looks exactly like Tai, I think these middle-of-the-night shifts are something I would miss.

It's like I feel closer to him every time the sun rolls around. I at least feel...grounded, even out at sea.

And the way he's been staring at me lately...I can't pretend I don't feel the heat in his eyes, and the curiosity behind that. It's a look that makes me feel alive, like I have something to look forward to, even though I don't know what it is.

But for all that Tai looks at me, and all that I look at him, there's nothing between us.

And so, I dream.

Daisy's Log: **Day 8**

Get me off this fucking ship!

9

DAISY

It's day nine on the boat, and I'm in charge of dinner.

It ain't easy.

I mean, it should be since I'm just opening up a can of chunky chicken soup, but that's hard to do when the boat is swinging from side to side, violently crashing down on the waves. It's been this back and forth action all day, but this up and down is something new. Feels like we're landing on the back of a turtle.

Smash!

Somehow I manage to get the soup in the saucepot without spilling, though that last impact nearly threw me off balance. I had a complete disaster with the eggs the other day.

Tai yells something inaudibly from up top, so I go up the stairs and peer into the cockpit.

It's soaking wet, like a wave just crashed over.

Tai is at the wheel, wearing a red Helly Hansen rain slicker. Richard is at the side of the boat, dressed in a yellow one that's too big for him, trying to pull in a sail.

Both of them have life jackets on, which is now required if you're going up top. Tai said earlier if this front gets nastier, anyone up top will have to be tethered to the boat with a cable, just in case.

I don't want to admit it, but I'm scared.

Lacey is scared too, that's why she went to her cabin to lie down, and took a bunch of her anxiety medication, pills that I very much want right now.

"What is it?" I yell at Tai. "Is everything okay?"

It's hard to keep the panic out of my voice.

"It's fine," Tai says gruffly, spinning the wheel like he's trying to gain control of the boat. "I need you to close any open hatches. Waves are getting bigger."

"Okay!" I tell him, happy to be doing something to help.

I go back downstairs and head to the open hatch over the couch. I get on the couch, reaching up for it but it's stiff, like the sea salt has rusted it in place.

I try with all my might to pull it down but no luck. It's like my muscles have atrophied from being away from the gym for so long.

I growl at the stubborn hatch, hating that I couldn't do it myself, further proving that I'm more or less useless, then head back up to Tai.

"It's stuck," I tell him reluctantly as a wave sprays over the side, nearly getting me.

"Oh for fuck's sake," he grumbles, just like I knew he would. We've been getting pretty close to each other on our night shifts, but when it comes to anything to do with the boat or the ocean, he gets pretty worked up. It's like the old man and the sea every day. Ahab and Moby Dick, except there is no whale, it's just the ocean.

"Want me to take the wheel?" Richard asks, ropes in his hands.

"No, I'll put her on autopilot for a second." Tai angrily pushes a button at the helm and then storms over to me.

I quickly go down the stairs and get out of the way before he jumps down.

"I could take the wheel," I offer. I know he doesn't like to use the autopilot on the boat because he says it can be finicky.

He gives me a loaded look—*yeah right*—and moves swiftly to the couch, just as grinding noise fills the cabin.

The boat suddenly lurches to the left, like we've swung halfway around.

Boom!

We slam sideways into a trough and water goes flying over the side of the boat.

Over the open hatch.

Down into the couch.

Drenching everything.

I can see Tai's face turn an angry shade of red right before Richard lets out a girlish yelp from up top, which would have been funny had this not been such a dangerous situation.

In a fury, Tai pushes past me and hoists himself upstairs.

Meanwhile, seawater continues to pour down the hatch.

And now Lacey is up, stumbling out of her cabin, her hair a mess from sleeping.

"What's happening? Where is Richard?"

I don't have time to tell her because I'm not sure what's happening.

I fly up the stairs to the cockpit, holding onto the handles so I don't fall, and see Richard at the wheel, trying to steer the boat, spinning it between his hands.

Tai gets him to move over and takes control.

"I almost fell overboard," Richard says, his face white as

a ghost, spray covering his glasses. "Thank god I held onto the boom."

He looks at Tai, whose face is furrowed in concentration as he brings the boat center again. Looks like we almost swung all the way to the direction we came from, though to be honest, with all these waves and this grey, dark sky, it's hard to tell.

"It's the autopilot," Tai says, smacking the wheel. "The fucker gave out." He looks at Richard. "You did the right thing by grabbing the wheel. Make sure you never touch the autopilot going forward, got it?" He looks at me and Lacey. "That goes for you both as well."

"Are we going to be okay?" Lacey asks as we hit another wave. She grips the handles by the stairs and I lean against the boat, distributing my weight for balance.

"We should be fine," Tai says. "This is the tail end of the front. Wind isn't too bad, there's no rain. The waves should ease a bit but even so, if anyone is up here, I think we should start clipping on to the boat. Just in case. There's another system moving in tomorrow and I have no idea how that's going to go. It's going to push us to the east, which is a shame. Might need an extra day to tack upwind and get to Suva."

We all nod silently. It's not the best news, but at least this is going to die down soon.

Only problem is that fucking hatch.

The entire couch is soaked.

AKA my bed.

I don't want to bug Tai about it, not now, so I motion for Lacey to head back down the stairs and then the two of us go about trying to close it. It's tough, and standing on the couch is like standing on a waterbed that sprung a leak, but together we manage to close the hatch.

"Some honeymoon, huh?' Lacey says, going over to the loveseat and sitting beside my luggage, leaning against it tiredly. There's a silly face on it now that someone drew with a marker. I wiped half of it off and then left it, figuring it's probably Tai's handiwork. Serves me right for packing so damn much, especially since I've pretty much been wearing the same clothes day in and day out.

"Well, you did want an adventure," I tell her, leaning against the galley.

Oh shit, the soup!

I turn around and start stirring it, though half seems to have burned at the bottom.

"Ugh," I moan. I'm not sure I can salvage this. I might have to start again.

"We never did learn the home domesticity skills, did we?" Lacey comments.

"Nope," I admit, dumping the soup in the garbage. "Though you have to admit that I do some mean scrambled eggs. And you do some pretty fine loaves of bread."

"I suppose that's the extent of what mom taught us," she says. "Though I learned how to make bread when I lived with my old roommate in Portland."

"And I learned my scrambled eggs from YouTube."

The secret is a dash of curry spice.

"I wonder what mom really wanted for us," Lacey muses, bracing herself as the boat slams down another wave. It's rare to see her this reflective and I like that fact that she's talking to me, so I don't want to screw it up like I usually do.

"I'm sure she just wanted us to be happy," I say carefully. "I mean, off the bat, both mom and dad knew we had no interest in the family business."

"None at all. You were all whales and I was all plants. Actually, at the time, it was roses."

"I remember your rose garden behind the house," I tell her. It was small but you could walk through it and Lacey had meticulously pruned all her roses to showroom status. I think she was maybe sixteen at the time.

Lacey is silent for a moment, apparently lost in the memory, as I get a new can of soup. Then she adjusts her glasses and looks at me.

"Are you?"

I glance at her. "Am I what?"

"Happy."

The soup slides out of the can and into the pan with a *plop*.

Perfect punctuation.

"Happy?" I repeat, not sure what to do with that question. "Of course I am."

Of course I am.

"That's what I thought," she says after a moment. "How could you not be?"

I want to bring up, you know, what I've been talking about since I got here which is my bad luck streak, but there's no point in bringing it up. I can tell that Lacey wants to argue, wants to prove some point, and I'm just going to let her at this point. I don't have it in me to fight.

So I just smile at her and start humming a song that's been in my head as I stir the soup, and she eventually sighs and goes to her cabin.

"Dinner will be ready soon," I call over my shoulder, but I don't think she cares.

Turns out, no one was hungry anyway, including myself. All the waves and rocking makes you feel extremely nauseous when you're down below, so I stay up top with my life jacket on, keeping out of the way. Tai and Richard are constantly running around and adjusting things, but other than that, the waves are getting smaller and things are starting to calm down.

Then night falls.

Lacey and Richard take their shift, both of them wearing lifejackets, clipped in for safety. Richard insisted on Lacey staying down below, but Lacey insisted otherwise and she's definitely the domineering one in that relationship.

That leaves me with a predicament.

"Where should I sleep?" I ask Tai as we get ready for bed.

"Take their bed," he says, heading into his cabin.

"Ew." I grimace. My sister's bed on her honeymoon? "*No.*"

He pauses and looks back at me. "Then sleep with me."

I want to give him the same answer but I can't.

Because it's definitely not *ew*, and I definitely don't want to say *no*.

"Or sleep wherever," he says. "All I know is that I need the sleep for this upcoming storm and that couch isn't an option."

Tell him to sleep in Lacey and Richard's cabin. It's not ew to him.

And yet...I don't want him to.

"Okay," I say. "So as long as you don't mind the company."

He gives me a wary look that says he actually does mind the company.

"I promise I won't snore," I add.

"Or drool," he says.

I blush. "Or drool."

"Or talk. Or move."

I nod. "I promise."

I quickly grab my night clothes and change into them in the tiny bathroom where there's barely enough room to turn around, my elbows banging into the walls. I use a makeup wipe to clean my face since the last time I used the sink I got water everywhere.

I have to say, getting into bed with someone that you're not going to have sex with can somehow feel even more intimate that doing the deed. It doesn't help that both Tai and I have to share the same sleeping bag spread on top of us, since mine got wet beneath the hatch.

Wet beneath the hatch, I repeat the thought to myself as I cautiously get under the covers. Suddenly everything seems lewd.

"Am I in the way? Drooling? Moving? Snoring?" I ask him as I place the pillow in front of me, which thankfully was spared the deluge.

"Not being quiet," he says to me, rolling over onto his side so his back is to me.

Hmmpf. Fine. No fun at sleepovers, I see.

I mean, he could at least be going to bed without a shirt on. I've only caught a glimpse at him shirtless this entire time and it wasn't long enough to really appreciate how magnificent his body is.

There's actually enough room in the berth that we aren't crammed up against each other, unlike his truck. Although it is a V-berth, which means our feet are more likely to touch than any other part of us. Maybe playing footsies is on the menu.

I decide to stick a toe out just to see.

I poke him right in the back of his calf.

"Daisy," he warns me, his voice muffled.

"Was just adjusting myself," I tell him, flipping over on to my back.

A pause. "Then how come I can hear you smiling?"

"I'm not smiling," I protest with a gasp, but it's a lie, because I am. How can he tell?

"Go to sleep Daisy," he says.

As if I can just fall asleep sharing the same bed as him.

Yet, somehow, I do.

I'M HAVING A MOST excellent dream.

I'm on a beach somewhere. A deserted island, the kind you see in travel brochures. You know the one, small and round with a green jungle interior, fringed by white sand, shallow blue glass-like water, palm trees dipping over the sand like hammocks.

I'm lying back on the beach, and it feels so real that I *feel* the sand hot and soft against my skin.

I'm completely naked but I'm not alone.

Tai's head is between my legs.

I don't see him. From my perspective I only see sky.

But I know it's him.

My fingers are wrapped in his hair, luscious thick hair, and his stubble is scraping against the sensitive skin of my inner thighs.

His tongue is a work of art.

He laps at my clit like a cat at a bowl of cream, each powerful stroke sending shockwaves through my body. He's so good that I'm on the verge of coming right away and then my body is shaking and he keeps going.

Again and again.

I stare up at the bluest sky and it's like being born all over again.

And then...

My dream starts to dissolve.

Like the sky is suddenly brighter and brighter until it's all white and...

My eyes open.

For real.

I'm lying on my back in the cabin, the cover off of me, my heart pounding especially loud in my ears, my breath ragged.

One of my hands is in my underwear, a few fingers inside me.

The other hand is at my breast, my nightshirt pushed up so that they're bare.

Tai is beside me and staring at me with the most intensely primal gaze, his focus on my open mouth.

OH MY GOD.

I jolt, as if suddenly coming back to life, ripping my hand out of my underwear, pulling down my shirt.

"Oh my god," I whisper, reaching for the covers and yanking them over me. "What...what was..."

Tai clears his throat. "You were having a dream," he says, his voice sounding thick and throaty.

Turned on.

"A sex dream," he adds, as if that wasn't obvious.

I swallow, feeling my whole body go hot and red.

Shit, shit, shit.

I am never going to live this down.

"And so you just sat there watching me?" I ask him, avoiding his eyes.

"Your moans woke me up," he says in a murmur.

"And so you just sat there watching me?" I repeat. I risk a better glance at him. He's on his side, head propped up on his elbow, as if he was just so casually watching me get myself off.

I mean, yeah...it's hot. It's fucking hot as hell.

But it's also mortifying to have someone like him see me in such a vulnerable state, no matter how hot it seems.

"I turned on the light to wake you," he says. "It worked."

I narrow my eyes at him. "Uh huh. And how long did you watch me for first?"

"Well, it was hard to see with it being so dark," he says. "Also, you come pretty fast. Each time you came, I figured it was over and then you just started up again."

I can't EVEN.

I close my eyes, putting my forearm over them for good measure.

"Don't be embarrassed," he says, and I know he's mocking me. "You finally got to show me your tits. Definitely worth the wait."

My arm flies off my face and I stare at him. "What the hell does that mean?"

His mouth curls slyly. "Don't you remember the wedding? When you wanted to go skinny-dipping, you spent a good amount of effort trying to remove the top of your dress. Then you tried to take off my shirt, to no avail."

I don't think my face can burn any hotter. Even my chest feels like it's on fire.

"Well then you should take your shirt off," I whine. "Make things fair. Even things out."

He bites his lip but makes no move to indulge me.

God, why does he have to be so hot?

"Fine. Fine, you saw me get off," I grumble. "You happy now?"

"Very."

I cock my brow, the words taking a moment to rest on my tongue before I spit them out. "Did it make you hard?"

Yeah. I said it.

A bold look flashes in his eyes, more intense than the darkest coffee. "What do you think?"

I think yes.

"Are you still hard?"

I don't know where the hell I'm getting the gumption to ask him these questions, but fuck it. It's only fair now.

The look in his eyes intensifies and I watch his throat as he swallows.

"Why don't you find out," he manages to say, his words measured.

Maybe he's taunting me, maybe he's serious.

But it doesn't matter because before I know what I'm doing, I'm rolling over to my side closer to him and reaching down over his stomach to his crotch and...

Yeah.

I mean, that's a very big yes.

A very big, hard, thick yes.

Hot and pulsing gently against my palm, even through his boxer briefs.

I shouldn't be doing any of this to begin with, but I give him a hard squeeze, feeling every inch of him in my hand.

A soft moan falls from his lips, flooding the cabin, making me ache between my legs.

Oh, fuck...

I glance up at his face and he's watching me through his dark lashes, his breath uneven, mouth open, and I want nothing more than to pull his cock out of his briefs and—

KNOCK KNOCK KNOCK.

The door to the cabin rattles.

Both our eyes widen in unison and I immediately snatch back my hand. It felt like it was God knocking on the door, telling me I'm making a big mistake.

"Yes?" Tai asks, his voice hoarse.

"Everything okay?" asks Richard from the other side of the door. "It's three-thirty."

"Shit," Tai swears under his breath. "Uh, sorry about that. Must have overslept! Be right there."

He quickly sits up, swinging his legs over the edge of the berth, taking in a deep breath through his nose. "Sorry," he says briskly. "My alarm went off, but I guess I didn't hit snooze. I was...distracted."

"I didn't even bother with mine," I tell him as he pulls his jeans on. I briefly get to admire the look of his ass in his boxer briefs. Just like his cock in the front, it's spectacular.

"That's your first mistake," he tells me, and I can tell from his tone that he's back in grump mode, and whatever sexy little escapade just happened between us is over. Maybe for good. "Don't rely on other people."

Then he heads out of the cabin.

I sigh, and slowly sit up. It's tempting to go back to sleep, but I know that if I lie down again, I'll never get back up, which means he'll have a reason to be mad at me.

Yet I am in no hurry to go on night shift with him after what just happened.

But I don't have much of a choice. It's not like I can avoid him.

I get dressed and then head out into the rest of the boat.

I pass by Richard in the galley who is grabbing a can of soda from the fridge, looking bleary-eyed and annoyed.

"Sorry about that," I tell him.

The look he gives me tells me he doesn't believe me.

I have to wonder if he heard Tai's moan when I palmed his dick.

I hope not, though I know that sound will forever be the soundtrack of all my future sex dreams.

On deck the air feels different than normal, though I can't quite put my finger on it. Electric and alive, but not in a good way.

Tai is already at the wheel, looking uncomfortable as he stares at something on the GPS plotter. He's forgotten to make coffee tonight, so already this shift is starting off on the wrong foot.

"What's wrong?" I ask, just as the wind starts to blow, rattling the sails.

"That front is here quicker than I thought," he says.

"Are we in trouble?"

He shakes his head, looking around him. There are no stars out tonight and the sky is dark and murky. You can't see much beyond the lights from the boat, but it looks like white caps are starting to form. "I don't think so," he says.

"Should I go downstairs and make coffee?" I ask him.

He manages to give me a quick smile. "Sure. Thank you."

Maybe he's feeling bad for being curt earlier.

I head downstairs and put the stove on, waiting for the water boil and arranging the French press. The wait gives me some time to think about what happened.

If Richard hadn't knocked on the door…

I don't know. Tai was looking at me like he was not only going to kiss me, but that he was going to take both my arms and pin them above my head and fuck the life out of me.

God, it would have been so easy too.

So needed.

Just to have someone touch me.

And not just anyone.

His touch. With those hands.

All over.

I gulp, feeling sexually frustrated again, wondering if there'll be another opportunity before we get to Fiji.

I have to say, as much as I am dying to get off this boat, I don't think I'm ready to say good-bye to him.

Which is funny, because days ago I couldn't wait.

As long as he doesn't turn into an ass again, I think. It's a big if.

When the coffee is ready, I pour it into the thermos, grab the mugs and head up top.

The wind is even stronger now, the cable that runs up the side of the mast making an incessant clanking sound.

He's busy figuring stuff out on the touch screen, so I pour him a mug and put it in the holder beside the wheel.

"Thank you," he says, giving me an appreciative glance before going back to whatever he's trying to do.

"You're welcome," I say. Then I hesitate, because I feel like something needs to be said about earlier. "I'm sorry I touched your dick."

He chuckles. "I'm not. It's my one redeeming quality."

I take a sip of my coffee and smile. "I wouldn't say that. I'd list them all but I wouldn't want to give you an ego. And yet something tells me it might be too late."

The smile he gives me is a little more rushed. He's frowning.

My heart sinks. I hope it's not me.

Then again, I hope it's nothing related to the boat, either.

Suddenly, BAM!

The wind slams into us from behind and I'm nearly knocked over.

It didn't seem possible, but the sky behind Tai has

turned even darker, the waves even choppier. The wind is relentless all of a sudden.

"She's here," Tai says warily.

My heart thuds and I have to sit down to keep my balance. "Who?"

"The storm."

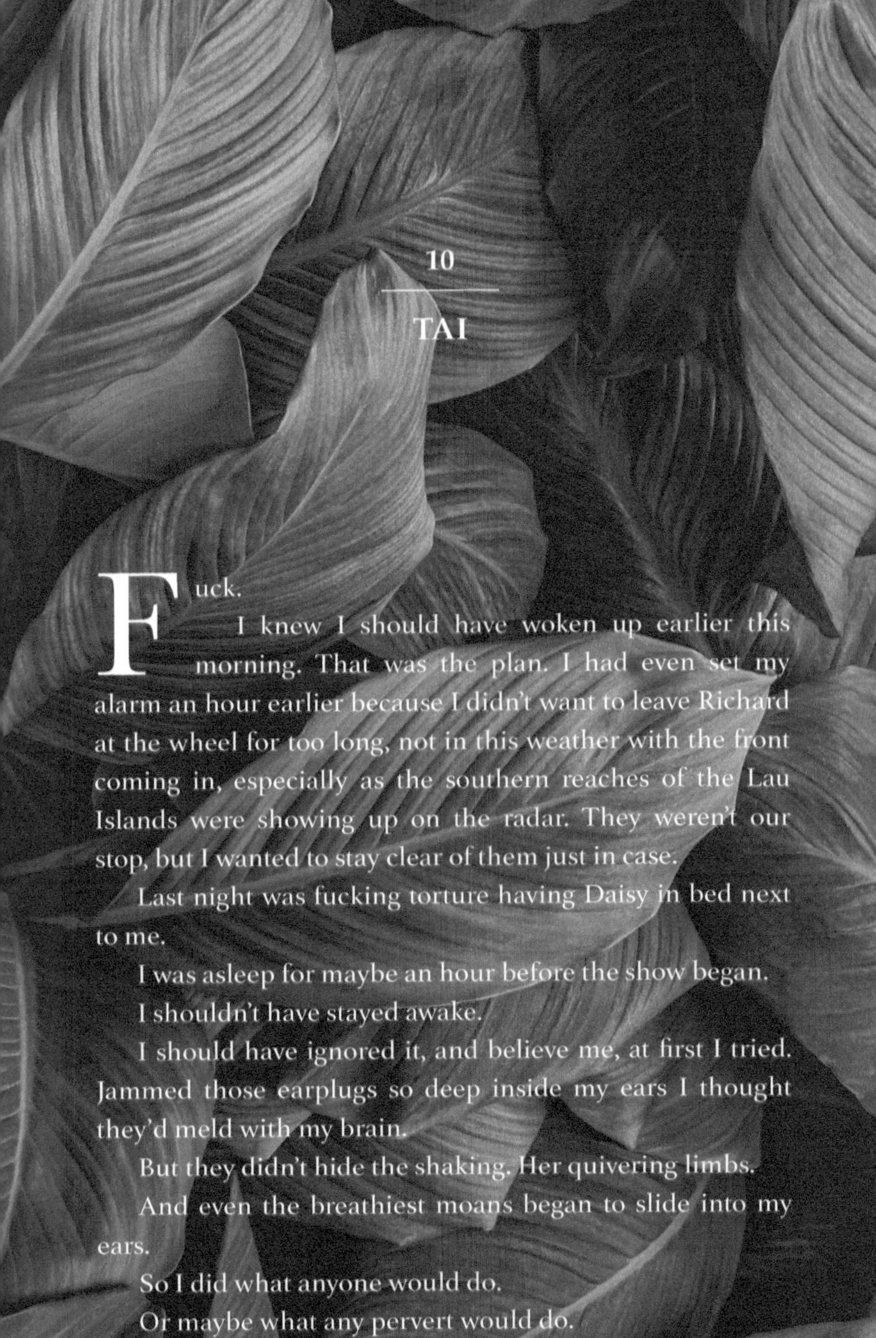

10

TAI

Fuck.

I knew I should have woken up earlier this morning. That was the plan. I had even set my alarm an hour earlier because I didn't want to leave Richard at the wheel for too long, not in this weather with the front coming in, especially as the southern reaches of the Lau Islands were showing up on the radar. They weren't our stop, but I wanted to stay clear of them just in case.

Last night was fucking torture having Daisy in bed next to me.

I was asleep for maybe an hour before the show began.

I shouldn't have stayed awake.

I should have ignored it, and believe me, at first I tried. Jammed those earplugs so deep inside my ears I thought they'd meld with my brain.

But they didn't hide the shaking. Her quivering limbs.

And even the breathiest moans began to slide into my ears.

So I did what anyone would do.

Or maybe what any pervert would do.

It was pitch dark in the cabin, so I just listened.

Listened to the wet sounds her fingers were making as she stroked herself, listened to her moans and the gasps and the way she'd cry out, "Oh yes."

I listened and imagined and I got off myself.

Couldn't fucking help it.

It was impossible to not touch myself, to not come alongside her, aiming up on to my belly in a thick stream. I was terrified that she'd wake up and find myself jerking off beside her, but it didn't stop me.

It's what I needed after all this time spent with her, all those times I wanted to kiss her when I didn't feel like arguing with her.

That's when I fell asleep again.

Maybe for ten minutes.

Must have turned off the alarm.

Then I woke up again.

She was still going at it.

A fucking machine.

This time I turned on the light hoping to wake her.

And in that time she was going at it again, in full glorious view of me.

Her top was bunched up above her tits and she was squeezing one nipple in such a way that it took every ounce of control not to lean over and take her other nipple between my teeth, pinching first before licking, then pulling it into my mouth.

Her other hand was down in her underwear. Pink satin knickers that were drenched with her own enjoyment.

I could have watched that all night. I started taking mental notes, thinking if I'd ever get my chance with her, I'd know all the right moves. She likes it soft at first, her fingertips just teasing her clit, teasing her length, then she slowly increased the pressure, the speed. When she seems like she's about to come from that alone, she nearly puts her whole fist inside herself.

My little gingersnap is greedy.

And needy.

I could fulfill all her needs.

Then...she woke up.

Flushed and embarrassed and bold all at once and, fuck, I would have been up for anything. The feeling of her hand on my dick was incredible, and I knew there and then how much she wanted me too.

And then Richard started banging on the door, bringing with him reality, and I realized what a colossal mistake I made. I let Daisy distract me from my job, the job I have in keeping everyone on this ship safe.

I'm still mad at myself for it, though I have to be careful so that Daisy doesn't mistake that for me being mad at her. I don't want to damage whatever trust we have between us, especially since I caught her (over and over again) in such a vulnerable position.

That said, I don't have any time to dwell on it.

We're in a situation.

Thankfully it's not the worst, but it's still something I need to stay on top of.

When I first got on deck the wind was just starting to whip up and I could feel the front coming from behind us, the way the sails changed and the boat started objecting to the direction. There was enough time for Daisy to make us some coffee, but I only had a few sips before things got gnarly. There was a lot of running around as we put on foul weather gear. I had to give Daisy the wheel for a bit so I could put mine on, plus life jackets.

It was a risk since the sails were up and the wind was

coming from the southwest. We have to stay as north as possible, especially with the Lau Islands to the right of us, which means fighting the wind a little.

Luckily Daisy was great behind the wheel, holding course.

That gave me enough time to start taking in sails and clipping us onto the lifeline. The wind kicked to forty knots, accelerating the boat to nine knots, and sending us skipping over waves. With each rise and fall over the waves, the whole boat shudders and shakes, like a bronco trying to buck us from its back.

"You're doing good," I tell Daisy, coming back to relieve her of the steering.

In the faint cockpit lights, she practically has to pry her white-knuckled grip off the wheel.

"Are we going to be okay?" she asks, before a wave whips over the side, skirting us both.

"We'll be fine, just a squall," I tell her. "A pain in the ass, that's it."

I glance at the instruments.

The rain is pouring now, messing with visibility, so the radar is blazing away looking for the next squall to tear through and, more fearsome on a night like this, freighters.

Daisy wasn't my ideal partner to have on a night like tonight. Not that she's incapable, just that this is risky sailing and I'd rather have her below deck where she's safe.

But with the autopilot out of commission and Richard needing his sleep, I don't have a choice. I need her.

She seems to get that. She's taking this seriously, if not fearfully.

"What else can I do?" she asks.

"Just be present," I tell her. "Have a seat, hold on."

She sits down beside me and I glance down the deck at

the sails. They're supposed to be halfway in, or reefed, in order to keep us from being where the wind wants to take us. But they aren't quite there yet.

"Sorry, can you take over again?" I ask her. "Just keep it steady as you were before. You might be getting more resistance now."

She nods, face grim and serious, and takes the wheel.

I head up to the front, carefully, taking slow steps and keeping low. The boat shudders with each slam of the waves and I train myself to walk in a similar rhythm. I'm almost at the bow when a wave comes over the side and soaks me, causing me to slip.

I hear Daisy yelp in the background and I reach out for a handle, holding on as my legs want to slip over the side of the boat. It takes a lot of upper body strength to pull me back up. I know I have the cable on, but they aren't always foolproof. The last thing I want is to go overboard in a storm, the chances of me being brought back into the boat, even with a lifeline, are pretty slim.

Don't focus on that, I tell myself.

I look back at Daisy who's obviously freaking out. Luckily she's still holding onto the wheel.

"I'm fine!" I yell at her. "Can you hit the deck lights?"

I glance back at the sail. It does seem to be stuck halfway but it's too dark to make out. I'll have to take some time to figure out what's wrong.

"What?" Daisy yells, and it's still dark.

I motion to where the switch is just as another wave nearly knocks me off balance. I grab onto the railing before I pitch over. "The deck lights, hit the deck lights, by your hand!"

"Okay!" she cries out uneasily, and hits the deck lights.

Except no lights come on.

Instead, there's a terrible grinding noise audible beneath the roar of the ocean and the whipping wind.

And Atarangi immediately starts going to the right, to the direction I've been trying hard to keep her away from.

"What's happening?" I yell at her, trying to make my way back to Daisy without falling overboard.

She's frantically trying to spin the wheel but nothing's happening.

The boat isn't changing direction.

"I don't know what happened," Daisy says, her voice breaking. "I just...I hit the..."

She stares at the panels and she doesn't have to say anything.

She slowly pushes a button and the deck lights go on.

Her eyes meet mine just as another wave crashes over me, but I hardly flinch.

Because I know what she's done, and she knows it too.

She accidently hit the auto-pilot switch instead.

"No!' the word explodes out of me and I start running down the deck, slipping and banging up my knees and scraping my hands, and I don't care.

I fling myself into the cockpit and practically shove Daisy out of the way. She plunks down in the seat, staring at me with huge, frightened eyes.

I grab the wheel and attempt to correct the boat. The wheel gives easily, too easily, and it does nothing to change the direction. I can feel the electronic connection between the steering and the wheel has been severed, shorted out, broken by the use of the autopilot, this fucking autopilot!

"Fuck!" I roar, slamming my fist into the wheel. "Fuck, fuck, fuck!" I grab the wheel and throw my head and back and scream into the wind.

"I'm so sorry, I'm so sorry," Daisy says.

"You idiot!" I scream at her. I don't care if this hurts her fucking feelings. "Do you even know what you've done? Is there any room in your brain to comprehend it?"

Now she's crying, her tears mixing with the rain falling off her hood.

"I'm sorry, I panicked, I thought I was hitting the deck lights!"

"You hit the autopilot!"

She presses her hands together in a praying manner. "I know," she says in anguish. "I know, I didn't mean to."

"You know what it looks like, you've seen it before. It says fucking autopilot on it, it looks nothing like the light switch!" I am livid, I am pure, raw anger.

"I panicked!"

"You didn't use your fucking head! Just out to fucking lunch, aren't you?"

"Tai," she sobs. "You don't have to be so mean."

"Be so mean?" I scream at her, spittle flying out. "This isn't the time to protect your precious princess feelings, okay? Do you realize what's going to happen now?"

She shakes her head. "No...no...can you, maybe you can fix it?"

"There is no fixing it right now! We are in the middle of a squall and we are drifting, okay?"

"Put the sails up! We can sail."

"To the east! The wind is pushing us east and do you know what's east of here? Land!"

She stops crying. "Really? That's great! We can get help."

She doesn't get it.

"When I say land, I mean islands. Atolls. Mostly uninhibited. You tell me what we're going to do in the dark, without any steering, huh? Let the wind magically push us into a harbor and right up to a fucking dock?"

A wave crashes over the side and into the cockpit as the boat continues to be pushed along. If I put the sail up now, we would be moving at breakneck speed but there's no saying where we'd end up.

I glance at the GPS, see the radar flashing. We're about 10 miles out from what looks to be an atoll, something small and without a name on the chart. And when I say 10 miles out, I mean we're heading straight for it.

I look up at Daisy. She's shaking slightly, staring at nothing. Perhaps she's in shock. Perhaps I shouldn't be yelling at her.

Even though it's all her fucking fault.

You're the one who put her in charge, I tell myself. *Maybe this is your fucking fault. Just like so many other things are.*

"What's happening?" Richard appears at the top of the stairs, throwing on his lifejacket. "I woke up to yelling, and my internal compass says we've changed direction."

"We're fucked!" I yell at him, letting go of my confident captain persona. "Absolutely and completely fucked!"

Richard frowns and I don't bother throwing Daisy under the bus. She can do that herself.

"I..." she begins, reluctantly looking at Richard. "I panicked, he was trying to get the sail in and I thought I hit the deck lights but..."

Richard's eyes widen beneath his glasses. "No. Please don't tell me you hit the autopilot."

"I hit the autopilot."

"I said please don't tell me that."

"It was an accident!"

Richard shakes his head in disbelief and motions for Daisy to undo her lifeline.

"Go downstairs and tell Lacey what happened," he tells her. "I'm staying up here."

Reluctantly she undoes her clip and gives it to Richard, then heads down the stairs.

She looks at me before she disappears into the cabin but I give her nothing in return.

"Is that true?!' Richard yells as he comes closer. "Did it shut down?"

I spin the wheel to show him. "We've got nothing."

"Shit."

He peers around at the navigation. "We're going eight knots with the sail reefed," he says, noting the instrument readings on the monitor. "What is this?" He points at the blob on the radar.

"That's an island."

"We're heading straight for it!" He blinks at it and then looks to me in shock.

"I know."

He shakes his head again, rubbing at his forehead for a moment before he's almost knocked off-balance by a wave. "This can't be. We have to do something. Maybe we can fix it?"

"I'm going to have to try," I tell him. If it's an electronic thing, I'm probably out of luck, but maybe there are few wires that need to be crossed, something, anything.

I can't do nothing.

"How much time do we have?" Richard asks as I move out from behind the wheel. He instinctively goes to it, even though it'll do no good.

"You're the one who loves trigonometry," I tell him.

I leave him up top to puzzle over it, even though I know the answer is in the range of "way too fucking soon."

You don't have time, I tell myself. *You need to prepare everyone for what's going to happen.*

I go down into the cabin and see Lacey leaning against

the table, seemingly in disbelief, and Daisy sitting down beside her giant piece of luggage and for some reason the sight of that thing taking up half the boat makes me want to rage and throw it overboard.

I can't do that right now. I already let it all out. Now I have to pull myself together and do what I can for the ship.

"I'm so sorry, Tai," Daisy whimpers quietly.

"I don't want to hear it," I snap at her. I look at Lacey. "I take it she caught you up to speed?"

To my surprise Lacey isn't crying. She's not even blinking.

"Lacey?" I repeat.

"What's going to happen to us?" she says eventually, slowly meeting my eyes. "Are we going to be okay?"

I tap the side of the stairs where the engine compartment is.

"The only shot we have is if I can get the steering fixed. I don't know how I'll do that, but I'm going to try."

"And if you can't? Then what happens?"

I take in a deep breath, trying to steady my voice. "I'm not sure what happens. But...I do know that we are at the mercy of the wind right now. It is pushing us in one direction and there is no stopping it. The good news in this is that we are heading downwind, which means we are going with the waves. It could be worse. We could be drifting and being battered from the side. If that happened, there's a good chance the boat would capsize."

Daisy gasps at that, bringing her hands to her mouth.

"Yeah," I say. "It's pretty much my worst nightmare."

"So if there are any freighters out there..." Lacey says.

"They aren't the biggest concern right now. We can pick them up on radar. We could call ahead and tell them we can't get out of their way, and maybe there's enough time for them to get out of ours."

"What is our biggest concern?" Lacey asks carefully.

"Ten miles in front of us is an island. It doesn't have a name, it's just a blip on the map. Could just be an atoll with some sand or maybe not even that. But it is land and there is a reef around it and in about a half hour, we're going to collide right into it."

Lacey's mouth drops open.

"So what do we do?" Daisy asks.

"What do we do?" I repeat.

"Yes. We have to prepare ourselves for the collision. So run us through the scenarios. Tell us what you think will happen, step-by-step, so we know how not to die."

Huh. Guess she's on top of things now.

I nod at her and then pop my head up into the cockpit and tell Richard to come back inside.

"What about keeping watch?" he asks.

"You can stay down here and keep watch," I tell him, pointing at the navigation table. "I want us all to be in earshot of the oh shit plan while I try to fix the steering."

With Richard at the table watching the radar, and Daisy and Lacey watching me, I lift up the stairs and access the engine. I know when I first got the boat it had no autopilot, so I had a friend install one. The fucker was cheap but it never worked quite right, so I'm wondering if it was fucked to begin with.

There are some wires. What to do with them, I don't know. I've hotwired a car before and this is nothing like that.

"So, the plan?" Lacey says, finding her voice.

Right.

"Let's do worst-case scenario first," I say, poking through the wires. "Run the simulation. That would be that we hit a rock far from shore. Something small enough that doesn't come up on radar. The start of a reef. Something like that. It breaks through the hull, more like rips through it at the speed we're going, and we quickly take on water. We have to abandon ship. We grab what we can—the satellite phone, water, high caloric foods, medicine, whatever. We get all of that, then we deploy the life raft and get in. And hope that the waves don't capsize us, hope that the wind takes us to land and not away from it. The boat sinks to the bottom of the South Pacific."

I have the deepest, coldest chill as I'm speaking these words. It's hard to believe this is most likely our reality. There seems to be a disconnect with my brain, maybe out of protection.

"And then what happens if we're lost at sea?" Daisy asks, her lip quivering.

I shake my head and get back to figuring out the wires, though I know it's no use. "No point entertaining it. But how about we go through the best-case scenario? That would be that the wind pushes us in through a natural opening into the island. No reef. We run aground, preferably on a sandy beach with minimal damage to the boat. With any luck there's a resort on the island. You girls can have a mini vacation while Richard and I and the locals get the boat back in the water. Then, when the weather clears, we continue sailing to Suva, which is only twenty-four hours away. Lacey and Richard would miss some work, but it's not the end of the world."

"I like this scenario best," Lacey says.

"We all do. But that's not the one we should prepare for." I pause, remembering what Daisy once told me. "Expect the worst but hope for the best."

"We're eight miles out," Richard announces.

I sigh and lean against the engine cover, closing my eyes.

Time to expect the worst.

"Okay," I say, shutting the compartment. I turn around to face them. "I'm not going to be able to fix this in the little time we have left. Lacey, Daisy, go grab a small bag, and Daisy, I mean small, okay, and fill it with whatever necessities you need for a week at sea. Medication, sunscreen, hats, more sunscreen, toothpaste, clothing to protect you from the sun, a deck of cards, stuff that can get wet and survive. Lacey, do the same for Richard."

Both sisters are staring at me with fraught eyes.

"Go, now," I tell them.

Suddenly, they scamper apart, Lacey heading past me to the back cabin, Daisy running to the front.

I look at Richard. "Keep an eye on the radar and gather charts and emergency equipment. The satellite phone. Put the portable radio in a waterproof bag. Take the first aid kit. And tell me when we're five miles out. I'll put in the distress call." I open up the fridge. "I'll be in charge of food and water and I'll get the life raft ready."

Richard swallows hard and then nods. "Aye, aye Captain Wakefield."

"Richard."

"Yes?"

"Please don't start with that right now."

I get to work, getting the smallest amount of food and water so that it won't weigh down the life raft, while being the most calorie dense and nutritious.

This is fucking crazy, I tell myself.

It's all I can tell myself.

I can't allow myself to really think about what's happening because if I do, I will lose it. And if I lose it, I can't keep my friends safe.

After Atarangi's death, I swore I would never be afraid of the ocean. That I wouldn't let it take that power from me. As if the ocean was a sentient, malevolent being that wanted to harm her. I felt like I made a bargain every time I stepped on a boat, and now I'm afraid that maybe that bargain has run its course.

It's time to collect.

I shove those thoughts away. I can't right now.

I have to fix this.

When I'm done with the food, I head up top and look around. The waves are bigger, the cockpit is filled with an inch of water that barely has enough time to drain before it's filled again.

Once I'm clipped in, I make my way to the life raft at the back. There's the dingy too, that's been hauled up for the voyage, resting on its side on the starboard side of the boat, but it's smaller and there's not enough time to get it ready.

When everything looks ready to go, Richard pops his head up briefly.

"Five miles," he says grimly.

I go back downstairs and sit at the navigation table. Lacey and Daisy have gathered around us.

I pick up the VHF receiver, searching for a signal.

I hold down the button and say something I never thought I'd say.

"Mayday, mayday, mayday. This is the sailing vessel Atarangi."

11

DAISY

My phone.

I know Tai just said to grab whatever essentials we needed for a week at sea, but I have to take my phone. Sure, there's no signal out here but maybe on whatever island we might crash on there will be. What if there is wi-fi? I could make a castaway Instagram account. At the very least, my phone could keep us entertained.

Better grab a charger, too.

I stick the phone and the charger in a Ziploc pouch, sealing it tight, then shove it in my Louis Vuitton Speedy, which is the size of a small duffle bag and already stuffed to the gills with everything else I've deemed an essential item. For a moment I'm worried that the salt water will damage the patina but then I realize how stupid of a concern that is when we all might die.

I haven't been letting myself think that way. In fact, I'm trying not to give much thought to anything right now. My heart is pounding and I feel like I'm floating as I run around trying to pack for what could be weeks at sea.

There are so many "what ifs" that want to tear through my brain right now.

What if the boat sinks before we can abandon ship and we drown?

What if the life raft doesn't work and we're stuck on top of the ship, waiting for help?

What if the life raft sinks?

What if we fall overboard and are eaten by sharks?

What if no one will rescue us?

It doesn't do me any good, so I just bat each hysteria-inducing thought out of my head, and focus on anything else I need right now.

"Do you have everything?" Lacey asks frantically as she pops her head in the cabin.

My heart sinks. "I don't know. I don't want to leave any of this behind. What about my Kindle, my laptop? I have an expensive crossbody bag in my suitcase, I…"

She shakes her head and gives me a vicious little glare. "Really? That's what you're worried about right now? Your fucking purse? Maybe stop being shallow for a moment and realize what's happening."

"I know what's happening, okay?" I yell. "I'm trying to, just, handle this!"

"Ladies," Richard calls out from the nav table. "We're at five miles."

Shit.

I grab my bag and we head back into the main cabin, while Richard pokes his head into the cockpit. "Five miles," he warns Tai.

Tai appears a second later, soaked to the bone, a lock of wet dark hair sticking to his forehead. He avoids my eyes and sits down at the nav table, eyeing the radar.

Picks up the VHF radio receiver.

"Mayday, mayday, mayday. This is the sailing vessel Atarangi."

The words make my stomach churn.

"Mayday, mayday, mayday," he repeats. "This is the sailing vessel Atarangi. We are in a distress situation. Steering has gone out. We are being pushed toward land, five miles out. We are at..." he pauses to read the chart. "18°13'53.2 south and 178°46'22.0 west. There are four people on board. I believe we are in danger of running aground a reef near one of the Lau Islands. Over."

Silence.

Tai eyes us all.

"What's happening?" Lacey asks.

"Have to wait a minute for it to go through," he says.

It's the longest minute of my life.

Finally.

"Can you...repeat..." A garbled voice comes through and then is buried by static.

"Fuck," Tai swears and then switches the radio to another channel.

"Mayday, mayday, mayday. This is the sailing vessel Atarangi. Do you copy?"

We wait. No one dares to move or breath, all of us straining to hear any response over the constant roar of the ocean, the hull slamming against the waves.

Tai repeats the call again, louder this time.

"Uh," Richard says, and we follow his gaze to the portholes. All we see outside are waves, but the difference is now you can actually see the waves instead of the blackness of before.

Richard turns and runs up the stairs to the deck, while the rest of us wait for an answer from the radio.

Tai sighs, getting visibly frustrated, his hand gripping

the mouthpiece so hard I'm afraid he's going to break it. He makes the call again.

"Mayday, mayday, mayday."

"Comrades?" Richard says, and I look at Lacey as if to say, *What is wrong with your husband? Comrades? Can't he say, you guys?*

"You're going to want to see this," he adds.

"I'll keep trying," Tai says quietly. "Be careful."

Lacey and I quickly head up to the top.

Richard is standing on the side of the ship, holding onto the railing for balance, facing forward.

Neither Lacey or I stray far from the hatch, instead we peer through the clear dodger at the horizon.

There is a horizon now. Somewhere in the east the sun is rising, breaking through low dark clouds in some places, making the faintest grainy light shine across the ocean. On one hand, that's great, because it means the storm is breaking up over there.

On the other hand, we can see exactly what we're getting into.

There's a mass of island rising right before us.

"Oh my god," I whisper.

We're still far out but we're moving fast and, more than that, the light is shining on the tops of the waves breaking just a few hundred meters in front of the ship.

"It's a reef!" Richard yells. "Collision eminent!"

Again, does this guy think he's in charge of the Starship Enterprise?

That snarky little thought feels good before the feeling of immense dread sets in.

We're fucked.

"What?" Tai says, bounding up the stairs and onto the cockpit. He stands beside Richard and stares at the sunrise.

Atarangi.

The morning sky, showing us our fate.

"We're going to hit," Tai says. He looks to us. "Go down-stairs, get everything and throw it up here!"

I don't hesitate. I scramble down the stairs with Lacey in tow.

I'm panicking, as I think anyone would in this situation, when the boat you're on is going to collide with a reef and you all might potentially die. I'm not even thinking, I'm just doing, grabbing everything we all had gathered and passing it to Lacey who is throwing it all up top.

"Is this it?" Richard asks when we come back up.

We nod. We all have our own bag, plus a bag of food and a bag of supplies. We're wearing rainproof gear and lifejack-ets. We're ready for something.

Or, we should be. I glance at the bow of the boat again just as we slam down another wave and the landmass looms larger, a murky sun behind its silhouette. The island seems fairly big, though with the way the boat is moving, it's hard to say. In the distance I can see another glimpse of a much smaller island.

But it's the reef that terrifies me. The way the waves are breaking, indicating how shallow it is. In fact, the body of water between the reef and the island, the lagoon, isn't as rough as it is out here in the deep.

The deep.

I feel so scared I might pee my pants.

"We're going to collide soon, another twenty metres," Tai yells at us, going back toward the life raft, which is housed in a large cylinder. "If anyone is clipped in, you need to unclip now. We can't afford to be dragged if that's the case. We need to get in the raft, now."

"Hold on!" Richard yells, and with a groan flips open the

bench seats, revealing the storage underneath. He grabs a fishing pole.

Tai nods at him. Good idea.

Meanwhile I'm thinking our survival might depend on Richard's fishing skills.

Then Tai lifts up the life raft cylinder, which must be at least four feet long and wide as a tree trunk, and raises it above his head with a huge feat of strength, tossing it in the water where it's immediately swallowed by waves.

It pops back up, and Tai begins to tug on the line attached to it as it drags behind the boat

"Come on, come on!" he yells, yanking at the line, trying to get the cylinder to open and inflate.

"Tai!" Richard yells, and then his words disappear as the most horrific screeching noise, the sound of wood splintering and fiberglass being punctured fills the air and I am thrown to the floor.

I land on the bench just opposite of the one Richard opened, my hands trying to break my fall as the waves start washing over the boat as it starts to pivot to one side. The sound continues to fill my head until I think that's all that's left of the world.

Then I hear screaming.

Lacey!

I manage to get up and look to see her slipping off the side of the boat, one hand desperately reaching for the railing before she goes over.

Without even thinking I lunge forward, landing on my elbows and sliding forward on the teak deck, splinter city, as the waves rock me in her direction. I reach for her hand, grasping it.

Then she throws her other arm up and I grab the other hand.

Her legs are in the water when the waves hit and my grip is slipping.

So am I.

I'm tumbling, almost going over the railing and losing my contact with her but I manage to keep my ass low and place the soles of my feet at the railing bars for leverage.

I pull her up as much as I can, straining, using every inch of my underused abs and muscles for balance and strength.

Then, just when I think my legs are going to give out, Richard is behind me, pulling me back by the waist. It gives me enough momentum to pull Lacey back on board and into the cockpit.

"Are you okay?" I ask her, even though it's obvious none of us are okay right now and that all looked rather painful.

She nods, giving me a meek, grateful look. Then she looks over at Richard in surprise.

One of the lenses in his glasses has cracked, blood pouring out of his mouth.

He smiles at her in relief.. He's missing a front tooth.

"Get in, get in!" Tai yells from the back of the boat, distracting us from Richard's face, and motioning down into the water. "Now!"

Oh my god.

No.

I can't do this. I can't leave this boat and get in a raft. I can't!

But then I get a good look at the boat.

We're no longer moving forward which is good, but we're twisted enough to the side that the waves keep crashing over.

Then there's the matter of the inside.

I stumble over to the stairs leading into the cabin.

There's at least two feet of water down below, sloshing to the level of the couches, cushions starting to float. The water seems to be coming from the fore cabin, the door twisted off.

Oh god, it's sinking.

We're sinking.

"Come on!" Tai yells. "Abandon the fucking ship!"

Lacey pulls at my arm and it's enough for me to snap out of it.

I follow her and Richard down the cockpit to the back where Tai has unfastened the railing. The life raft sits on the water, fully inflated, a little canopy over it. It looks like a cheap floating house that kids would play in, albeit with a flashing beacon on the top.

How the hell is that going to protect us?

"Get in!" Tai says, reaching forward and grabbing me by the arm, pulling me to the landing at the back of the boat, where once upon a time I would sit on calm days and watch the water pass beneath my dangling feet.

Seems like a lifetime ago.

The raft is tied up against the ship, but with the waves threatening to tip us all over, I'm scared to death to try and jump in it.

"Jump!" Tai yells. "You'll be okay, you have your life jacket."

I almost want him to push me but I don't think he would.

Instead, I take in a deep breath, conjure up all my courage, and leap.

I miss, of course.

Half of me lands in the water, so much colder than I thought it would be, but most of me (my boobs) lands in the raft, so I'm able to work that weight load to my advantage and tumble inside.

Some of our bags are already inside, so Tai must have some pretty good aim. I wait under the plastic tarp, the bottom of the small enclosure moving violently with the waves, and then Lacey manages to get inside the raft, then Richard.

It's tight in here and smells like chemicals, and I hold hands with Lacey, more me wanting to be comforted than the other way around, as Tai starts throwing the rest of the bags to Richard.

Then one doesn't make it. Richard's bag. It bounces off the raft, just missing the opening and lands further away in the water.

"Fuck!" Tai yells. "Sorry Richard!'

"It's fine!" Richard yells back.

Tai quickly climbs down to the bottom of the boat's platform, with the fishing rod in one hand, and the rope attached to the life raft. Then he ties the rope around his waist, tight.

He closes his eyes and jumps straight down into the water, sinking beneath the waves, only the top of the fishing pole visible.

"Tai!" I scream, as his life jacket pulls him back up the surface. "What are you doing? Get in!"

He shakes his head and shoves the rod in the raft, then starts to swim up alongside the boat, away from us.

"What is he doing?" I cry out.

"This raft is only for four people and we have too many supplies," Richard says grimly. "If you haven't noticed, Tai is all muscle. If he came in here, we would sink."

Oh, I noticed all right, but now's not the time to dwell on it.

"He's trying to swim to shore," Lacey says. "Pull us all in."

"A modern-day He-Man," Richard comments.

"But that's crazy!" And yet, that's what Tai is attempting to do, he's swimming, making powerful strokes and we're actually moving away from the boat a little, I guess because the boat could suddenly collapse on us, or we could be bashed against it.

The land in front of us is getting closer and when I chance a look over the side into the water, I think I can see the coral reefs just below the surface. No wonder we ran aground, the reef is so close to the surface, I—

A scraping sound fills the raft cavity, then a hiss. The raft seems to stop moving for a moment, then we're lurched forward as Tai pulls us.

"Shit!" Richard swears. "I think we punctured on the reef."

He leans out of the raft and Tai is swimming back to us.

The raft starts to deflate in one corner, water starting to seep in right behind Lacey.

"Stay where you are," Tai yells at us, spitting out water as we bob up and down in the waves. "Stay in the raft until you can't."

He starts swimming again, trying so hard to get us closer and closer to land.

It works.

We're about fifty meters from the beach.

But the raft doesn't have enough buoyancy anymore.

"Time to get the fuck out," I say, grabbing my bag.

Lacey and Richard do the same, grabbing the rest of the stuff.

One by one, we awkwardly, reluctantly pile out into the water.

I think this is the point where my adrenaline runs out.

The moment I'm floating in the water, I barely have enough strength to hold onto my LV, let alone swim. All of us are struggling. We're just slaves to the life jackets at the moment.

But then I see Tai coming back for us, walking, lit from behind by the light of dawn. He grabs me underneath my shoulders and hauls me up onto land until he leaves me on the beach.

He does the same for Lacey and Richard.

Then he goes and collapses on his back further up on the sand.

The waves are breaking on me now, so somehow I manage to get to my knees and then crawl up onto the shore, away from the water, collapsing on my side.

It's hard to breathe. I spit out water. Everything aches and burns.

I don't know how long I lie there, but eventually my breathing slows and the sky lightens enough that I can make out the colors in the shadows.

A white beach.

Dark green jungle.

Clear blue water.

We made it.

But where?

"We need to take shelter," Tai says, helping Lacey to her feet. "Just over here."

I get to my feet and stagger forward, following, Richard behind me.

The sand gives way to coconut palms and flowering bushes and ferns and a dark, earthy smelling jungle beyond.

I collapse again to my knees, finding a soft spot in the sandy dirt, laying my head against my bag.

"Everyone okay?" Tai asks.

We all make sounds that either sound like yes or no, but obviously none of us are dying.

Yet.

"What do we do now?" I ask, my voice sore and hoarse from screaming and swallowing salt water.

"We wait for the storm to die down a bit," Tai says, leaning against a palm tree, watching the horizon.

Watching where his boat is.

Or what's left of her.

My heart sinks for him. As glad as I am to be alive, what happened to Atarangi is all too much to handle.

"Then," he says, "I'll use the satellite phone to call for help."

"Will that work?" I ask, thinking of the VHF.

"It will, as will the locator beacon that activated when the raft opened up. No matter what happens, people will know where we are. People will find us."

"Do you promise?"

He turns his head ever so slightly, though I can't read his expression in the shadows.

"I promise. Get some rest."

12

DAISY

I wake up with my face pressed against wet dirt, my eyes focusing on an ant that is hurriedly crossing in front of me, heading somewhere on a mission.

I'm also drooling. I guess some things don't change, no matter where you find yourself.

And where am I, anyway?

I blink, my eyes burning from the dried salt water on my lashes, and I slowly, carefully sit up, my head woozy. My muscles ache like I've been passed out on the hard ground for a few hours, which isn't a lie.

The sun outside this thicket of ferns and bushes is bright and I have to shield my eyes for a moment before I focus on Lacey and Richard. She's sleeping with her back against a coconut palm, Richard is on the ground with his head in her lap. Both of them are snoring.

My first thought is that I am so happy that they're alive.

Things could have gone so much worse than they did.

My second thought is that Richard snores like a banshee, and Lacey is drooling on his forehead. My god, it must run in the Lewis family.

And Tai...

I look around, slowly getting up.

He's nowhere in sight.

I try not to panic, looking around.

The jungle behind me is thick with foliage and the sound of birds and buzzing insects. The air is so humid that it takes me a moment to realize my clothes are still wet from the ocean and my skin is damp. The jungle looks like a dangerous place, and by dangerous, I mean full of insects and gross things that I don't want any part of.

I walk past the row of palms and fragrant flowers between the jungle and the beach, and step out into the sand.

Holy crap.

In the burning light of what must be mid-day, it's apparent that not only is the storm completely gone, but it's dropped us off in the lap of a quintessential deserted island.

The sand is blindingly white, the water the palest of blue. To the right of us, the land slopes upward until it forms steep rock cliffs. To the left, the beach continues in a flat track, on and on.

In front of me is Tai, sitting on the sand where it meets the water, gentle clear waves lapping his feet, as if a storm never passed through here at all.

His back is to me and he's looking out across the blue lagoon, toward the reefs.

Toward Atarangi.

She's still there! She's on her side and the sails are ripped to shreds, but she hasn't sunken into the depths. She's still there.

Something about that warms my heart.

I want to go and say something about that to Tai, but I

think he's probably still mad at me, since this thing is pretty much all my fault.

At the very least, I need to use the washroom.

I quickly turn around and start looking around where we slept. Lacey and Richard are still snoring away but a quick search of our bags proves that nothing stayed dry.

I'm looking for tissue, to be precise, since none of us had the smarts to bring toilet paper.

Who knew it was one of the essential items?

So I head into the bush, trying not to go too far because, got to admit, it's kind of scary being on an island like this. Maybe people do live here, which is great, but I don't want them to watch me pee. Or maybe there are some crazy lizards that bite your butt or something. I don't know.

What I do know is I squat and go about my business and...

I feel eyes on me.

Hear a snuff of air.

From the side.

You know that scene in *Jurassic Park*, when Robert Muldoon, the sexy Australian warden, is hunting for the raptors and the raptor suddenly appears from the side and he's all "Clever girl"?

Well, yeah. I just looked over and there's a fucking pair of eyes looking at me.

A motherfucking *goat*.

I scream and fall over, scrambling to my feet and yanking up my pants and then I'm running, I don't know in what direction but I don't care, I'm so disoriented.

That was a goat, right? Goat eyes are so damn creepy, it could have been some demon!

"Daisy?" I hear Lacey's voice.

I run toward her voice, nearly knocking her over when I crash through some bushes.

"What's wrong?" she asks, holding onto me, her eyes wide. "What happened?"

"A goat!" I manage to yelp.

She frowns. "A goat?"

"Was watching me pee!"

"What? Where?"

I try to point where I came from but I have no idea anymore. "I don't know but I was going to the bathroom and minding my business, and I looked over and a fucking goat face was staring at me."

Clever goat.

"Well that's a good sign," Lacey says. "Means there might be people here. Goats are an introduced species."

Even so, I get the feeling she doesn't believe me.

"Come on, let's go back to camp."

"To camp?" I repeat. "It's like we already live here now."

She gives me a look that says, *We do.*

Back at *camp*, Richard is now awake, leaning against the palm tree and rubbing at his head.

"Are you okay?" Lacey asks, dropping to her knees beside him.

"I have an atrocious headache," he says, slowly looking up at us. "And a face to match."

Yeah, so Richard isn't looking the best right now.

He's pale, his tooth is missing, his one lens is still cracked, he's got a spreading bruise under that eye, and a split upper lip.

"You look great," I tell him adamantly, crouching down.

"Don't be facetious. I look like a Benzite."

"I don't know what that is," I admit.

"It's from Star Trek," Lacey says.

I shake my head. I guess when Richard gets stressed, he goes to his happy place.

"Can you see without your glasses?" I ask him.

"Blind as a caecilian."

"Is that a Star Trek reference again?"

"It's a type of amphibian that lives underground," Lacey informs me.

"Can you give him your glasses?" I ask her. "You can see without yours."

She pauses, brows coming together. "No I can't."

"You weren't wearing them the other day and I saw you read the back of my book just fine."

The book in question was a historical romance novel about a reformed rake I burned through in a day. I picked up a bunch of paperbacks in the airport gift shops, and managed to pack some last night since I wasn't sure my Kindle was going to hold out. Kindle, paperback—it's good to have your reading materials covered on all bases.

Before Lacey can protest again, I reach out and snatch her glasses off her face, putting them on.

I can see perfectly, which means there's no prescription in these glasses.

Just as I suspected.

"You don't need glasses!" I yell gleefully. "I knew it!"

"That's preposterous. Of course she does," Richard says adamantly.

Lacey snatches them back, slipping them on. "I do. Maybe *you* need glasses."

Right. "I don't and you know it. You had perfect vision growing up, you were always bragging about it. Then you graduated high school and suddenly you said you were nearly blind. I always figured you wore them just so you'd seem smarter."

Lacey is turning red. She shakes her head and looks away.

Richard holds out his hand. "Give them to me."

She shakes her head harder.

"Lacey Loo," he says. "Give me your glasses."

Reluctantly, she takes them off and hands them over.

Richard then takes off his broken pair and slips hers on. Frowns. "Lacey…"

"Okay, okay, fine!" she suddenly cries out, getting to her feet. "So, I don't need glasses." She puts "need" in quotation marks. "I have to wear them. People won't take me seriously if I don't."

"It's okay," I tell her, getting to my feet. "I totally get it."

"It's not okay," Richard says grimly. "How could you lie to me?"

Uh oh.

Time for me to skedaddle.

I grab my Speedy duffel and then head to the beach, ready to start unpacking it and drying stuff out.

To my complete surprise, Tai is in the water, swimming across the lagoon toward the boat.

"Tai!" I yell at him. "What are you doing?"

It's not like it's a casual swim out to the boat, the lagoon has to be at least three hundred feet across to the reef.

If he can hear me, he doesn't show it. He just keeps going, his bronzed back and arms a contrast against the clear turquoise waters as he makes his powerful strokes toward Atarangi.

Now that the water is flat and the weather is calm, it does look like a beautiful place to swim, but I remember enough about marine biology to know that atolls aren't immune to sharks. Great whites are rare here in the South Pacific, and we're most likely to find hammerheads, nurse, and reef sharks, generally harmless, but that doesn't mean tiger sharks aren't lurking about, especially after a storm where the water beyond the coral reef might be murkier.

"Leave him be," Lacey says from behind me.

I jump, whirling around. She's not wearing her glasses anymore.

"I thought you were fighting," I tell her.

"I'm done." She shrugs. "He'll get over it."

I look back to Tai. "I saw him sitting on the beach earlier, just staring at the boat. Now he's swimming to it. What's he doing?"

"Probably going to see if he can salvage anything."

"I worry about him," I admit. "I know how much that boat meant to him."

She eyes me carefully for a moment.

"What?" I ask.

"I don't think you do," she says knowingly.

I fold my arms across my chest, hating this game she plays where she knows something and doesn't come right out and tell me. I'm awful at this game. I tell everyone everything, whether they want to hear it or not.

"Lacey, what's going on?"

She wriggles her lips, deliberating. Finally she says, "It's not my place to tell you this so please just forget I told you. But, Tai had a sister."

I blink. *Had* a sister?

"He doesn't talk about her. No one in the family does. Her room in their house is still preserved, hasn't been touched since the day she died."

"Oh my god," I say softly, my heart aching for him. "I had no idea."

"I know you didn't. Like I said, he doesn't talk about her. Ever." Quietly she adds, "I wish he would. I think that's why he used to be so into boxing when he was younger. You've seen his knuckles, right? Only way he could get out the rage."

"What happened to her?"

Lacey exhales sadly, her eyes going to Tai as he swims further and further away. "She was sixteen. They were at Piha beach, it's near Auckland. Beautiful place, but dangerous swimming conditions. His sister was a surfer, almost pro. Really, really good. She was out there for a competition and a wave completely knocked her out. Tai was there watching, he was a part-time lifeguard so he had the skills. He ran out into the water to save her, as did a few other people when it became apparent that she was drowning, but..."

Fuck.

I feel like the wind has been knocked out of me. "My god. That's horrible."

She nods. "You'd think it would have scared Tai from the ocean, but he still went back to being a lifeguard, still got into sailing. Sometimes I feel like he thinks he's made some kind of bargain with the ocean, at least there have been one or two occasions where he's gotten drunk and said something like that."

I stare numbly at Tai as he almost reaches the boat, looking so small in the water compared to it. "He shouldn't be doing that. It feels dangerous."

"He'll do it anyway. He won't give up on that ship. Atarangi. That was his sister's name."

I glance at her, my eyes wide. "No... He named the boat after her?"

Lacey nods. "That's why I said to let him be. He's obviously going through something right now. We all are but, I think he might be taking it worse than any of us."

"So why should I let him be? Right now he needs us."

She gives me a wry look. "I know you don't know him like I do, but you at least get that he's the strong silent type who wants to be left alone. You know what happens when you get in his way. And," she pauses, "I think you're the last person he wants to talk to right now."

Because this is all my fault.

I close my eyes and let the guilt wash over me. I've been trying to ignore it but that's probably the worst thing you can do.

Lacey puts her hand on my shoulder. "I don't blame you for this. Neither does Richard. Everything was a mess and accidents happen." She nods in the direction of Tai. "But he's going to need some time. He's reactive even on a good day, and right now we all need to keep a clear head. So just stay clear of him, okay? Don't meddle, don't get in his way."

"Just let him stay mad at me and blame me for wrecking his boat named after his dead sister? For almost getting us all killed?" I spit out indignantly.

"Yes," she says. "Live with it and let him live with it. You'll know when the time is right." She starts walking off in the direction of the cliffs.

"Where are you going?" I call out after her.

"Want to see the cliffs up close," she says. "I'm curious about the fauna growing on it."

Ugh. I really don't want to be alone right now, especially after what I just learned about his sister, but it seems that's what everyone wants. Tai, Lacey, Richard, they're all off on their own and figuring things out, and here I am not wanting to be alone with my thoughts.

At least you're off the ship, the voice in my head speaks up, the one that so desperately wants to focus on the positive, even though there is no positive other than the fact that we're not dead.

And yeah, at least we're off the ship, but now we're stuck together on what looks to be a deserted island.

Or is it?

I open up my bag, which is completely ruined and saggy, and vigorously dump the contents out onto the sand. Naturally, everything is soaked. I've got a pair of jean shorts, a gauzy knee-length skirt, a bikini, several pairs of clean underwear, a bra (why did I pack a bra?), a sports bra (did I think I was going to the gym?), leggings, a flannel shirt, a peasant top, a tank top, two t-shirts, flip flops, a pair of socks, a small makeup bag, a candle (what?), a paperback, nail polish, tweezers, sunscreen, a baseball cap, sunglasses, my vibrator (don't even ask), and finally, my phone and charger in a Ziploc pouch.

The phone and charger seem to be okay. Granted, there's no way to charge the charger but at least the phone can get one jump out of it.

Excitedly I take the phone out and turn it on.

It works!

"Yassss," I cry out at the sight of my now familiar wallpaper, a sunset shot I took during the wedding.

But there's no signal at all. I expected that, but I'm still disappointed.

Still, I open up the maps and try to find our location.

The GPS is slow and there's a lot of grey grid as it tries to load. I can see the blinking blue dot, I just can't see where it's located.

I wait for the map to load, occasionally stealing a glance at Tai. He's reached the boat, standing on the reef to try and get aboard. Normally I would tell someone off that's standing on a reef because they're damaging rare coral that may never grow back again, but he's too far to hear me and I'm sure he wouldn't appreciate it. I'm also sure he knows that himself.

I glance back at the phone, but the grid is still loading. I carefully place it on top of my bag and then set about laying everything out in the sun so it can dry. I make sure to hide the vibrator inside one of my reef shoes. I'm honestly not sure why I packed that, guess I'm not really using my head during a crisis.

Once I'm done, I check my phone again. It's loaded, showing our location.

Which shows a long blob of an island with no name. No roads or any other markings either.

It's rather phallic looking. Rounded at one end, like two humps melded together, skinnier at the other, widening just a little at the tip.

Dong Island.

Doesn't really matter what its real name is now—it's Dong Island.

"What are you doing?" Lacey asks me, trudging through the sand toward me. "You have a phone?"

"Yeah, I have a phone. It's my most prized possession."

"You're supposed to only pack essentials," she says and then eyes my massive spread of clothing, looking aghast. "Daisy, did you pack your entire wardrobe?"

"No," I reply testily. I had to leave *a lot* of clothes behind. "I'm sorry I didn't want to spend days at sea in a raft wearing the same clothes and stinking up the place. And why wouldn't I take my phone? How is that not an essential?"

"Is there a signal?"

"Does it matter?"

"What use is it then?"

I gasp. "Are you kidding? Please don't tell me you used your phone only for phone calls."

She narrows her eyes. "I also write emails. Which is worthless if you don't have a connection."

"Well for your information, the GPS on my maps works and I found the island, so there."

I thrust my phone out and she takes it from me, peering at it.

"You're burning, by the way," I say, grabbing the sunscreen beside me and offering it to her.

She sighs dramatically and we swap, phone for the sunscreen.

"Why did our mother have to have such fair skin?" she whines as she slops some on.

"You saw the island, right?"

Dong Island.

"I did." She hands me back the sunscreen and I quickly slap some on myself. "There's no name. Nothing useful."

"Did you zoom out though? It shows that we're right at the bottom of the Lau Islands."

"Tai already mentioned that."

"Yeah, but a lot of those islands don't look that far from here," I tell her. "Maybe you and Richard can use Atarangi's dingy and check them out."

She gives me a dry look. "Want to get rid of us that bad?"

"Worth a shot," I say, even though I know those other islands are probably hundreds of miles away.

"We need to explore *this* island," she says.

Dong Island.

"I agree," I tell her, getting to my feet. "But we should probably wait for Tai to return."

Lacey makes an impatient huff. I have a feeling she's trying to avoid Richard.

"Why don't you help me make an SOS sign out of shells and stuff," I tell her.

"You go right ahead. I'm going for a walk."

"More fauna catch your eye?"

You can't ignore your husband forever.

So, while she goes for another walk, I go about trying to build an SOS sign big enough to see from an airplane. Unfortunately math isn't my strong suit.

With Lacey heading down the beach, and Tai standing on the wreck, I head back into the jungle toward "camp."

Richard is riffling through Lacey's bag and hanging stuff on branches.

"Hey Richard," I say.

He jumps, lets out a high yelp.

"Sorry," I apologize. "Didn't mean to scare you."

"Oh, it's not your fault," he says, hand to his chest. "With my vision limited, my senses are on overdrive attempting to compensate."

Uh huh. "How are you feeling?"

"Still a bit of a headache but I had some water, feeling a trifle better now." He pauses. "Where's Lacey?" he asks lightly, trying to sound blasé.

"She's looking at plants. Tai swam back to the boat."

"He did!"

"It's still there, stuck on the reef." I peer at him. He looks a little pale. "Maybe you should get out of the bush and go get some sun or something. Nothing will dry in here."

He gives a quick shake of his head. Probably still mad at his wife for her lying about needing glasses thing.

"You think you know someone," he starts.

"Listen," I say, quickly talking over him, not wanting to be dragged into their first marital quarrel. "How big do I need to make an SOS sign? Or is HELP a better option? More letters though…"

"I doubt you need to make one of those," he says.

"They do it on all the survivor shows. Except Survivor."

"The raft had a beacon, Tai gave the distress call, and we have a satellite phone…I just can't seem to find the latter."

Great.

"Look, I want to do something. How big do I make the letters?"

He sighs. "As big as you can. And SOS is a better choice, if you ask me. Though of course, if you wish to keep with the original maritime notation, you need a line placed over the SOS and—"

"Okay thank you," I tell him, turning around before he can give me the history behind it. "Oh, and if you hear anything in the jungle, it's probably a goat."

"What?" he asks, but I'm already running to the beach.

I spend the next hour trying to use my clothes and items, plus various sticks and branches and coconut shells trying to spell out SOS. Because of the size, I have no idea what it looks like or if it's even legible, but it's probably good enough.

By the time I'm done I'm exhausted and starving, and both Lacey and Tai have returned from their expeditions.

"What on earth are you doing?" Tai asks me, hauling a duffel bag over his shoulder, soaking sleeping bags hastily tied to it.

My heart skips a bit, that he's actually talking to me. It's good to see him.

And I mean, like, really good.

He's shirtless, wearing just his boxer briefs, zero hint of modesty whatsoever. Instead his golden brown, built as fuck, taut and muscled body is on full display. I hadn't even noticed that he has a Polynesian-looking tattoo across his chest. I want to ask him about it, I want to take my time admiring him. I especially want to let my eyes drift down to his junk.

But this isn't the time or place.

"I'm building an SOS signal," I tell him.

"No need." He waves the satellite phone at me. "I talked to rescue."

"You did!" I exclaim.

"Oh thank god," Lacey says, wiping her brow.

He nods. "Yes, well there's good news and bad news."

"Bad news first," I tell him.

He sighs. "We have to call back in a few days."

"What?" Lacey exclaims. "Who did you call?"

"It's complicated," Tai says. "I had to not only swim back to the boat so I could actually pick up a signal, but there really isn't any protocol for figuring out who to call. You can't just call 911 here."

"So who did you call?"

"I eventually got through to a search and rescue out of Suva. They were able to see where we were because of the phone's GPS, but because we're all alive and we don't have any life-threatening injuries, they said we're low on their priority list. Apparently that storm was a wild one. Lots of people worse off than we are on other islands, not just other ships."

"Maybe call back again, try someone else? Maybe a private company?" Lacey asks.

"I don't think it would be any different," he says, "and it's important we don't waste the battery. Took me ten minutes to finally get through."

"So, what's the good news?" I ask.

"I managed to salvage some stuff from the boat." He pats

the duffel bag "And at least they know we're here. If we're placed low on priority, well that makes me think the situation isn't half-bad for us."

"Isn't half-bad?" Lacey exclaims. "We're shipwrecked!"

"We're going to have to rough it for a few days," he says, walking past us. "Could be worse."

I have to say, with everything Lacey told me, I expected Tai to be taking this a lot worse. Now that I know he's not *that* worried, it makes me feel less scared.

"Hey," I call after him. "My phone works. I was able to pull up the island on the map."

He reluctantly stops and turns slightly toward me. "And?"

"It looks like a dong."

He flinches and I swear I see a hint of a smile on his lips. *Worth it.*

Then he shakes his head and keeps walking to the camp.

"Grow up, Daisy," Lacey hisses at me, following him.

I shrug.

13

———

DAISY

Our first day on the island passes by somewhat comfortably, given the circumstances of us being shipwrecked.

Other than the fact that Richard is still giving Lacey the cold shoulder, and that makes her mad at *him*, for some backwards reason.

And Tai, of course, is still mad at me. He's not ignoring me completely, but I can tell he tries not to address me, and he definitely doesn't want to look at me. There have been numerous times that I've wanted to pull him aside and apologize profusely for what happened, as well as talk about his sister, but I know when to keep my distance.

Besides, he can't ignore me forever. Where is he going to go?

Actually that's a stupid question. I can't really tell how large the island is, but I know that it's big enough (and phallic enough) to show up on my phone. I suppose if he wanted to, he could head down to one end and create a separate "No Redheads Allowed" camp. That is what happened on *Lost*, isn't it? Half the people stayed on the beach, the other half went into the jungle. Live together, die alone?

At any rate, we're stuck together for now, having just finished eating heated up cans of beans. We weren't spared Richard doing an overly dramatic "I have made fire" Tom Hanks impression after he created the fire, but it's easy when you have a lighter.

"How long was Tom Hanks on that island in *Castaway*?" I ask.

We're all on the beach, sitting around the small, crackling fire. The sun set just a few minutes ago, a beautiful golden show, and it's still light enough to see, with the first stars starting to appear above.

"He was stuck there four years," Lacey says. "God, I hope that's not our fate."

"It's not," Tai tells her sternly. "Tomorrow I'll set out to explore. For all we know, there's a resort on the other side of the island."

"Can you imagine?" I sigh happily, hugging my knees to my chest. "Like, a Four Seasons or something? They'd have Egyptian cotton sheets, and turn-down service, and those little bungalows over the water."

"That's not too different from this," Richard says.

"Uh huh," I tell him. "We just ate beans out of a can, like a bunch of hobos. The only reason we have something even remotely nice to sleep on is because Tai went back to the boat and managed to get two sleeping bags. For the four of us. We don't even have pillows."

"Or toilet paper," Richard says.

"Just use leaves," Tai mutters. Then he adjusts himself and winces.

"Are you okay?" I ask.

He clamps his mouth shut and nods. "I'm...fine."

I frown and then exchange a look with the other two. They shrug.

"You know the first thing I would do if there turned out to be a resort?" Lacey asks.

"Complain to the manager?" I quip.

She rolls her eyes. "No." Then she smiles. "I would order the biggest, juiciest cheeseburger they had with loads of fries. McDonald's fries. And then I'd wash it down with an ice-cold glass of white wine. Oh, maybe a pina colada."

She's practically drooling.

"You'd think you were stranded here for weeks, not twelve hours," Tai says, wincing again.

"Uh, we've been at sea for ten days," I point out. "That's a long time to be away from civilization. Though I wouldn't go for a cheeseburger. I would get a big greasy bucket of fried chicken and a beer."

"That's the ticket," Richard muses. He's still wearing his broken glasses and looks off into the distance happily, obviously day-dreaming. "Make it a six-pack."

Too bad no one had thought to pack alcohol as an essential item, although we had pretty much run through the supply already. I did have my bottle of vodka I won in poker, and a couple of bottles of New Zealand wine in my suitcase, but I didn't think to take them.

"Anyway, I don't think this is the island from *Castaway*," Richard says. "More like *Gilligan's Island*. Hey Tai? You're Gilligan and I'm the Skipper."

Tai gives him a wary look. "Excuse me?"

"Well, Daisy is obviously Ginger," Lacey says. "She's got the boobs and the hair and the attitude. I'll be the Professor."

"You're Mary-Anne," Richard protests.

"Mary-Anne isn't a blond, and anyway, how sexist do

you have to be to assume that I can't be the professor just because I'm a woman? I *am* a professor, Richard."

"So am I."

"And you're definitely not the Skipper," Tai says, adjusting his seating again.

"So then who am I?" Richard asks woefully. "The professor's wife?"

"You're Gilligan," Lacey tells him.

He seems more offended than he should be. "I am *not* Gilligan. Gilligan is the hapless imbecile that keeps screwing everything up." He jerks his chin at me. "Daisy is Gilligan."

I gasp. "I am not! I'm Ginger! One hundred percent."

"Well, this whole thing *is* your fault," Tai says under his breath.

No. No. He. Didn't.

I give him the sharpest daggers I can muster with my eyes, hoping they'll burn holes right into his sexy head. "I said I was sorry a million times. What do you want me to do? Get on my knees and beg for forgiveness?"

He tilts his head thoughtfully, trying to weigh that option.

Jerk.

"Okay, so maybe it's not *Gilligan's Island*," Lacey says quickly, trying to calm the volcano that's about to go off inside of me. She knows that look I get. I'm already Tomato Zone 2.

"It's the island from *Lost*," Richard interjects. "No, better yet, *The Blue Lagoon*."

"Ew," Lacey says, scrunching up her nose. "That movie is about incestual cousins screwing each other."

"It's the island from *The Baby-Sitter's Club: Super Special Four*," I tell them, just as Tai lets out a low moan.

We all turn to look at him.

"What on earth is it, Tai?" Lacey asks.

He seems beyond uncomfortable.

He shakes his head and then gets to his feet awkwardly.

"Tai?" I ask.

He looks at me, then looks to Lacey.

Then he goes to Richard, leans over to whisper something in his ear.

Lacey and I exchange a glance, having no idea what's going on.

"Oh," Richard says, eyes going round as Tai tells him something obviously shocking. "Oh my." He suppresses a smile, and then gets to his feet and whispers something back into Tai's ear. Tai nods, and then Richard eyes Lacey. "Lacey Loo, could you come here?"

I guess the use of the nickname means they aren't fighting anymore.

"What is going on?" I ask, getting to my feet too.

The three of them start whispering, ignoring me.

Finally Richard runs off to the bushes.

"Can you show me?" Lacey asks Tai.

Tai looks revolted. "Hell no."

"I am a doctor."

"Of plants!"

"Which is part of the issue!"

"What the hell is going on?" I practically yell, putting myself in between them. "Is this the Island of Secrets?"

Lacey gives me a steady look.

"We think Tai wiped his ass with some poisonous leaves," she says bluntly.

"For fuck's sake, Lacey!" Tai yells at her, his face darkening.

I burst out laughing.

"He did what?" I cry out, tears nearly falling down my cheeks.

"Ah shit," Tai mumbles, covering his face with his hand and turning away from us.

"Speaking of shit," Lacey says. She's trying to bite back a smile. "We'll have to see what leaves you used. This will help us treat your, uh..."

"Oh, please stop," Tai whimpers.

I'm still laughing. Like the kind of laughing where I slap my knee and can't breathe. I don't know if I'm going insane or what, but I literally can't stop. This is the funniest thing.

"I've got the book," Richard says, holding a flashlight and a botany identifier book that I always see my sister flipping through. "We just need to see the leaves."

Lacey reaches out and grabs Tai's arms. "There's nothing to be embarrassed about. Show us the leaves that did this to you."

Tai groans, avoiding looking at me. He walks off to the jungle, Lacey and Richard following.

"Do you want me to come too?" I call after him.

He shoots me a warning glance over his shoulder. "Don't you dare."

I giggle and sink down into the sand again, wiping the tears from my face. I'm glad I packed my diary. Once it's dry, I'm making another log.

Log.

And I'm giggling again. I think I've regressed back in age about twenty-years, but as my father used to say, if you're not laughing, you're crying.

Or, doing both.

THE NEXT MORNING I wake up just after dawn. I barely slept at all.

We had unzipped the two sleeping bags, that were unfortunately still a little damp, and laid them out side-by-side. Since it's so hot and humid here, we didn't need a top sheet, and it was nice to have the layer of fabric between us and the ground.

I slept at one end, Tai at the other, with Lacey and Richard in the middle. When they returned from their mini jungle expedition last night in search of Tai's evil toilet paper, Tai did a great job of ignoring me. He was embarrassed, of course, and it was quite obvious he wanted nothing to do with me.

Meanwhile, Lacey and Richard were lovey dovey all night, making up for their fight. They didn't have sex, *thank god*, but the cuddling and sweet talk was enough to make me sick and wish I had the foresight to pack earplugs.

Regardless, as soon as the sun was up, I was up too.

I roll over and look at the row of bodies. Lacey and Richard are snoring away, as usual, and Tai is gone.

I get to my feet and quickly get changed into my shorts, bikini top and flannel shirt, bring my ratty gross hair into a ponytail and stick on a ball cap. Oh, my kingdom for a proper shower.

I need to brush my teeth and do my business, but after what happened to Tai, I feel like I need a little advice.

Stepping out onto the beach, I spot Tai crouching down by the charred logs, trying to get a fire going again, the morning sky fading from fiery pink to pale blue.

I especially like what he's wearing this morning, a rich aqua shirt that matches the color of the lagoon, framing his muscles very nicely. I take a moment to appreciate his hands as they adjust the logs. Part of me wishes that Richard had never interrupted us that night, though if that were the case, we would have barrelled right into the reef while screwing each other senseless.

But what a way to go.

"Hey," I say to him. "Did you watch the sunrise?"

He glances up at me briefly and grunts in response.

"So very caveman like," I comment. "You haven't been in the wild very long and you're already reverting."

"That's funny," he says mildly.

"I've been told I can be," I say, hugging my arms across my chest. Even though the heat and humidity are starting to creep up, there's a bit of a chill out here, the wind blowing lightly. "How are you feeling?"

He gives me a look that tells me to back off, but of course I don't.

"I'm just wondering what leaves I can use," I add. "You know.."

"Use a book," he says, gesturing to the torn-up pages in the fire. "Makes good toilet paper *and* good kindling."

I'm horrified. He's torn up a book? That's sacrilegious.

And then I get a closer look at the book.

"Oh my god!" I cry out. "Where did you get that?"

He bites his lip, avoiding my eyes.

"Tai! Is that my book? Is that *The Devilish Rake*?"

"Look," he says defensively. "I saw it lying on the beach, I didn't know it was yours."

"Yes you did! I had put it on the beach along with all my other stuff, trying to signal for help!"

"It's just a book," he says, and I gasp even louder. "You already read it, I saw you read it!"

"We're on a deserted island, it may be one of the only books I'll ever get to read again!"

As if to make his point, the pages catch fire and start burning.

"I can't believe you did that," I practically whimper, watching the pages curl.

"Give me a break," he says with a roll of his eyes. "Do you want to wipe your ass with poisonous leaves or not?"

I gesture to the jungle. "I'm sure there are other options!"

"Suit yourself," he says, reaching into his back pocket and pulling out the copy of the paperback, a lot of the pages already torn out. "Here, you can have it back. Probably did the book a favor by making it shorter."

"Now you're just trying to be a dick. Book burner."

"Boat sinker."

Asshole. He knows he's got me with that one. It hits deep, right between the ribs. I don't even have anything to say to that except sorry and I know my apologies are worthless to him.

So I turn around and start walking off, down the beach to my SOS sign to see what else he ruined.

It all looks fine.

Until I realize he replaced the book with my vibrator, making up part of the S.

Dear god.

I whip around and storm back across the beach to Tai, who is trying not to laugh.

Asshole again.

"You found my vibrator!" I yell, knowing I'm probably waking up Lacey and Richard, and boy, what a way to wake up.

"I don't know what you're talking about," he says, rubbing his lips together. His poker face is still terrible.

"Yes you do! I hid it in my shoe!"

"Gingersnap, there was no hiding that thing. Sweet Jesus, way to give a guy a complex."

"You know perfectly well that your, uh, that it's comparable."

A dark brow arches. "Oh is it?"

"I'm not comfortable complimenting you right now."

"I see," he says, taking a step toward me. "It's hard not to do, isn't it?"

"Shut up."

"I am curious as to why you had to pack *that* for the life raft. Were you going to use it as a paddle, or...?" he trails off, licking his lips.

Ugh. Can he please stop being sexy for like one second so I can be mad at him?

"I panicked, okay?" I smile wickedly. "Don't tell me you're threatened."

"Whatever makes you sleep at night," he says, heading back to camp.

"I didn't sleep!" I yell at him. "Lacey and Little Dicky were being nauseating."

"Don't be jealous!" I hear Lacey yell from beyond the palm trees. Guess they're up.

I sigh and look at the book in my hands. Well, since it's already been ripped apart, if you can't beat them, join them.

It isn't until after breakfast, which is tomato soup and crackers, not the worst of the meals but not the best, that Tai announces he's going to go on an expedition across the island.

"I'm coming," Richard says, raising his hand like he's in class.

"You're not," Tai says. "You can barely see. You'll be a danger to yourself and I am not carrying you back here. Maybe later, when I get a better look at the terrain."

"Then Lacey should go," Richard says. "She knows the fauna here." He adds in a low voice, "You obviously can't be trusted around it."

"I'm not leaving you," Lacey says. "You're still a bit dizzy from," she gestures to his mangled face, "all this."

"I'll go!" I say, jumping to my feet.

Tai's brows knit together. "You? Gilligan? I don't think so."

"Stop calling me Gilligan," I tell him, following him as he walks back to camp. "I'm going with you."

"Only if I can call you Gilligan," he says, drinking from a bottle of water. He hands it to me. "And only if you don't talk to me. I'm not really in the mood."

"You're never in the mood," I tell him, taking a sip. "Thanks." I eye the rest of the water supply. "We're going to run low soon, aren't we?"

He nods grimly, wiping his mouth with the back of his hand. "Another reason to head inland. This place is big enough, and the elevation over there high enough, to have a stream, maybe even a pond or a lake. Don't know how long it will be until the next weather system passes through and gives us rain. Least if we find some water, we can use the purification tablets."

"So what should I bring?"

He glances down at my flip flops. "Those won't do. Wear your running shoes, or those water shoes I found your dildo in."

"It's a vibrator, not a dildo. A dildo doesn't vibrate."

"Don't think you bought the waterproof version, Gingersnap."

"I thought it was Gilligan."

He waves me away and starts walking off into the jungle. I quickly shove my tennis shoes on, still soggy from having worn them the night of the wreck, and run after him. Squish, squish, squish.

With Tai leading the way, the jungle isn't so bad. If there are any spiderwebs in the way, he deals with the brunt of them, and he deals with them a lot. To his credit, he doesn't flinch or complain. The only thing that's separating him from Michael Douglas in *Romancing the Stone* is a machete.

I'm sure Lacey and Richard would have a field day in this jungle, with all the different ferns, and trees with hanging vines and twisting bark, a million shades and shapes of green leaves. But for me, it's all just one hot, sticky blur of vegetation. You can barely see the sky in places.

"How do we know how to get back?" I ask him, staring at his back, the way his shirt is sticking to his skin, the sweat at the nape of his neck.

"I have a compass, I'll get us back," he tells me without turning around. "How are you holding up back there?"

"I'm fine. Just hot. Sweaty. Tired. Have a crazy amount of chub rub happening."

He stops in his tracks and I collide right into him.

"I'm sorry, what?" he asks, turning around. "Chub rub? Is that some wankfest innuendo?"

I laugh. "No, it's when your thighs touch and it's sweaty and well...friction happens. In other words, I shouldn't have worn shorts." I point at my legs.

"But then I wouldn't be able to ogle you," he says, totally deadpan, and turns around and starts walking again.

"Yeah right," I mutter. "Where's the ogling?"

He doesn't say anything to that.

We keep walking.

And walking.

It's not all horrible, there are a ton of colorful birds singing pretty little songs.

Pretty soon I'm humming a song of my own.

"Please stop that," Tai says, still marching forward.

I hum it louder.

It's the theme song to *Gilligan's Island*.

"Can't," I tell him. "It's stuck in my head."

"Well, can you keep it *in* your head?"

Then he stops suddenly and shushes me.

"Don't shush me," I cry out.

"Listen," he whispers harshly.

So I stop humming and listen.

I think I hear the sound of running water.

We both look at each other with wide, hopeful eyes.

Tai even manages a quick smile.

"Come on," he says, leading the way, heading a little more to the left, and following the sound.

It's not long until we come across the source.

It's not just a stream, but a large pool of water, complete with a low waterfall on one end, and a stream running off on the other.

"Oh my god!" I gasp, wanting to cry tears of joy.

It's beautiful, like something out of a movie. Cue the uplifting music.

The water is a deep blue-green and fairly clear where the sun splices through the open canopy above and lights up the depths. The rocks are slick and black, volcanic, and flowers and ferns grow along the sides of the pool, framing it like a picture. The smell is earthy and green and wet and wonderful.

Tai doesn't even hesitate. He drops his backpack to the ground and immediately starts to tear off his clothes until he's completely naked.

I mean all of it, off.

I don't even have time to react, my eyes glued to his gorgeous round ass, a couple of shades lighter than the rest of his bronzed brown body. It bounces firmly as he runs right into the pool, disappearing into the water.

He dives under, and then pops his head up, shaking his hair from side to side. He's smiling so wide, it pulls something out from under me, like I'm suddenly unstable, unprepared. For what, I don't know, but it has something to do with him.

"What are you waiting for?" he yells at me, treading water in the middle of the pool. "Get in here!"

"How do I know what's in the water?"

"I'll protect you," he says with a wicked grin, which tells me he will do no such thing. "Come on. You shy?"

"You know I'm not," I tell him. "I just don't want my feet nibbled by mysterious water things."

"Mysterious water things, huh? Didn't you want to be a marine biologist?"

"That's the ocean! Marine!"

I sigh and start undoing my shorts, taking off my tank top. I'm wearing a bikini top and blue underwear that does nothing to cover my generous ass, nor my boobs. This isn't the time to be insecure though. When I was younger I used to let body images dictate the activities I did. Nowadays, I don't let that stop me, even though I haven't been to the gym in weeks.

Especially when Tai is gazing at me in such an intense, almost primal way, like I'm the hottest thing he's ever seen. It's hard to feel anything but desired.

God, I hope that's not all in my head.

I am starting to flush though, just from his gaze, so I

quickly get to the edge of the pool to cool off.

"Careful!" he cautions me as I step on the slick rocks.

They're as slippery as ice.

Before I know it, I'm falling.

I pitch forward, so I fall right into the water.

On my stomach.

SPLAT.

Ow.

I haven't done a motherfucking belly flop since I was a kid, and with boobs it's a whole new painful ballgame.

I lift my head, trying to swim, my skin burning.

My face is burning too, from embarrassment. So much for the water cooling me off.

"Are you okay?" Tai asks, though he's also laughing as he swims over to me. I guess it serves me right.

"I'm fine," I mumble, trying to find my footing, my toes skirting over the slimy rocks at the bottom. Ick.

"Not the most graceful, are you?" he asks, grinning at me. A lock of hair has flopped on his forehead and I kick forward to reach out and brush it off his face. My fingers tingle as I touch his skin, my breath catching in my chest, not just from treading water, but from how close we are to each other. He briefly dips his chin and mouth into the water, his eyes alternating between flirty and intense.

I don't mind either look.

"Hey, I'll have you know that I was able to do yoga on your boat. How many people can say that?"

He spits out a bit of water and grins again, those pretty white teeth against his skin, his eyes crinkling in the corners. "I watched you do yoga. You fell over a lot."

"The boat was constantly moving!"

"Any excuse," he says.

I'm about to ask him to do yoga on dry land, just to see if

he can do a standing split without falling over, when some-thing BRUSHES AGAINST MY LEG.

"Ahhhh!" I scream, and with rapid-fire kicks I manage to lunge at Tai, wrapping my arms around his neck, my legs going around his waist.

"What is it, what is it?" he asks as I hold on tight, trying to get as much of my body above the water as possible. I'm aware that he's having to tread water extra hard, now that I'm clinging to him like a bear climbing a tree.

"Something touched my leg!"

"Are you sure it wasn't your other leg?"

I'm not sure. "It wasn't my other leg! It was a thing!"

"A mysterious water thing?"

"Shut up," I growl in his ear, holding him tighter. I have to say, it's making me feel better.

"It was probably a fish," he says. "That could be our lunch."

"You didn't even bring a rod."

"I can spear fish."

I pull back to look at him, our faces just inches apart. He's gazing at me through black wet lashes. Lucky bastard. I can't get that look even with a million coats of mascara.

"You spear fish?" I ask, my voice quieter now, since our lips are so close.

"Mmmhmm," he murmurs, his weighted gaze on my mouth. "I can spear a lot of things."

Oh jeez. I'm suddenly, painfully aware that if I let myself lower on his waist, just a little, the tip of his dick will touch me in just the right place. That's assuming he has a hard-on, and from the way he's looking at me, I'm pretty sure he does.

I'd wager...

Before I even know what's happening, I lean forward, my body operating on instinct only.

And I kiss him.

I can't help it.

All these weeks of wanting to do this, wanting to know what his lips feel like against mine, it was inevitable that I'd lose control.

He stiffens at first, hesitating, then I feel the muscles in his back relax as he kisses me back.

And...shit.

I mean...wow.

He's a *good* kisser.

Lips soft but firm, his tongue slow and teasing at first, then as his mouth opens, becomes hungrier, greedier, I feel like I'm about to be devoured, god *I want* to be devoured, and...

We both slip under the water, submerged, still kissing, Tai unable to keep us both afloat.

Then we break apart, coming up for air.

I stare at him.

He stares at me.

A goat stares at the both of us.

"Oh my god!" I cry out suddenly at the goat who has appeared in the foliage behind Tai.

Tai whips around. "Oh. Hello. A goat."

The goat opens its mouth and lets out a horrible bleat that sounds more like a human scream.

"Holy shit," I swear, my heart racing fast for so many reasons. "What is up with that goat?"

The goat does another bleat, then turns around and runs back into the trees.

Tai watches it go, his back to me, and in that moment I realize he's trying to put distance between us, between what had just happened.

I kissed him. He kissed me back.

Maybe he needs time to process.

"Tai?"

He slowly turns around, treading water. He looks at me. The expression in his eyes has changed. It's harder somehow. Distant.

"It's just a goat," I tell him, half-joking.

He doesn't smile.

Shit. Did I screw everything up?

"I'm sorry," I say quietly, my stomach all swirling with knots.

"Why are you sorry?" he asks. He doesn't swim any closer, his voice is flat.

"For kissing you."

"You have to stop apologizing for those things."

"Then I'm sorry...for whatever has made you turn cold like this."

He frowns, his gaze turned away. "I'm not *cold*...I..."

"If you're still mad about the boat, I get it. I hate myself for what I did and I'm so, so sorry. It was an accident, I—"

"*Stop*," he says sharply. His brow furrows sympathetically, face softening. "I'm not mad at you Daisy. I was mad. I was...scared. And I'm sorry I took it out on you, I shouldn't have, and I know you obviously didn't do it on purpose. I know it was an accident." He pauses, worrying his lip between his teeth. "I should have told you this earlier and I'm a dick for not doing so. Sometimes my stubbornness gets the best of me. Sometimes I get so wrapped up in my head...it's like I can't see the big picture anymore."

My chest feels lighter, like it suddenly has wings. I can't help but smile at his forgiveness. I mean, yes, it would have helped if he told me this earlier, but still.

"I totally get it," I tell him.

"You don't," he says softly. "I never hated you, Daisy, but I hate myself. Because I know it's my fault."

"Your fault? I'm the one who pushed autopilot."

He shakes his head, the pool reflecting in his eyes. "I should have been more prepared that night. I shouldn't have even gone to sleep, should have stayed up with Richard. You...I let myself be distracted by you, Daisy. I went to sleep because I wanted to at least sleep with you. Beside you. Just once. You make it so hard to think about anything else. And that's my job. I need to be thinking about everything else. I'm the captain and it's my duty to look after the ship, to look after everyone and make sure they're safe. And that night, I couldn't do it."

Oh. Well, jeez.

"You *did* make sure everyone is safe, Tai. We're all here, we're all alive. I know you didn't save the boat but it's still on the reef, it can be salvaged."

"No," he says angrily. "It can't be. It's gone. She's gone."

I'm not sure if he's talking about the boat or his sister. It might be both.

I swim toward him, placing my hand around his waist.

"Please, Daisy," he murmurs, closing his eyes. "I can't..."

I ignore the sting of rejection.

"You did your job, Tai. You saved us. You got us off that ship. Now we're here and we're alive. Let yourself feel that. Let yourself be alive, too."

I watch him closely, the way he's breathing heavily through his nose, the pain on his brow. I'm probably making things worse. I should probably let go.

"I was married," he says. The words come out heavy, sinking into the water.

I let go of his waist, shocked. "What?"

He glances at me briefly. "I was married. For three years.

Her name was Holly. Is Holly. She's still out there, married again, with kids. Which is fine, that's something she always wanted. Can't say I did."

I'm so stunned, I don't even know how to file this information into my brain. He was married? What else is he keeping from me?

"Why didn't you tell me?" I ask.

He shrugs with one shoulder out of the water. "Wasn't important."

"It's kind of important."

"Why?"

"Because...maybe it explains why you're so grumpy." One of the explanations anyway.

"Can't a man be a grump? Does he need a reason?" he says half-heartedly.

"How long ago? I mean, when did you get divorced?"

"Four years ago or so? It was amicable."

"An amicable divorce? That's hard to believe. What happened?"

He sighs. "Nothing happened. One day she decided she didn't love me anymore. She never cheated, I don't think. She just decided I wasn't worth fighting for. She wouldn't do couples counselling, wouldn't listen to my side of things. The side that told her I loved her. She just...suddenly didn't care anymore."

"God," I whisper.

"I'm over it now," he says. "But it took some time. Not only to get over her but to get over the damage she did. Makes it really hard to trust someone, you know?"

Yeah. I know.

"I'm sorry," I tell him.

"Me too. But it's for the best at any rate. You want to know the funny thing? I'd been screwed over before that. I thought Holly was different. Special. She worked at the marina with me, she was low-maintenance, she was one of the boys. She wasn't..."

"Like those *other* girls?" I fill in wryly.

"Yeah."

"Girls like me?"

He gives me a puzzled look. "She wasn't anything like you, Daisy."

Then he dives under the water, swimming past me, heading for shore.

I decide to stop being a pervert for once and not watch him get dressed. Besides, my mind is tripping over what he just said. I don't know what any of that meant.

What I do know is that he thinks I'm a distraction, and apparently not in the right way. Not a distraction he wants.

You're not what he wants, I tell myself. Part of me thinks that maybe that's just because we're on this island. Maybe when we get back to Fiji...

And then what? Even if he gives into you in Fiji, he's going back to New Zealand, to his life there. And you're going...who knows where.

Besides, he didn't just drop the marriage bomb on me for no reason. That was his way of saying not now, not ever. As if the reason before wasn't enough.

I can't help but feel completely deflated and disappointed. I kissed him. What the hell was I thinking?

I get out of the water and get dressed, while Tai fills up water bottles from the stream, popping in some purification tablets.

"Should we head back and tell the others?" I ask him when we're ready to go.

"I think we should follow this stream, see where it leads. If there's anything on this island, people will take advantage of a water source." He peers at me. "You up for it?"

"Up for anything," I tell him, though really I just want to get back to camp and have some alone time, try to make sense of everything that just happened.

Even though more time to dwell on the rejection will just make me feel worse.

He nods and I follow him down the stream for about twenty minutes or so, the refreshing dip in the pool undone by sweat and grime, until the forest seems to open up.

Suddenly we find ourselves on a beach.

Another side of paradise.

"Bloody hell," Tai says in awe.

I have to agree.

The lagoon on this side is much bigger and is peppered with islands. Some of them look like tiny little outcrops of sand and a few palm trees, the water shallow enough to walk to, others are larger and further away. It's like a whole new world over here, with a million shades of blue.

"This is incredible," I say, looking down the beach. There are plumeria flowers everywhere here, pinks and whites and yellows, their beauty and fragrant smell peppering the beach. I stop by one of the trees and take a deep whiff of a blossom. Heaven.

"Daisy," Tai says with urgency. "Daisy, come here."

I turn to where Tai disappeared in the opposite direction, behind a grove of palm trees.

I duck around them and see what he's staring at in disbelief.

My god.

It's a building.

TAI

The building that Daisy and I are gawking at looks like it was erected in the 1970s and never used again. It's a bungalow, raised a few feet off the ground with a short flight of stairs heading up to a deck, the wood gray and faded from the elements.

"It's a leftover from the Dharma Initiative," Daisy whispers from beside me.

She might not be far off there.

"We should look around for a hatch," I tell her, "see if there's a Scottish guy down there pushing a button."

She gives me an impressed look.

"You're not the only one who watched *Lost*, Gingersnap," I inform her, walking toward the building.

"I'm surprised you're not calling me Freckles," she notes. "Considering."

"Have to be original with my nicknames, don't I, Gilligan?"

I can practically feel her roll her eyes from behind me.

I'm glad we're back in this space again, where we can talk and poke fun at each other. I hated being mad at her, and I really had no reason to. I knew she had made a mistake, I knew that the boat running aground was an accident. At the very least, she didn't do it on purpose.

I've spent the last couple of days trying to grapple with my anger, most of it directed at myself, some at Daisy, and some at the ocean itself, for trying to take more lives that matter to me.

I've been in rough shape, to say the least, even though I've done my best to hide it. I have to. I feel responsible for my crew, for my friends...for Daisy. Now that we're on land, I feel it's my purpose to keep everyone safe until we get rescued. My job as captain isn't over yet.

"Who wants to go inside first?" Daisy asks, before she quickly adds, "Not it."

I stare at her for a moment, at the cheeky smile on her peach-colored lips.

Lips that I tasted, lips that left me hungry, starving for more.

Kissing her was probably the highlight of my year, if I'm being honest. I can't remember the last time I felt so ravenous for someone, not just physically, but emotionally. On another level. Like I've had this cage built inside my chest for far too long, rusted shut from the sea, and someone has finally found it. She hasn't made her way in yet, but I think she's trying, and I desperately want to let her.

But I can't. Because I'm not built that way. Because Holly did such a number on me, I know if I give into Daisy, there would be no turning back. She would own me, all of me, and I would be at her feet—hook, line, and sinker.

I can't let that happen.

For one, I need to keep my head on straight until we're rescued. There is no way around that.

For two...I'm afraid.

I've had my future dashed before. I've had my hopes and my heart ground up into dust. Call me a coward, but I'll do anything not to go through that again.

Even if that means saying no to Daisy.

Even if all I want to do is say yes.

"What?" she asks me. "You're looking at me weird."

I clear my throat, giving her a quick smile. "Just trying to figure out when you became such a chicken."

Good job, Tai. Deflection.

"Chicken?" she repeats. She laughs. "That's rich."

She puts her hand at my shoulder and pushes me forward.

"You're the brave spear fisherman Maori warrior. You go check it out."

I shrug and walk through the overgrown grass to the bungalow, carefully going up the stairs alongside vines that have wrapped themselves around the railing. So far they seem to hold.

The deck seems to hold too, and I poke my head in through the doorway.

It looks like no one has been in here in a long time, though it's not as bad as the outside.

There are three sets of bunkbeds, one against the back wall, the others on either side of it. The bunkbeds are bare, just wood slats, which is probably for the best considering a whole world of creatures could make their home in old mattresses.

There's nothing else in the room except a low table against the opposite wall, and there are four windows, the shuttered kind with battered screens. The door is off the hinges, and while some vines have snaked in across the floor and there are bugs scurrying about, I think I may have found our new sleeping quarters.

"It's not the Four Seasons," I tell Daisy as I exit and come back down the stairs. "But we can make do."

She scrunches up her nose. "Anything gross?"

"Not really. Go take a look."

She hesitates and then goes up the stairs. I can't help but stare at her ass as she goes, the way they look in those jean shorts turns my brain to mush.

You idiot, I can't help but think. *She had her legs wrapped around you, talking about spearfishing while you were naked, inches from your cock, and you didn't do a fucking thing.*

She pops her head back out of the bungalow. "It's okay...Doesn't look very comfortable but at least it's off the ground. I may need you to kill all the spiders though."

"I will slay whatever dragons you wish," I tell her. I walk around to the front of the bungalow and peer around it. There's another building a few yards away.

"Hey, I found the hatch," I tell her.

I walk through the mix of grass and sand until I come to a squat, low concrete building surrounded by frangipani flowers. The door is missing on this one. Beyond it I see another, smaller concrete block.

I go in the bigger one first. There's dirt inside, covering up what used to be the floor, and vines are growing up the walls. In the middle are a bunch of tables and steel chairs. On the walls, covered by the overgrowing foliage, are old charts and maps. A relic of a printer sits in the corner, gathering dust.

"What is it?" Daisy asks, poking her head in.

"I dunno. Could be an old research station. This place definitely isn't a resort."

"Whatever it is, it hasn't been used in forever. Guess they don't have a phone or internet, huh?"

I look around. There's a stack of brown papers beside an

old-fashioned calculator. It's impossible to read what's printed on them, but there's a faded stamp in the corner that reads Nature something or other.

"I think maybe this island was used as a protected wildlife area," I tell her, turning around. "But whoever was stationed here has been gone a long, long time."

We step back outside, and I head over to the other building.

Turns out to be a shower block and toilet. Both not up to anyone's standards.

"Don't even bother," I tell Daisy as I come back out.

"No toilet paper?" she asks, her eyes dancing.

I'm never going to live that down, am I?

"For your information, I'm completely fine now," I tell her. "Just a little…"

"Raw?"

"Shut up."

I was going to say embarrassed.

She giggles and I do my best to ignore her.

We both look across at the lagoon. It really is stunning here, like a completely different ecosystem than the other side. The water is so clear and so shallow, it looks like you can walk across it to all the islands. Or at least it would be an easy swim. I wish I hadn't left my binoculars back at camp, I'm curious to see if there are any remnants of buildings on the other islands, though at first glance there don't seem to be any. This place not only looks deserted, it feels deserted, too.

"So I guess we go back and tell the newlyweds to pack up," I tell her.

"You really want us to move here?"

"We've got shelter, we've got a fresh-water stream, and there seems to be a rainwater catchment on top of the old shower block. I think we're better off here, more protected from any storm surges or the like."

Though to be honest, I feel weird about leaving the Atarangi where she is. Not that she's going anywhere, but I feel like I'm abandoning her when she needs me, as silly as that seems. Maybe if I can just get Daisy, Lacey, and Richard over here, I can stay at the other camp...might be better having Daisy at more of a distance, too.

Though, even if that's what I need, it's not what I want.

We head back to camp, following the stream back to the waterfall, then the compass guides us the rest of the way. By the time we make it to the other side of the island, it seems like we've been gone most of the day.

"Where have you guys been?" Lacey cries out as we stumble out of the jungle and onto the sand.

"I was going to send out a search party," Richard says. "Consisting of Lacey."

We fill them in on what we found, from the waterfall and pool, to the stream, to the abandoned research station.

"So the desert island becomes the *deserted* island," Richard muses. "Nice twist."

"Not very helpful for us if it's uninhabited," Lacey points out. "What kind of research is it?"

"Not too sure. Something to do with nature. Maybe marine, maybe bird, maybe insects."

"Maybe it's like the Island of Dr. Moreau," Richard says.

"More like the Island of Dr. Boner," Daisy says, biting back a smile.

Lacey puts her hands on her hips and gives her sister a *look*. "It's Bon-Air. Okay? Doctor Bon-Air. It's derived from the phrase "de bonne aire," literally meaning of handsome or of good bearing."

I stare at Richard, who right now does not look of very good bearing.

"Is that what he promised you?" I say to Lacey, unable to stay out of it.

Lacey flinches like I slapped her. "What? It's true."

I glance at Richard, brow raised. "Hey Dick, you want to tell her the truth about her new last name?"

His skin seems to pale before my eyes, and he adjusts his broken glasses. Clears his throat.

"Richard?" Lacey asks imploringly. "Tell me he's wrong."

He looks at her, chin raised. "Remember when you lied to me about having to wear glasses?" he says.

She blinks at him.

Shit's about to go down.

I glance over at Daisy. "Hey, I'm hungry, you hungry?"

I motion over to the fire and she giggles as we quickly walk over there, leaving the newlyweds to start on the second epic fight of this island.

"Island of Dr. Boner," I say to her. "I like where your mind is at. Filled with cocks."

"Hey, you've seen the island's shape," she says. "Besides, you're the one who had your cock out today."

"You peeked?"

She blushes, looking away. "I didn't. But now I wish I did, just to hold it over you."

"Oh, you can hold it all right. You did such a good job before."

She bites her lip in such a way that I'm immediately brought back to that moment on the boat when I caught her getting off.

Fuck, I have *got* to stop thinking like this.

I have to stop flirting like this, too.

Even though it's painful to stop.

I give her a quick smile, trying to put a bit of distance between us.

"So, lunch," I tell her, rather awkwardly.

She watches me for a moment, really studying my face, and I can't ignore the flash of disappointment on hers. Then she manages a fake smile. "Let's go get some beans."

I AUTOMATICALLY WAKE up just before sunrise.

Atarangi.

Always for Atarangi.

It's still dark when I get up off the sleeping bag, careful not to step on anyone. Richard and Lacey are snoring, but even without earplugs, I don't really hear them anymore. They've turned into white noise machines.

I glance over at Daisy, who is on her side, back to me. I watch her for a few moments. She looks especially tiny all curled up like that and I'm struck by this irrepressible urge to protect her. Not just in the way I've felt all along, as a captain, but as something more than that. I want to shield her from whatever dangers might lurk on this island, but I also want to shield her heart from any more sorrow. She's been dealt a shit hand lately, losing her job, her dickface ex, this whole being shipwrecked thing.

I want her to be happy.

Which is why it's better she doesn't get involved with you. You're a mess. You live in New Zealand and she lives in America. Even if you did give in to her, you know there'd be nothing beyond it.

The thoughts are pessimistic, but they're true. No use denying them.

I ignore the sour feeling in my chest, and head out across the sand. I sit down near the water, watching the sun rise, coloring the sky behind Atarangi into shades of lavender and orchid. The morning has a purple tone, washing the lagoon with a lilac tint.

Every sunrise has meaning. Every sunrise is a chance to start again.

These days, it's the only thing I have to count on.

After our expedition to the abandoned research station yesterday, we decided to wait until today to move there. It took a long time for Richard and Lacey to stop fighting after she found out her last name was actually Boner, not Bon-Air. Lacey Boner does have a certain ring to it, though.

There's part of me that wants to stay behind here, so I figure I'll come back later. I'll probably sleep here at night. Just hope none of them take offense to that.

When I'm done watching the sunrise, I start lighting the fire for our breakfast, expecting to see Daisy again. When she doesn't show, I can't help but feel disappointed. Maybe she's decided to stay away.

It's for the best.

Eventually everyone gets up, we eat, taking our time to get ready for the day, then we all go about packing up our stuff for the journey across the island.

"What are you doing?" I ask Daisy, who keeps darting in and out of the forest with sticks and palm fronds.

"I'm creating a new sign," she says. "Since I have to pack up my shit and what not."

"Don't forget your vibrator," I yell at her.

She gives me a dirty look.

The trek inland takes longer this time, with Richard only able to see out of one eye and stumbling every couple of minutes, doing his best Jerry Lewis impersonation.

Everyone is tired and hot from carrying their gear, and the mosquitos are out in full force. Plus, Lacey feels like she has to stop and identify every single plant she comes across, from guava (which we pile into our bags to eat later), to weeds with antiseptic and antibacterial properties. Naturally, she takes samples of those too.

Finally, we come to the waterfall.

The payoff is worth it.

This time we have soap and shampoo with us, so everyone jumps in the pool and cleans the hell out of themselves, myself included, then we proceed to do some laundry as well so we can dry it out on the beach later. After ten days at sea and a few days shipwrecked, we all need it.

We even manage to have lunch at the pool, just some crackers and dried fruit. Richard tries his hand at fishing after Daisy told him about the mystery fish, but we don't have any bait. I tell them I'll look for some clams later in the ocean and see what we can do. Fresh caught fish over an open flame would be a good way to welcome in our (temporary) life at the new camp.

When we finally get to the bungalows, everyone is exhausted. We have just enough energy to dry things out on the beach, choose beds, and explore a little.

"I've never seen so many different types of plumeria in one place," Lacey marvels, as she touches the frangipani (which is what we call it in New Zealand).

"I thought you hated flowers," Daisy says to her.

Lacey gives her a disgruntled look. "I never said that."

"You never said that, but you purposely used zero flowers at the wedding. Which was weird, but you know, you're a plant person."

"I used to grow roses, remember?" she says.

"So it has nothing to do with my name being Daisy? A flower?"

Lacey rolls her eyes. "Oh my god. You would think that, wouldn't you?"

"How could I not?"

Ah, fuck. The sisters are about to go at it again. Every day there's a different fight. Maybe everyone sleeping in one building isn't the best idea.

I glance at Richard to exchange an *oh boy* look with him, but he's staring over my shoulder in shock.

It's probably that damn goat, I think, turning around.

Nope.

It's a man.

"Hello there," the man says.

All four of us jump at once. Lacey screams.

"Sorry, didn't mean to frighten you," he says in an American accent, holding his hands out as if to calm us. "I was curious about the castaways and here you are. The name is Fred, by the way. Fred Ferguson."

Fred Ferguson's a short guy, paunchy, with a bushy white mustache, balding grey hair at the top. He's got big reflective sunglasses that look straight out of the '80s, wearing a dirt-stained T-shirt that says "Beer Me" and red cargo shorts. No shoes.

"Hello Fred," I say warily. "Where did you come from?"

So suddenly, into our lives.

Fred chuckles and gestures behind him. "Got a dinghy on the other side of those palms. Down the beach. Came from over there." He points far across the lagoon to one of the longer islands. "Noticed the two of you yesterday, looking about." Nods at me and Daisy. "Heard about your boat. My condolences."

"How did you know about the boat?" I ask.

"Not much to do out here except count bird eggs and listen to the radio, and the birds ain't laying right now."

"Are you a scientist?" Richard asks. A good question, because he doesn't *seem* like a scientist.

Fred nods. Puts his hands in his pockets and rocks back on his heels. "Yep. Been stationed here for about, well let's see...three months now."

"Three months!" Lacey exclaims.

"All alone too," he says. "Hope you fellas don't blame me, but when I picked up the transmission that a yacht had wrecked on the reefs, I was grateful for the company. Been by my lonesome an awful long time."

"Don't they usually station you with another researcher?" Richard asks.

"They had. Dale was his name. Good guy. Smelled like garlic. But his wife was pregnant, went into labor two months early. He had to go back. Wife and babe are doing fine now, no worries there, but he's not coming back and they haven't found a suitable replacement. I'm staying on until the next batch of researchers come over. Should be a few weeks from now, but they've been saying that awhile." He pauses, squints at us. "You guys have any beer?"

"I wish," Daisy says.

He looks deflated. "Shucks. I could really go for a Rolling Rock about now."

"Who are you working for?" Lacey asks.

"Nature Conservancy," he says. "They're working with the Fijian government to try and study the population of the sulphur-crested myzomela here, after rats were eradicated a few years ago."

"And where is here?" I ask. "There's no name on the charts."

"Here is Plumeria Island. And this whole area," he gestures wide to the lagoon, "is the Plumeria Atoll."

"I knew it!" Lacey cries out. We all look at each other. She shrugs. "Well, I knew that the species of plumeria were notable."

Daisy is shaking her head and I know she's doubling down on Boner Island in her mind.

"So, what's this?" I gesture to the barracks.

"Back in the day they were studying all sorts of things. This place was never inhabited, so, aside from rats that escaped from boats, the atoll has a lot to offer in terms of wildlife."

"Well, how do you explain *that*?" Daisy says dramatically, pointing at the goat that has come wandering up from behind Fred. The goat stands beside him like a dog.

"You mean Wilson? No idea how he got here. Though he says he's been here quite some time." Fred looks down at the goat. The goat looks right back at him.

I frown, worried that perhaps Fred has been in the sun too long. "I'm sorry. You said the goat told you this?"

"Yep," Fred says, reaching down and patting Wilson on the head. "We get along just fine."

"What else has the goat told you?" Daisy asks suspiciously.

"Uh, sorry to be direct, Fred," I say to him, interrupting Daisy (because who knows where that conversation was going), "but is there a way you can put in a rescue call for us? We're supposed to call the search and rescue back from our satellite phone, but maybe you have better connections, *and* a better connection."

"Of course," he says, though he does look a little disappointed. He gestures behind him. "My dinghy can take two of you over with me. I've got a nice bungalow. Flush toilet."

"Flush toilet!" Daisy exclaims, like she was told he had Oscar Isaac chilling over there or something.

"We would love to see the research you're doing," Lacey speaks up, sticking her thumb at Richard. "And help in any way. We're both botanists at the University of Otago."

"Are ya now?" Fred says, stroking his mustache. "That is interesting. And most welcome, of course." He glances at me and Daisy. "You two don't mind? I can come back for you later."

"Don't worry about us," I tell him. "We'll be fine."

Fred, Lacey, and Richard wave, and then disappear behind the coconuts.

Wilson stays where he is.

Staring at us.

"Why did you do that?" Daisy moans dramatically. "Flush toilets, Tai!"

"Relax," I tell her. "You'd rather hang out with Fred "The Goatman" Ferguson than me?"

"I'd rather use a toilet and actual toilet paper than hang out with you."

"Fair enough."

But secretly I'm pleased she has to stay.

Which bodes well for no one.

DAISY

Daisy's Log: Day...what are days?

Dear Diary,

It's been awhile since I've written in you. I guess there's no point in doing a recap, because I'm just talking to myself and I know what the recap would be, even though it's future Daisy who will read this, but there's no way in hell that future Daisy will ever forget the last few days. Still, if I ever have to write a memoir based on my time here, this will be my fact-checker.

But anyway, to recap, the boat reefed (my fault, legally), and we swam to shore and Tai contacted the rescue people and they were all like chill out man, we'll get to you when we get to you, and then Tai and I went exploring and swimming and I kissed him and I shouldn't have and now things are weird between us.

Oh, and I learned he was married. How crazy is that? I really didn't expect it. Not that people need to talk about their exes—though lord, I know I talked enough about mine—but you'd think it would have come up in conversation. Even Lacey didn't mention it, then again she barely wanted to tell me about his sister. Next I'll find out he's a secret agent or something. Definitely has the body for it.

Now we're living in what he calls the barracks, which is this old research station. The Goatman, a scientist (not an actual goat man), lives across the lagoon (we're on the south side of the island now). Yesterday he took Lacey and Richard to visit his digs on some other island. When they came back, they said that he placed a call for help and that we'll get rescued in two days! Yay!! They also brought some supplies that Goatman gave them, like an extra sleeping bag and pillow, towels, and some cooking stuff. Just watch them hog it all for themselves.

So that's that. I'm lying down on the bed, which is just wooden slats and as uncomfortable as it sounds but, with the sleeping bag beneath me, it's okay. Still no pillow for me, but rolled up clothes work fine (though they still smell like diesel, even after washing them).

It's just after sunrise. I should probably get up, but I know Tai takes this time for himself and after I kissed him, I feel like I'm a pest. A sexpest. Although yesterday, we did have a good time putting all the stuff away, kind of like old times.

But who am I kidding? Even the old times were never easy. If we weren't flirting, we were fighting.

For once I'd like to do neither. I'd like to just...be with him.

I sigh and close the journal.

The symphony of Richard and Lacey's snoring is amplified in this room, though I have to say last night was the best sleep I had yet. Lately it's taken forever to fall asleep because

I felt like bugs were crawling on me (and they usually were), and my mind has been racing over the whole being shipwrecked thing, going over all the possible horrible scenarios in this endless anxiety spin. But last night I must have passed right out. I was even trying to stay up to see when Tai came back to bed. He disappeared around ten and that was that.

I sit up and eye his bed in the dim light. Not sure he even slept on it, his sleeping bag is gone.

I get to my feet, pull on my skirt and a tank, and step onto the deck.

Wow. What a view.

From this side of the island the sunrise isn't as prominent, but it doesn't make it less of a show. Just like Tai said, the sun rising is the one thing you can count on when you can't seem to count on anything else. No matter how uncertain the future, the sun still rises.

Then I see him.

Swimming half-way across the lagoon to the little island.

He looks like he's on a mission, swimming fast.

Then I see what he's swimming toward.

Glinting in the rising sun is my suitcase, washed up on the shore.

Oh my god!

Without thinking I pull down my skirt and run into the water in just my white tank top and underwear, sloshing through it. It gets as deep as my chest after a while, and it becomes easier to just swim.

Tai reaches the tiny island's shore and turns around to see me swimming toward him. "Daisy, look," he says, going over to the suitcase. "When I last checked the boat, I didn't see it. I figured it went out to sea with the hole in the hull."

He's grinning like he won the lottery, so you can understand how I feel, given that's my suitcase.

"Oh my god," I cry out breathlessly, splashing through the water until I collapse into the baby-powder white sand right beside the suitcase. I throw my body on it, hugging it. I don't care. "And you made fun of me for bringing it."

"Don't get carried away yet. Everything might be ruined."

But I know I invested in the right sparkly rose gold luggage. I quickly unzip it and push the top open and it reveals the smaller suitcase inside, like a nesting doll.

Totally dry.

I let out a whoop and Tai helps me bring the carry-on out. We plop it down on the sand.

"I never thought I'd be happy to see these again," he says.

I laugh and unzip the smaller suitcase.

You know the briefcase in *Pulp Fiction*, how when Sam Jackson opened it, all you'd see is the gold reflecting on his face?

That's what this feels like. Except, replace the gold bars with bottles of alcohol glinting in the sun, and there you have it.

Nirvana.

"Shit," Tai says. "There they are."

He reaches in and picks up the bottle of vodka I won during poker, while I bring out a bottle of sauvignon blanc. Beneath that are two bottles of pinot noir. None of them broke, thanks to all the clothes they're nestled in.

Clothes! I gleefully pull my favorite worn sweatshirt and hold it up to me, feeling the cozy dry fabric. I don't care if it's too hot to wear it here, it's comforting.

Tai is sitting beside me in the sand, watching me. I can't

quite read the look on his face, but I think he might find me endearing.

"What?" I ask him.

"Nothing," he says, giving me a soft smile. He starts unscrewing the top of the vodka. "What else do you got in there?"

I start rummaging. "Books, that you will *not* use as toilet paper." I glance up to see him drinking straight from the bottle. "What are you doing?"

"Getting drunk. What does it look like I'm doing?"

"It's like 7AM."

"Gingersnap, deserted island time is like airport time. There are no rules."

"Is that so?" I reach out for it. "Give me that."

I take the bottle of vodka and have a shot, some spilling down my chin. It burns, especially since I've barely eaten anything, but it also feels *really* good.

"Hey, easy there, don't waste it," he says, taking it back.

"Tai, we can't sit here and drink this vodka."

"Why not?"

I look across at the barracks in the shadows of the jungle. "Because..."

"Your sister and Richard went with Fred yesterday and they came back with a pillow and a sleeping bag. I don't see either of us with pillows, do you?" He gestures.

"No. But I noticed you didn't sleep in the bungalow last night," I tell him. I don't know that for sure, but I'm testing him.

He presses his lips together and nods, looking away as he hands me back the bottle. "I slept back at camp. Was just getting back here when I saw your suitcase."

"Why?"

He shrugs. "Don't know. Just felt like I had...unfinished business."

Ah.

I clear my throat, sticking the bottle in the sand between us.

"You know, Lacey told me about your sister."

He doesn't seem surprised. Just nods.

"I'm really sorry. I know that this must be tough."

He shrugs again with one shoulder. "No tougher for me than anyone else."

"Do you want to talk about it?" I ask, hoping he does, but expecting he doesn't.

"Not really." He picks up the bottle. "Would rather do this."

I watch as he takes an even deeper gulp.

He passes it back to me. "Stop judging," he says. "Join me. We can at least celebrate getting rescued."

"Cheers to that." I take the bottle and tip it back. Already feeling pretty buzzed.

When Fred, Lacey, and Richard returned from their expedition yesterday, Fred told us he was able to contact Suva Search and Rescue again. They, once again, said we were low on their priority list. After all, we aren't exactly in danger anymore, they had other people to attend to, and if they did finally come for us it would be a massive expense at this point. Then Lacey had Fred contact his team at the Nature Conservancy. They were way more helpful. Said they'd be sending in a plane in a couple of days to drop off a new scientist and that they'd take the rest of us back to Fiji.

Just a few more days and we're out of here!

"Can you imagine being stuck here for as long as Fred has, all by yourself?" I muse.

Tai doesn't hesitate. "I could do it."

Of course he could. I lean back on my elbows, stretching my feet out in front of me in the sand. The water is gently lapping the shore just below. "Strong silent type, no need for company."

He shrugs, his eyes resting on my breasts which I now realize are practically on display in my soaking wet white tank top.

Way to choose white this morning, Daisy.

"Can't say I wouldn't mind some company," he says, voice on a lower register.

I gulp. Watching his eyes as they take me in, then drift up to my face.

"Fred's not so lucky," I remind him.

"Neither am I."

Well, you could be.

"You know, for a man who pretends to not be attracted to me, you're looking at my breasts like you were looking at that vodka earlier."

He doesn't say anything to that. Just makes a disgruntled sound. Grabs the bottle, and gets to his feet, walking over to the small grove of palm trees that make up this tiny island, the sand sticking to his skin.

He leans against a palm, back to me, and drinks, looking out over the east side of the lagoon.

In any other situation, this would be the perfect set-up.

Me, on a private island, with a perfect man, in paradise.

Not that Tai is perfect. He's obviously not. But I know he's perfect for someone. And if I really let my mind run away on me, he might just be perfect for me.

He just doesn't know it yet.

He doesn't want to know it. Girl, get the hint.

I should leave him alone. I should get the hint.

But this back and forth dance is getting frustrating.

I reach into my suitcase and find a small jar wrapped in tissue. It's just a jar of Manuka honey I picked up in Russell. Sounds lame, but I was going to keep it wrapped and give it to myself as a present when I was feeling blue. You know, when we got back home.

I unwrap it and twist off the lid.

I dip my finger into the liquid gold and stick it in my mouth.

There's nothing sweeter.

I close my eyes for a moment and take in the bliss. The taste dances on my tongue.

Honey is such a simple substance, something we've eaten for thousands of years, a straightforward pleasure, a gift from the gods that our body instantly recognizes.

It's unbelievable right now, especially having eaten nothing but canned goods for days.

I get up and take the jar over to Tai, who is still drinking the vodka, staring off into nothing.

"Tai," I whisper, sticking my finger into the jar.

I stand right in front of him, holding my finger out, the honey dripping on the end.

He blinks at it. "Where did you get that?"

"Open your mouth."

His eyes meet mine and for a moment I think he's going to be a real hard-head and refuse.

Then he does as he's told.

Opens his mouth.

That gorgeous, sensual mouth.

Wraps his lips around my finger, and gives it one, long deep pull that I feel all the way to my toes. His eyes never leave mine, if anything they intensify as his tongue rolls over the sides of my skin.

A moan vibrates through him, and I think it might be the sexiest sound I've ever heard.

Slowly, without breaking eye contact, he grabs my hand and slowly pulls my finger out and oh my god, I'm already wet between my thighs, fighting the urge to squeeze them together.

This. Is. Intense.

The bottle of vodka drops from his hands and into the sand.

He then takes my hand and dips my finger into the honey again.

Runs my fingers across my collarbones.

Oh god.

His eyes flash, devious. He dips his head and slowly runs his tongue along my clavicles.

I'm hit by all senses in full force. I *smell* the shampoo he used from our waterfall shower, *see* his thick, gorgeous hair, I *taste* the honey on the roof of my mouth, *hear* my own heart pounding loudly in my head, *feel* his lips and tongue as they suck at my sensitive skin, the nip of his teeth.

I shiver inwardly, overwhelmed, and his head moves lower, *lower*, down my chest.

He pauses, pulls back, looking up through his lashes at me.

I suck in my breath, tensing, recognizing the dark carnality in his gaze.

He wants me.

There's no denying it. Not this.

With one hand still around my wrist, his other hand goes to my breast. Palms it gently, my nipple already hard through the wet tank top.

I am dying on my feet.

His thumb brushes lightly over my nipple, then rolls it beneath his touch.

My breath hitches as his hand moves up to my shoulder, slides the strap down, before he does the same to the neckline, my breast popping out.

He leans in as if he's going to kiss me on the lips. His breath smells like honey and vodka, his breathing raspy, gaze hungry. He licks his lips while staring at my mouth, then dips my finger in the honey again and runs the tip of my finger across my nipple.

Fuck.

I gasp as he lowers his head, cupping, squeezing, kneading my breast while he sucks the sweetness off the hardened tip.

Melting. I am melting in his mouth, I am melting between my legs. My head goes back and I stare up at the sky, that early morning sky, my breast thrust forward as he devours me, his lips sucking and pulling, his tongue licking, swirling, teasing.

"Oh god," I whisper.

I'm going to fall to my knees if he keeps this up.

And yet I don't want him to stop.

He moans into my breast, then yanks down my top so both breasts are exposed.

"Fucking gorgeous," he murmurs against them, hands full, mouth exploring both, gentle and teasing one minute, ravaging me the next.

Then, he suddenly stops.

I am *aching* for him.

He pulls back and puts one of his hands to the back of my neck, holding me in place as he rests his forehead against mine. His eyes are pinched shut, he's breathing hard. Trying to control himself.

I don't want him to control himself anymore. He's done too much of that already.

Maybe it's the vodka. Maybe it's the honey. Maybe it's that we're getting rescued.

Maybe it's because it's Tai Wakefield, a man who has me completely undone and obsessed.

But I let go of the honey, the jar falling to the sand. I don't even care.

I place my hands on either side of his face, his stubble rough, on its way to a full-on beard now.

I wait until he opens his eyes. Looks at me.

"Fuck me," I tell him, my voice hoarse from pleasure.

I can see the fight in his eyes. The want to say no, the urge to say yes.

His urges win.

So do mine.

In a flash he whips me around so I'm pressed up hard against the palm tree, the rough bark digging into the back of my head.

He's kissing me roughly, with impatience, teeth, lips, tongue all in a frenzy, creating a hurricane that will gladly consume us. Hands pinch my nipple, they make a fist around my ponytail. They skim over my hips, then slide between my thighs.

The kiss deepens, hot, messy, the kind of kiss that makes my eyes roll back in my head, cause my toes to curl in the sand. It deepens and intensifies, spurring on a hunger on a very thorough level, as his fingers shove aside my underwear, already soaked from the ocean and from my own need.

I'm practically begging for it by the time his finger slides along my clit.

Ah.

What I've been dying to feel.

I cry out into his mouth, wanting, needing more of it. My legs part another inch.

"Fuck," he murmurs against my lips. "You're drenched."

"That shouldn't surprise you."

He grins. I know he's remembering my sex dream, while his finger slowly glides along until it slips inside me.

There is no turning back now.

I gasp, a pornographic sound that surprises even me, and I immediately clench around him. Then another finger. Then another.

"How many do you want?" he asks, lips going to my neck now, leaving quick, sharp kisses. "How many fingers until I'm at your pussy's standards?"

I let out a breathy laugh. "My pussy's standards are high, but your cock will do."

"Patience, Gingersnap," he says, licking up my earlobe, causing me to shiver. He's found one of many sweet spots with that one. I have goosebumps.

"Think I've been mighty patient," I manage to say.

"Maybe." He starts thrusting his fingers in and out, slowly. "I want you to come on my hand. I want to know what that feels like. To make you do that, right here."

My knees are starting to give out as I try and accommodate his straining arm. "Pretty sure if I come on your hand, you might have to catch me."

"I'm already in a good position to do so," he says, working me harder. He leans in and takes my bottom lip between his teeth before slowly pulling it into his mouth. Teases the inside of it with his tongue.

Shit. I don't think I'm going to make it long, I—

The thought falls from my head as his thumb rubs against my clit.

The pressure inside me goes over the threshold.

My skin flushes like I'm on fire and then…

I'm falling.

Sinking against the palm tree.

Falling into his hand.

Letting go.

Coming hard.

Barely coherent noises spill from my mouth as my body feels like it's being torn with pleasure. I quake and tremble and hold onto Tai as everything turns to comets and shooting stars, my heart and soul blasted through a prism.

I'm never coming down from this.

I don't even know where this is, but I'd like to stay.

Eventually, somehow, I come back to reality. The sun is so bright and Tai is still stroking me softly with his large hand, those skilled fingers easing up. He's biting his lip as he grins at me, his eyes flickering with savagery and want that have only deepened.

I'm still pulsing as he pulls his fingers out from inside me. My eyes barely focus as I watch him lick up the side of his forefinger. "Can't tell what's sweeter," he says huskily. "You or the honey."

This man knows to say all the right things.

He deserves all the right things, too.

With my top half-off, and a lazy, sated smile on my lips, I reach down and grab his cock inside his swim trunks, thick, long and hard. His mouth drops open, a moan escaping.

I drop to my knees in the sand, undoing the Velcro at the top of his shorts and then tugging them down enough so his cock pops out.

Nearly takes my eye out.

But my god, it's gorgeous. I've seen enough dicks in my day to be an expert of sorts, and I know I'm probably biased, but Tai's is the most perfect penis I've ever seen. As big and intimidating as possible, without looking like a cervix-basher, his cock is thick, mean, and pretty.

Impulsively I lean in and lick up the tip, my tongue reveling in the salty hit of his precum, my fist tight around his wide girth. I have small hands, and I can barely contain him.

"Fucking hell," Tai swears, wrapping my ponytail around his hand.

I stare up at him, making sure he's watching me, and then I begin.

TAI

I don't think I've ever seen a more beautiful sight than the sight of Daisy Lewis on her knees, staring up at me intently with those big, wicked eyes of hers, my large cock firmly placed in her tiny hand.

Any doubts I had about this have been completely eradicated by the time she opens her pert little mouth and slides the tip inside.

What are doubts? What is life?

My eyes pinch shut and I moan, unable to keep my cool. I desperately want to grab the back of her head and start fucking her mouth, just go to town on her, but I'm still a gentleman at heart, and I know I need to save that savagery for later.

For now, though, I tug at her ponytail, indicating I want more.

She gives me more. Pulls down my swim togs, grabs onto my bare ass, digging her nails in. Works my cock with her tongue until I can't remember my name, sliding me in and out of her wet mouth, her grip perfect and tight. She razes the pulsing underside with her teeth, eliciting another breathless groan from deep inside my chest, then sucks off the tip.

I will not last long if she keeps this up.

"Stop," I manage to say, my voice croaking. I sound like I'm dying, feels like I am. My body is fighting against me, wanting her to continue, to shoot my load straight to the back of her throat.

But I'm all about patience at heart. I've waited this long for her, after all.

Daisy, meanwhile, doesn't listen.

I glance down at her and she's staring up at me with a wicked glint in her eyes, daring me to come.

"Don't make me," I tell her hoarsely, using her ponytail as leverage and yanking her head back, a trail of spit from the tip of my cock to her mouth.

Fucking hell.

I must be crazy to stop this, but I do have other plans.

"You want me to stop?" she says sweetly, though there's a hint of trepidation in her eyes, like she thinks I'm rejecting her. Can't say I blame her for thinking that way.

"What did you ask me earlier? If I'd fuck you?"

She purses her lips. "I believe I told you to fuck me."

"You know I have a hard time taking orders."

"Even from your first mate?"

First mate. The idea of her as a first mate lights up something inside me.

It also makes me harder.

"First mate bows to the captain," I tell her, widening my stance, folding my arms. I'm very aware of what I must look like to her, standing in front of her like this, naked with my cock jutting out, her on her knees in front of me.

"Hard to bow when I'm on my knees."

"It means, the first mate does what I say. Under all

circumstances. Take off your top. Show me those gorgeous tits of yours."

A visceral thrill runs up my spine as I watch her dutifully comply, peeling that wet tank top off like I'm living in a fucking porno.

My god, she's a dream come true. She's incredible.

Every inch of her, inside and out.

"This good enough?" she asks coyly.

I realize I'm living out any man's desert island fantasy.

New name for this place: Fantasy Island.

I clear my throat. "Get on all fours. Turn around."

Her brows raise, followed by one of her naughty smiles.

"Aye-aye Captain," she says, obviously relishing this role playing. Or perhaps it's not playing at all.

She falls forward, her tits swinging, then turns around until her ass is facing me.

I take a moment to admire the view, running my hand up and down my cock, thinking how easy it would be to just come right here, all across her back.

But I don't want easy right now.

I go to my knees, putting my hands at her hips. She flinches a little at my touch, anticipating my next move.

My fingers slide beneath the edges of her underwear and pull them down, down, down over her ample thighs and calves. Her skin is so creamy and pale, she nearly matches the sand. But there's a luminosity about her skin, it glows, like the warmth inside her radiates outward.

You're a fucking lucky bastard.

About to get luckier, too.

I lower my head and place a quick bite on one ass cheek.

She yelps.

I grin.

I then spread her cheeks and go to town on her, my tongue licking, searching, everywhere.

Perhaps a bit forward but I have no qualms doing this with Daisy. I know her enough, and I can make some pretty good guesses as to what she likes.

And she likes this.

She pushes herself back against my mouth, moaning loudly.

"Fuck, Tai," she cries out.

I mumble against her, making sure she's close to coming, then pull back.

Before she has a chance to catch her breath, I grip her hip with one hand and position my cock at the other, teasing her wetness.

"Guess this would be a good time to ask if you're on the pill," I say, feeling a little sheepish that I let things go this far before it even occurred to me.

"Yes, yes," she says impatiently. She glances at me over her shoulder, her face flushed. "I'm protected, I have an IUD, I'm clean."

"Just got to be sure." I pause, no need to tell her how long it's been since I was with someone, nor that I usually take every precaution. Condoms were the one thing I didn't think to pack.

"Tai," she whines, sounding breathless, impatient.

"It's Captain Wakefield," I tell her, grinning.

"Captain Wakefield. What are you waiting for?"

Nothing.

I suck in my breath and with one swift, hard thrust I plunge my cock deep inside of her.

"Fuck!" Daisy yelps, and I realize I may have been a bit rough.

I'm about to apologize when she cries out, "Keep going."

That I can do. I slowly pull out and then spear her again, my cock sinking into the hilt as my fingers make bruises on her hips.

Now I'm groaning, my eyes falling closed as my head goes back to the sky. We slowly build up a rhythm. The slow drag of me pulling out, the hard thrust as I piston my hips into her.

Her ass shakes and jiggles with each deliberate thrust, spurring me on to go harder, deeper. I tighten my hold on her, tilting her and adjusting myself so that I'm grinding against her in all the right places, my balls swinging against her ass.

"Oh god," she says through a moan. "Yes, keep going."

All the encouragement I need.

I bite my lip and keep pumping into her, my glutes getting a workout as I rhythmically pound and pound and pound. Sweat is pouring off of me, splashing onto her skin, the humidity mixing with my exertion.

Without losing cadence, I reach down with one hand and find her clit, soft and silky, aching for my touch.

"Tai," she whimpers. "I'm going to come."

I knew she would. If I learned anything from those dreams of hers, it's that she doesn't take long at all.

And, despite all my efforts to keep myself back, it's not going to take long for me either.

With my finger slipping and sliding all over her swollen clit, I stroke that sensitive bundle of nerves until she's tense and ready to explode. Then, as she yells out my name and begins to shake and shudder, clenching around my cock, I let go.

"Fuck, fuck, fuck," I growl, thrusting in harder and deeper, faster, like I'm trying to impale her right into the sand. Everything inside me tenses from my balls to my chest and then I'm being walloped by a tsunami, the orgasm ripping me apart and dragging me out to sea.

In these depths I don't even know what I'm doing, just that I'm an incoherent mess, a man who is sinking faster and faster, until everything is black.

"Fucking hell," I manage to say, partially collapsing on top of Daisy, whose face is already pressed against the sand, unable to keep herself up, her ass raised.

What even was that? How was that even possible?

Damn.

It feels like it takes forever for my heart rate to slow and for my breath to return to normal, but time ceases to have meaning. I am in no rush, all I need is right here. My cock still inside of her as she softly pulses around it, my hot, damp skin against her skin, the both of us burning up underneath the rising sun.

Eventually, though, we have to part.

I straighten up, running my hand down over her back, placing little kisses on her spine, before I grab her hips and pull out.

I'm not sure what to say to her. I don't know if there is anything to say.

Except that part of me wants to thank her.

Thank her for being so persistent. Thank her for opening up my eyes.

I knew it wouldn't just be a casual fuck with her, and as the reality is slowly comes back in, I know I want more.

I want us to be together. Just like this.

Again and again.

Until when? The voice in my head asks.

I don't have an answer.

But I know what I want.

"I think this is the first time I've ever gotten sandburn,"

she says to me, turning around and getting to her knees. She shows me her palms, which are all red.

"Sorry," I tell her, not really sorry at all. I get to my feet and grab her hand, pulling her up. I gesture to both our knees, also red. "Looks like a work hazard."

She grins, then suddenly turns shy. I guess because we're both standing here naked in the stark light, though perhaps it's because I just nailed her like a madman.

I bend down and pick up her clothes, handing them to her. "You may want these. As much as I would like to stay on Naked Island all day, I'm not sure your sister would appreciate it." I pause. "Richard might."

She snatches the clothes from me, laughing. "Naked Island," she says as she slips her clothes on and I yank on my swim trunks. "I like that. Please tell me it's a private island."

"Only two members, Gingersnap," I tell her.

You and me.

She looks delighted.

Then she sighs loudly. "I guess we should get back before they wake up and think the worst."

"You sure they won't think we're off somewhere screwing each other?"

"That is the worst. Sorry. I just...let's just keep this between us until we're off this damn island and in Fiji. I feel like I'm barely getting along with her and I dunno..."

I get what she's saying. Lacey would probably give her shit. Would probably give me shit too. Not that I care, but it matters to Daisy.

"No problem. Keep things simple. And secret. I'm good at that."

She gives me a soft grin. "Thank you." She looks past the

palms to the suitcase. "Well, we better pack up. Hopefully it doesn't get wet again."

"Listen, just in case, I'll carry it out of the water, as long as you grab that vodka."

She nods, grabbing it, and we quickly shove everything back in its place, zipping it back up before we enter the water.

I carry the suitcase above my head. Not so easy when it weighs a ton and the water is almost too deep to walk in spots, but I manage to get across the shallows of the lagoon just as Lacey and Richard come spilling out of the bungalow.

"Where have you been?" Lacey says and then sees the suitcase as I dump it on the sand. She points frantically. "Where the hell did that come from?"

"It washed ashore like a message in a bottle," Daisy says proudly, as if she had something to do with the suitcase coming back to her like a boomerang. "Any guesses what that message is?" she asks.

"That stupid designer bag you kept moaning about losing?" Lacey says.

Daisy rolls her eyes, and then reveals the bottle of vodka she had hidden behind her back. "The message was, let's get crazy!"

While Lacey and Richard freak out over the booze, practically snatching the bottle from her hands, Daisy gives me a faint wink. Which is to say, we already did the crazy part.

Not that it was crazy, per se. I should feel ashamed for finally having sex with her, or at least a little guilty, but surprisingly I feel neither. I told myself I needed to stay away from her because she was a distraction, a road with no future, a chance at heartbreak, something to steal me away from redemption.

But at the moment, I just don't care.

Because that was better than I could have even imagined. Not only was it a long time coming, but it was something I never even knew I needed. Not just in a physical way, though god knows it's been way too long since I last got laid, but in a spiritual way. Like that release was for those darkened, hardened bits inside me, the ones I try to keep buried and locked away. It helped shed light on those places, helped to give me hope that I could one day be free of them.

Or maybe I'm looking into it too much. Either way, I have no regrets. The only thing I have is this pressing need to do it again, immediately. A swift return to Naked Island.

But any hopes of that are dashed now that Lacey and Richard are all over the vodka. I never thought I'd see either of them drinking hard liquor straight out of the bottle, but there's a first time for everything, and being isolated on this island is apparently bringing that out of everyone.

"We need to have a party," Lacey says adamantly.

Never thought I'd hear her say that either.

"We need to invite Fred and Wilson," Richard adds, passing the bottle back to her. It's already half-way gone from just the four of us.

"The goat?" I question.

"Of course," Richard says. "It's the man's only friend."

Uh-huh. "Don't you think it's odd that he talks to the goat?"

"People talk to animals all the time, Tai, it's called anthropomorphizing."

"I mean, the goat talks to him."

Richard raises a stern brow. "Tai, goats don't talk."

I can't argue with that.

Daisy takes the bottle back from Lacey and examines it. "At the rate we're going, we'll be drunk by noon."

"There's always the wine," I mention.

"You have wine?" Lacey exclaims.

"Yes," Daisy says cautiously. I can tell she doesn't want to share it and I probably shouldn't have said anything. "I don't want to burn through it but..."

"We're getting rescued the day after tomorrow," Lacey says. "Tonight we'll party, we'll drink. Tomorrow we'll pack and be all hungover. The next day we fly out of here. Fiji! You can buy more wine there."

Daisy seems to weigh that option. "You're right."

"I suppose we should go invite Fred," Richard says. "The question is, how do we get over there? We have no way of contacting him from here, and he's the one with the raft."

I'm about to volunteer to swim there, since a lot of it is shallow enough and there are a few other smaller islands peppered about, good places to rest if I get tired, when Daisy points into the distance.

"No need," she says. "I think that's him already."

I quickly grab my binoculars from the bag and look through them. Fred is coming across the water in his dinghy, with Wilson at the very front of the boat. He looks like he's got some equipment with him.

"It's like he knew," I comment.

It's not long before Fred is close to shore and the goat is leaping off into the water. It runs, splashing through, straight toward us, until he veers to the side at the last minute, disappearing into the jungle.

"Ahoy," Fred says. "Permission to come to your island."

"The Island of Dr. Boner," Daisy says.

"*Stop*," Lacey warns her.

"Ah yes, it is rather phallic-shaped, isn't it?" Fred says, getting out of the dinghy into ankle-deep water, and pulling it on shore. "Dale used to call it The Schlong but that was

Dale for ya. Weird guy. I miss him. Don't miss his smell. Oh, what in god's green earth is that?"

Fred has spotted the vodka bottle.

"I found it!" Daisy says, holding it out for him. "My suitcase washed ashore. Have vodka and wine. Even some honey."

"Honey?" Lacey says, sounding offended. "You never mentioned that!"

"I, er, left it on the island," Daisy says, avoiding looking at me. She's blushing. Fucking adorable. We'll never look at honey the same way.

"We were thinking of having a shindig," I tell Fred. "I was about to swim over and formally invite you."

"Shucks, I'm honored to be invited. But I'm glad you didn't swim over. Saw lots of sharks along the way. They're in a mood today."

"I'm sorry what?" Lacey says.

"Sharks?" Daisy repeats.

"Where?" I ask, not feeling so great about Daisy and I swimming to the island and back.

"Out yonder," Fred says, gesturing toward his island and to the west. "They tend to stay near one of the barrier islands. See this whole atoll is roughly in the shape of a fish. The west over there, that's the tail section. There are breaks in the reef where it opens to the ocean. That was done on purpose back in the day, when they wanted to open a channel up for boats to get through. Anyway, same current that brought your suitcase in also brought the sharks."

Suddenly this little slice of paradise doesn't feel so safe anymore.

"Is it just this side of the island?"

"Oh heavens no. I think there's more up where you wrecked."

And suddenly I need a drink.

Daisy must see this in my face because now she's passing the bottle to me. All the times I went swimming there...

"But don't worry," he adds. "For the most part, they're harmless. Mainly hammerheads, which look worse than they are. Don't think I've ever heard of an attack. Tiger sharks on the other hand... Anyway, just stay out of the water for a few days, you'll be fine. Okay, hurry up with that vodka son and pass it back. Been way too long."

I absently take a big swig, barely feeling the burn, then hand it back to him.

"Anyhoo," he says, eagerly taking the bottle. "Seems I had an inkling today was going to be special. I brought over some camping equipment and some extra food. Now that we have alcohol, I don't think we're missing a thing."

Food? All of us castaways head to the dingy and peer inside.

There's a camping stove, a small bottle of propane, and a grill.

And the food.

Which happens to be heaps of canned goods.

Shit.

I mean, we were running low so I am in no way complaining that we have food to eat, but at the same time, I know we're all tired of the same old thing. At least in this mix though, there are some wild card items such as sliced olives, diced tomatoes, corn, mushrooms, tuna, sardines, even some tins of Spam.

"There's a lot more where that came from," Fred says. "We have a whole bunker full of this stuff out yonder. None's expired either, so you can eat without worrying."

"This is very generous of you," I tell Fred. "But I can do better than the tuna and sardines."

I grab a tin of sardines and then go over to the tree my fishing pole is resting against.

"Now that I have bait, I'm catching us lunch and dinner," I tell them.

Daisy claps excitedly, like my number one fan. Hard to tell if she's a fan of me or the potential fish, though.

While everyone goes about getting ready for the day and prepping for the party, I take the fishing rod and head down the beach, toward the west. Figure that with the current being the way it is, more fish will be at that end.

This must be the "head" of the dick, if you're looking at the shape of the island. From here I can see where the land curves inward. If I kept walking along the beach it would eventually take me around and connect me to the other side.

I stick the sardine on the end and throw the line in the water. I don't want to go in deeper than my ankles thanks to Fred's warning about sharks, but I hope there're enough fish in the sandy shallows.

I don't have to wait long to find out.

There's a flash of silver in the water and then a tug at my line.

The fish puts up a bit of a fight, but in record time I pull it up out of the water.

A bonefish, about ten pounds, and a beautiful silver olive color.

"Yesssss!" I yell. I close my eyes, giving thanks to the ocean for providing us with the food, a little karakia or prayer.

When I open my eyes, I notice a shark fin in the water.

That's a sight that will never not chill you to the core.

But after getting over the initial shock, I realize it's just a small nurse shark, coming to check on what the commotion in the water was all about.

"Better luck next time," I tell the shark, then I head back down the sand toward barracks.

I feel like a soldier returning from war.

Everyone sees the fish and immediately swarms me, congratulating me like I'm a hero. I have to say, after feeling like I've majorly fucked up for most of this trip, it feels good to provide for them. Like I'm finally the captain again, after deeming myself unworthy.

I quickly kill the fish, then clean it on a large rock. On the camping stove, Fred heats up the diced tomatoes and olives. I grab the grill and put it over the fire Richard started, sprinkling the fish with liberal amounts of salt and pepper that Fred brought. While it grills, smelling absolutely incredible after a week of somewhat tasteless food, Daisy pours everyone pinot noir into tin mugs. Lacey sets out the plastic plates.

When it's all ready, we sit down on the sand, fresh caught grilled fish covered in tomatoes and olives in one hand, mug of wine in the other.

We raise our drinks.

"To Tai," Fred says.

"And to Fred," says Lacey.

"Before we dig in," I tell them, "I'd like to say a few words first. I...being here has made me realize I've lost touch with some things, a lot of the connection that my ancestors had to the land, so if you don't mind, I'd like to take a moment and give a proper thanks. A karakia, in Maori." I close my eyes. "Nau mai e ngā hua, o Papatūānuku, o Ranginui kete kai. Whītiki kia ora! Hāumi e. Hui e. Tāiki e! That is, I welcome the gifts of food, provided by the earth mother and the sky father, bearer of food baskets. Gifts bound together to sustain all of us. United and connected as one."

"Amen," everyone says.

"Okay, let's fucking eat," I tell them, taking a hearty sip of the warm but wonderful wine, and digging in.

It's the best meal I've ever had in my life. I know it's the same for everyone else, enough that we sound like we're all having an orgasm at once. Everyone looks so incredibly happy.

I catch Daisy's eye and that happiness spreads inside me.

I'm incredibly happy.

17

DAISY

Sore.

I am so *sore*.

I didn't think it had been that long since I last had sex, but having sex with Tai was obviously a first time thing. And my god, can that guy wear you out! I had no illusions of how skilled he would be with that cock of his, I could tell just by his hands that he'd know what he's doing and he'd give it to me good.

But he gave it to me maybe a little too good, if that's at all possible. Last night was crazy.

We got good and drunk on the rest of the vodka and wine, and we ate the most amazing meals in the history of cuisine (fish for lunch and dinner...don't really know what kind of fish it was, but it was good).

Then, when everyone passed out on the beach, we snuck into the jungle and ripped the clothes off each other, stealing what moments could find.

Then, after it got dark and everyone went to bed, we took a sleeping bag and headed down the beach, out of sight. We went at it all night long, barely getting any shuteye.

"Good morning," Tai says gently, his voice thick with sleep.

I roll my head to the side and see him staring at me, his eyes half-closed. How can a man be so hot and manly and pretty all at once?

"Hi," I tell him. I'm smiling. Of course I'm smiling. I'm lying on a sleeping bag on our own private section of the beach, naked, Tai beside me.

Also naked.

And hard. Very hard.

My eyes focus on his morning wood for a moment, the source of my pain and pleasure. The sun isn't up yet—you'd think we'd sleep in for once—but I can definitely make that thing out in the dim light. He's primed and ready.

"How did you sleep?" he asks, leaning in to kiss my jaw, reaching over to brush the bedhead off my brow.

I close my eyes at his touch and sigh happily.

"Good. When we did sleep. I am a little sore, though."

"It's the sand. Not so great for the back."

"No, it's your monster cock. Not so good for my cooch."

He snorts. "You sure about that?"

"Your monster cock?"

"I think it's been doing you a world of good. I'd go so far as to say you're pretty much insatiable. Been thirsting for it for weeks now."

I glare at him playfully. "Have I been that obvious?"

"Hey, I'm the one catching you having sex dreams about me," he says, slowing bringing his hand down over my breasts, gently teasing my nipple.

I'm starting to squirm. "I never said the dreams were about you."

"Who was it about then?"

"Okay, so it was about you."

"And what was I doing in your dream?"

I gnaw on my lip for a moment, debating if I should tell him.

"I see," he says with a nod. "You don't want to ask for it."

"Hey, I asked you to fuck me."

"No." He pinches my nipple hard and I gasp. "You *told* me to fuck you. It was an order, and I obeyed, a captain momentarily giving in. No matter though, I already know what I want."

He moves over on top of me and I will never ever get sick of the sight of his mammoth frame, his big, hard muscles bearing down on me. I'm already small but this makes me feel itty bitty, like I've been captured by this big bad beast of a man with the heart of gold, a man that takes me and ravages me and...hmmm sounds like one of my favorite romance novels.

My hands go to his back, relishing the feeling of his smooth, bare skin, his taut muscles beneath.

But he moves, sliding down and down, leaving wet, hot kisses from between my breasts, down my stomach, over my belly button, until he's firmly between my legs.

Big hands slide under my ass, bunching it, and I spread my thighs.

"Just like your dream?" he murmurs, flashing me a wicked grin.

Oh, what a sight. This will be forever framed in my mind gallery.

"Hmmm, I'm not sure yet," I say playfully. "Let's see what you got."

"Sounds like a challenge," he says before he dips his mouth, placing his lips around my clit.

Holy bejesus!

The feel of his warm mouth sends shockwaves and shivers through my limbs, from the top of my head, all the way to my toes. I start to lift my hips, wanting more pressure, more suction.

Tai pulls back instead.

Tease.

I lift my head and stare down at him. "What are you doing? Don't stop."

"Just making sure I'm living up to your dream."

"Well, you're not. In my dream you didn't stop!"

His mouth curls into an amused smile. Then, while keeping his eyes locked on mine, proceeds to blow gently on my clit.

Oh my stars.

My head flops back onto the sleeping back, and I stare up at the sky as it lightens above us.

I squirm beneath him, trying to raise my hips again, needing his mouth to put me out of this delicious torture, but he's not in a hurry. He slowly blows all the way down to my ass.

Fuck.

"Please," I whimper. "Tai...I want..."

Use your words, Daisy, I think, but it proceeds to come out in an unintelligible mumble.

He pauses. "If I remember correctly you came a lot during your dream. Very quickly. Can't have that happen now that I've finally got your sweet cunt in front of me. I want to take my time savoring each and every inch of your honey."

I lift my head again and stare down at him. Dirty mouthed bastard.

His long tongue slowly protrudes. The moment it makes contact with my skin, I'm hissing like a tea kettle.

"Patience," he says before he spreads his tongue wide, licking up my length in a long, slow stroke, giving my clit a flick at the end.

I throw my arm over my face in breathless despair. "You're killing me."

"What's the rush? You want to come, I want to take my time. I eat things slowly."

His tongue suddenly plunges inside me, causing me to jolt.

Damn it!

"You're a sadist," I mumble. "A secret Dom who wants to make a girl beg for it. The real Tai Wakefield is into torture."

"Never said I was an angel," he says. I look down at him and he smiles, his lips glistening. "But I promise you, Gingersnap, I'll make it so good for you. Just hold out a little bit."

"Jerk," I mutter, but it drifts off into a blissful sigh as his tongue begins to lap me up again, increasing speed and pressure.

Then one thumb curves around my bum and presses into me, just the tip.

"God, yes," I moan, my limbs straining, heart pounding louder. "More of *that*."

Yes, yes, yes.

His voice is muffled as he starts working me faster, his tongue flicking harder, his thumb sliding deeper.

Finally, he's giving me what we both need.

And in true Daisy fashion, it doesn't take long at all.

With his thumb and now his tongue both plunging up inside me, his other thumb rubbing circles at my clit, I'm coming...

I already know it's going to blow my world apart before it even starts.

It's like every little tightened knot inside of me, every little tense string of anxiety and worry and sadness, all of it, everything negative and dark and buried, has suddenly been cut with a pair of shears. I'm let loose, freed, exploding in all different directions at once, like a beam of light has opened up inside of me, throwing me out into the universe like a confetti cannon.

I am spinning and flying and it's all so much.

So much.

Too much.

At the top of this flight, where I don't even know my name, I only know that I have Tai for now. And that for now is not forever.

And as I realize that, I'm trying to hold onto this moment. This moment where I have him. Until now, the only thing I had was the rising sun. Now I'll do anything not to lose this.

"Oh god," I whimper. My bones feel hollow, my body weightless. I'm lying on the sleeping bag, bare and vulnerable and fileted to the soul. My feelings snuck up on me like a motherfucking freight train, running me right into the ground.

Fucking hell. He goes down on me once and suddenly it's like I can't live without him?

Get a grip, Daisy.

But other than my hands, which have frozen in place around the sleeping bag, I can't get a grip right now.

I thought this was just sex between us, I thought that's all I wanted.

That's usually all I want. I've kept my heart out of most entanglements because that's what it was, an entanglement. A net. A place to be caught and held before you're hurt. The only person I let myself fall for was Chris, and look what happened with that. Only proved my point, that it's not worth letting your guard down and letting someone in, because you're only going to experience pain in the end.

But Tai? I want Tai. All of him. And as much as I pretend that I can do this sex thing with him, I'm going to be devastated when we have to part ways.

I don't want to say goodbye.

"You okay?" Tai asks, coming up beside me.

I blink at him and realize I have tears in my eyes.

Shit.

I nod. "Yup. Good." Give him a small, shaky smile.

"You're crying," he says, running his finger underneath my eye, wiping the tear away.

"Guess I needed to," I tell him. "Nothing you did, just..."

"A release?"

"Yeah."

A release and the realization that this man is going to break my heart.

I'M HUNGOVER AND, I have to admit, there's something comforting about it. Like even though we survived a shipwreck, and we're stuck on this semi-deserted island, the hangover feels like an old friend. An old friend that likes to smack you upside the head and kick you in the gut, but an old friend nonetheless.

Everyone else is feeling it, too. It was the plan, after all. Morning sex with Tai helped, but we had to hurry back to the barracks before people realized we were missing, and then the hangover reared its ugly head.

We're all sitting on the beach around the fire. Fred is heating up a pot of coffee on the camping stove, and at the moment, Fred is our savior. We haven't had coffee since the shipwreck and we need it more than ever.

Finally, it's ready. Poured into the mugs we drank the wine from last night.

It's instant, but it's hot and heavenly.

"Never thought freeze-dried, chemically processed coffee crystals could taste so divine," Richard remarks. "Elixir of the Gods."

"I wouldn't go that far," Fred says with a chuckle. "You stay here long enough, drinking that stuff, you'll start having fantasies about a perfectly brewed espresso." His eyes go to a dreamy place.

"So do you think you'll leave with us when the plane comes?" Tai asks him.

Fred shrugs. "Don't know. Don't think so."

"You still have work to do?"

"I don't want to have to leave Wilson," Fred says. "Only true friend I got."

That's so sweet and sad at the same time. Maybe I've been too harsh with that little goat.

Suddenly Lacey starts snickering, looking at something over my shoulder.

"Whatcha got there, Wilson?" Fred asks.

I look over my shoulder to see Wilson just outside the bungalow.

Chewing on something.

Oh my god.

He's chewing on my vibrator.

Shit!

"Hey!" I yell, putting my coffee down and scrambling to my feet, kicking up sand as I go.

I start running after Wilson, who then thinks it's a game of sorts, and starts running around the bungalow in circles, the vibrator flopping in his mouth.

Everyone is falling over themselves, laughing, but I'm determined to get that thing back. It was expensive as hell and when you find a good one, you hang onto it.

"Daisy!" Tai yells, voice breaking up as he laughs. "Daisy, you don't need it that badly. Let it go!"

I mean, he's right. I have Tai.

For now.

And I have better standards than using a vibrator that a goat chewed on.

I stop, catching my breath, and Wilson joyfully runs off into the jungle, bleating in victory.

"Enjoy it, you pervert!" I yell after him.

Then I return to the beach, knowing how much I'm going red. Tomato Zone Four, maybe.

"Why Daisy, I'm not sure where your face ends and your hair begins," Tai jokes.

"Yes, you're very red," Richard explains bluntly, as if I didn't get it.

"I have to say, I didn't think Wilson had it in him," Fred muses. "Usually such a polite goat."

"Uh huh," I say, sitting back down and covering my face with my mug. There's no such thing as a polite goat.

The rest of the morning passes at a slow pace. Oh, the goat and vibrator jokes keep coming from all directions (that's what she said?), but everyone is taking it easy, and seeming to be in good spirits, despite the excess spirit of last night.

I'm sitting in the sand, reading a book about a mafia

princess. Lacey is beside me, scribbling something on a notepad. Tai and Richard are at Tai's fishing spot, hoping to get lunch. Fred has gone back to his camp to get some more sardines for bait.

Wilson is still MIA.

Hope he didn't choke on it.

"What are you writing?" I ask Lacey.

She sighs and puts her pen down. "Why?"

"Jeez, testy, testy. Just curious. Can't a sister be curious?"

"If you must know, I'm documenting our peril."

"Peril?" I repeat. I gesture to the paradise around us. "How is this peril?"

She frowns. "You know Daisy, sometimes I think you live in a different reality."

My hackles raise. Here we go again with the whole 'coasting by' thing. "I don't live in another reality. I'm trying to make the best of it."

"Make the best of it, huh? We all know what that means."

My brows shoot up. "What does that mean, then?"

"No wonder you don't mind being stranded in the middle of the Pacific when you've got Tai to fuck whenever you want."

"What!?" I exclaim. "What makes you think that?"

Oh god.

"Oh, come on," she says. "We all know it."

"All of you?"

"Yes, Fred told us."

"What?"

"Well, the goat told him."

The goat?

"*Wilson*," I seethe, as if he's Newman on *Seinfeld*.

"It's so obvious you wanted him from the start. Guess he finally gave in."

"Okay, fine. Fine." I raise my palms in surrender. Cats out of the bag. "We're together. But what difference is it to you?"

"You don't know him like I know him."

"Maybe not, maybe I don't have years of friendship with him, but I know him in my own way and I'm getting to know more of him every single day." My heart is drumming in my chest as I say this. "Besides, I don't have to have been friends with him for a long time to know just what kind of man he is. He's kind, he's funny, he's selfless, he's protective, he's broken and yet he keeps on going. He's fucking amazing."

"Which is why you should stay ten feet away from him," she snaps. "You're going to use him and break his heart, just like you've always done."

"*Always done*?" I cry out.

"You dispose of guys when you're done with them. Toss them away like they don't exist. Then you move on like nothing has happened, because to you, nothing *has* happened."

"How would you even know that? You've never taken any interest in my life!"

"Facebook tells me everything I need to know. In a relationship, single. In a relationship, single. You're never single for more than a month, it's like you're afraid to be alone, you just go from guy to guy and I've never seen you once look heartbroken over it."

"Maybe I'm not the type to profess my feelings all over social media."

She gives me a steady look. "You're right. I don't think I've ever seen you post anything negative. Another reason why life is just one fucking lucky happenstance to the next.

And why nearly losing your life in a shipwreck doesn't seem to have any impact on you."

"Doesn't have an impact on me?" I repeat. "This has been hard for me, too. But maybe, just maybe, I'm looking on the bright side, which is that we are getting rescued tomorrow. There's an end in sight to this. Maybe I'd lose my motherfucking mind if I stayed one more day here, but that's not happening, okay? And maybe it wouldn't hurt you to be happy about that, too."

She stares at me for a moment and then nods. Goes back to scribbling about her peril.

Jeez Louise. I don't know what it is about Lacey. Just when I think there's no more excess baggage between us, she finds even more. There's an endless supply of angst and resentment. Are all sibling relationships this complicated, or did I get handed a doozy?

"We are men," Richard announces as he and Tai walk toward us. Richard has the rod and a peachy silver fish at the end of it. He pounds his chest with one hand. "We bring food for you women."

I want to roll my eyes, but he *is* bringing food for us women, so I rein it in. Better this than his Star Trek talk.

"Right on time," Tai says, shielding his eyes from the sun as he looks across the lagoon where Fred is coming back with his dinghy. "You'd swear that guy has a sixth sense for food and booze."

But as Fred gets closer, his expression is grim.

Something in my stomach drops.

Shit.

I exchange a worried glance with Tai, not liking the look of this.

"Castaways," Fred addresses us, getting out of the boat.

Tai runs over to help him haul it up on the beach. "I'm afraid I have some bad news."

I swallow hard. I knew it.

He looks off to the west. "Seems another weather system is moving in overnight. Things are going to get pretty rough for us."

"What do you mean?" I ask. "Are we in danger?"

"Not really," he says, and I relax slightly. "This is a fairly good location. I have to say mine is better though. It's facing the east lagoon, more protected from the waves, less currents. I think it would be best if we all moved over there at some point today. Just till the storm passes."

"Sure," Lacey says. "I mean, that's not the best news, but we'll make it work."

"Oh, beg ya pardon," Fred says, taking off his ball cap and holding it between his hands. "That wasn't the bad news. Though I suppose it was part of the bad news."

"What's the bad news, Fred?" Tai asks gravely.

For a moment I expect him to tell me his goat died, but then I notice Wilson off in the distance. I have to admit, I'm kind of relieved, even though he still has the vibrator.

"They're not coming," Fred says.

Okay, that relief was short-lived.

"What do you mean they're not coming?" Lacey asks. "You mean rescue?"

He nods. "The storm sure done and messed things up for us."

"They're coming after the storm passes, though," I say. "Right?"

Right?

"Oh, for sure," he says. "Don't worry your pretty red head over that." He hesitates. "It'll just be in a few weeks from now."

"A few weeks!" I exclaim.

"You're kidding me!" Lacey cries out.

"Afraid not. The storm messed up their schedule and the availability of their planes. Believe me, I'm just as disappointed as you are."

No you're not, I can't help but think. *You have your goat, and now you have us.*

I'm starting to feel like whatever hope and good thoughts I had lately were just an illusion. I kept telling myself it would be over soon, that I needed to make it through one more day. I focused on the positive because there was an end in sight. I didn't let myself get too sucked in to anything negative because I had a feeling that's where I'd stay.

Now I feel like the rug has been yanked out from under me and I'm falling. No happy hopeful feelings to keep me up anymore. No inner buoyancy to keep me afloat.

We're really fucking stuck here.

And what if they don't come in two weeks?

What if it gets pushed back and back?

What if something awful happens to us in the meantime? What if someone gets attacked by a shark? Or gets sick and can't get medicine? What if I slipped on the rocks at the waterfall and split open my head? Who is going to help us?

I turn away from everyone, throw my head back to the sky and I scream.

"FUUUUUUUUUCK!!!!"

I mean, I am having an out-of-body experience right now, there's no other way to describe it. All the feelings I've pushed aside, all to try and keep a positive frame of mind are now coming out of me like a rushing torrent of despair and rage.

"Fuck, fuck, FUCK!" The words just rip right out of me.

"Daisy," I hear Tai whisper, and then feel his arms around me. "It's okay."

I yank myself out of his grasp, staring at him, staring at everyone else. They're all in shock, maybe because of the situation, maybe because I am finally losing my mind.

"It's not okay! You just heard what Fred said! We're stuck here for another few weeks. And then what happens after that? Another few weeks more? And more?"

"It's not going to be like that," Fred says calmly. "I promise you."

"You promise me!" I repeat. "You've been stranded here for three months! How long have they been promising *you* that someone else is coming?"

"We'll call Suva again," Tai says, raising his palms, trying to calm me. "We'll explain what happened. They will come for us. It's okay. You're going to be okay."

"I'm not okay, okay!" I yell. "None of this," I gesture wildly to the beach and the island, "is okay."

"You need to focus on the positive," Lacey says.

I blink at her, stunned that she's throwing that back in my face so soon, though her voice is a little shaky, like she doesn't really believe it. "You literally just told me that," she adds. "Remember? All your positive posts, the shit you say on Facebook?"

"Well, maybe that was shit! Maybe I put on that happy face on social media because that's the kind of person I wanted to be. It's the kind of person I wanted people to see me as. But I'm not okay, not now, and..." I trail off. "I've never really been okay."

"I find that hard to believe," she says. "You've—"

"If you tell me once more that I luck into everything, especially *now*, I'm going to find something really disgusting in that jungle and I'm going to put it on your head!" I snap at her. "Contrary to what you thought, I didn't have a perfect life. I kept people at a distance. I didn't get attached to my relationships. I stayed with a job because it was easy. I pretended that it was fine and lied to myself because admitting the truth, that I wasn't happy, would have been too hard. I kept up the persona and I fooled myself into believing it's who I was. But it wasn't."

I look around. Tai is watching me carefully. Richard seems to be hanging on my every word, while Fred wanders down the beach, head low, hands in his pockets. I feel for him, I do. I want him off this godforsaken place as much I want that for myself.

Amazing how things can turn from paradise to pain when your future is at risk.

"I don't even know who I am," I say softly, feeling tears well up inside my throat. "I don't. I thought I did but it was just the lies I told myself. So here I am, figuring it all out, and the most I got out of this is that I'm not okay!"

"None of us are okay right now," Richard says quietly.

"Right!" I yell. "We aren't. We're fucked! We're screwed! We're shipwrecked and we don't know when we're going to get rescued."

"But you could focus on the positive, that they know where we are, that help will come," Lacey points out, suddenly taking on my old persona.

"No. YOU focus on the positive," I tell her. "I'm choosing not to. I'm choosing to be a realist. I'm choosing, for once in my life, to put my hand up and say, I am not okay. I'm not okay with this, I'm not okay with my life, I'm not okay with anything."

"You could try a different adjective than okay," Richard mumbles.

"Fuck you, Mr. Thesaurus," I tell him, giving him the finger.

Lacey gasps.

"There's nothing wrong with using the same word," I tell him indignantly, "and there's nothing wrong with admitting to the world that you could use some help. Why, even here, do we have to look on the bright side all the fucking time?"

Okay, I realize now that I sound like a total hypocrite from what I was telling Lacey earlier but maybe I am a fucking hypocrite. Maybe I've always been one.

"Can't we just for a minute take in the reality as it is and say, you know what? This is some fucked up shit and I'm scared and I don't know how the hell we're going to get out of it."

"But we will get out of it," Tai says.

I exhale loudly and sink to my knees, putting my head in my hands. "I know," I mumble. "I know. We will. Because we're humans and that's what we'll do. We'll get out of this. But for once I would love to just admit that I'm scared and I'm worried and, at this moment, I'm weak. I don't want to be that person that smiles for the selfies and puts up some bull-shit inspirational caption when inside I feel broken. I want to be that person that admits, Hey! I'm Daisy and I'm broken and yet I'm still worthy too."

Everyone is silent.

But my tears don't come. I want them to. I want the release, especially as it feels like the greatest weight on my chest has been lifted, like I've had an anvil placed there my whole life. A weight that kept me carefully controlled, a weight that prevented me from opening up and taking a risk and becoming who I want to become.

I don't even know who I want to become.

I just know, as I'm on my knees in the sand, that I'm

ready to become someone else. Get through this shit and come out the other side better.

To become is better than being.

But will anyone love what I become?

Will I?

I get to my feet, feeling those tears now starting to come up again.

So I turn toward the jungle and run.

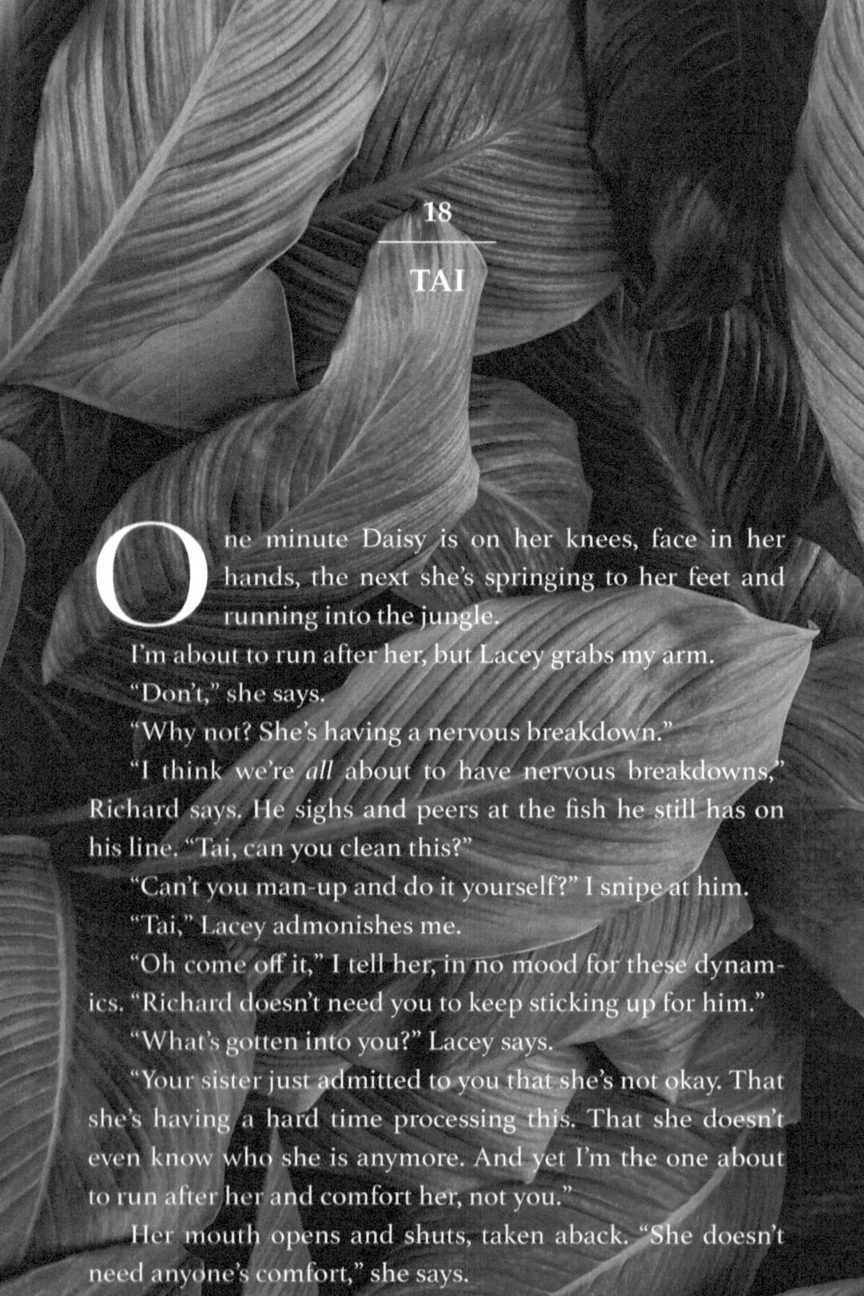

18

TAI

One minute Daisy is on her knees, face in her hands, the next she's springing to her feet and running into the jungle.

I'm about to run after her, but Lacey grabs my arm.

"Don't," she says.

"Why not? She's having a nervous breakdown."

"I think we're *all* about to have nervous breakdowns," Richard says. He sighs and peers at the fish he still has on his line. "Tai, can you clean this?"

"Can't you man-up and do it yourself?" I snipe at him.

"Tai," Lacey admonishes me.

"Oh come off it," I tell her, in no mood for these dynamics. "Richard doesn't need you to keep sticking up for him."

"What's gotten into you?" Lacey says.

"Your sister just admitted to you that she's not okay. That she's having a hard time processing this. That she doesn't even know who she is anymore. And yet I'm the one about to run after her and comfort her, not you."

Her mouth opens and shuts, taken aback. "She doesn't need anyone's comfort," she says.

"How could you say such a thing? Everyone needs that at some point. I don't care how strong you are." Or how much you keep it inside.

"Look, you don't know Daisy like I do," she begins.

"Apparently, you never knew her at all," Richard says quietly.

Lacey's blue eyes go wide. She turns to her husband in shock. "I *know* my sister."

"She doesn't even know herself," Richard explains. "Maybe you should stop being so hard on her for a minute, and just give her a break."

Lacey looks like he's just slapped her, skin paling. "Give her a break? She's only been given breaks her whole life! You know that!"

"I know what you've told me, and only that," Richard says. "Perhaps Daisy was born with a silver spoon in her mouth, perhaps not. What does it matter?"

"My parents were hard on me, and easy on her. That's why it matters."

"That happens, Lacey loo. It's very common. What should matter is whether your parents love the both of you, and they do."

"Well, why should I work so hard for everything, and she gets everything handed to her?"

"Because life isn't fair? Because it doesn't work that way? Because Daisy took the opportunities presented to her, just as you took yours? Yes, I'll be the first one to say that yours have been more challenging, but you fought for the life you chose. You fought for me. Daisy is only now admitting that she wants more for herself. Put yourself in her shoes for a moment, and just imagine working a job for ten years that you didn't even like all that much." He pauses. "And she failed at it. Isn't it better to fail at something you love than something you hate?"

"And you shouldn't be rooting for her to fail, at any rate," I tell Lacey. "Which tells me that whatever issues you have with your sister, it's all to do with you, and nothing to do with her."

I glance over at the west where Fred is standing on the beach and staring off into the distance.

Dark, angry-looking clouds are building on the horizon.

Storm's coming.

And moving fast.

"Now you can think about the fact that I'm right, or you can continue harboring resentment, but I'm going to get Daisy," I tell her.

I turn and run off into the forest, the deep musty smell of earth and foliage filling my lungs.

"Daisy!" I yell, leaping over fallen logs, dodging tangled roots. The canopy above makes the world dimmer, harder to see.

I pause and listen. I hear the stream burbling nearby, the constant birdsong, but beyond that, nothing.

I head toward the flowing water and then follow it, knowing this is probably what Daisy did.

I'm worried about her. I wasn't expecting for her to melt down like that, even though it was obviously a long time coming. I knew from the moment I first met her that she was wearing a mask, that beneath the makeup and the trendy clothes and that bright smile, was a little lost girl who was trying to be what the world wanted her to be. It definitely didn't help that she had someone like Lacey drilling those things in her head. If you hear something enough, you believe it.

You become it.

And now Daisy wants to become something else.

I want to help her become that person.

"Daisy!" I yell again, as the elevation gets slightly higher, the stream bringing me closer to the pool.

When I finally get there, I see a couple of crested iguanas on the rocks. They look at me with idle surprise, but don't dart off. Daisy is nowhere to be found.

I could have sworn she would have come here.

Maybe she went to the old camp?

To the boat?

The image of Atarangi sitting on the reef hits deep.

I'm about to run in that direction when I swear I hear her voice.

I stop and listen.

There's just the running water, the birds.

My heart pounding in my throat.

I *will* find Daisy.

And once I find her, I'm not going to let her go.

I mean that.

Not on this island, not when we get back to Fiji. Whether I have to go to the States, whether she'll come to New Zealand, I don't know, but I know that she's worth fighting for and that we can make it work, whatever it is.

If she wants to, I remind myself.

Other than the sex, she's given no real indications that she sees something long-term with us. Or perhaps I've been too afraid to look closely, to read into the wrong thing. We're both people who had our hearts broken and our trust shattered by the last person we were with. Just because I'm feeling one way doesn't mean she feels the same.

But it's worth the shot, anyway.

I cup my hands around my mouth and try again. "Daisy!"

Silence, except for the waterfall. Even the birds have stopped.

Then I hear it again, coming from the east, the direction behind the waterfall.

A very faint, "Tai!"

I take off, running alongside the pool, the iguanas scattering, then I'm scampering up a slope to where the stream runs and plunges over the edge.

I haven't explored this area yet, but I don't let that slow me down.

I keep running, battling through overgrown vines, wishing I had a machete.

"Daisy!" I yell again, catching my breath.

"Tai!"

I pick up her direction, head away from the stream, running deeper and deeper into the jungle.

"Tai!"

I see her. Standing in a thicket of ferns.

Her red head stands out like a flame amongst all the green.

"Daisy!"

I run right over to her and bring her into my arms, squeezing her tight.

"I'm so sorry." She's babbling into my chest. "I got lost, I didn't know where I was."

"It's okay," I tell her, running my hand down the back of her head, smoothing her hair. "I'm here now. You're fine."

She shakes her head.

Because no. That's the point.

Of course, she's not fine.

I pull back just enough to look her over, keeping my hands on her shoulders. She looks well, other than the puffy red eyes and the tears streaming down her delicate, freckled face.

"Gingersnap, you're breaking my heart here," I whisper to her, cupping her face in my hands. I pull her in and kiss her forehead, then the top of her head, and she throws her arms around my waist, holding me tight.

"I'm sorry," she sniffles.

"Don't be sorry. Whatever you're feeling is valid. Just... don't be afraid to feel it."

"I know. Or...I don't know." She takes in a deep breath that shakes her whole body. "Once upon a time I was that person that if anything remotely negative happened to me or to people I know, I'd push the negative feelings away. 'Focus on the positive' was my mantra. Count your blessings. Be grateful for what you have. Those were my stock answers every time I was presented with something less than happy, less than perfect. And you know what?"

She pauses, resting her cheek on my chest. "It was all bullshit. All it did was invalidate my feelings, *and* the feelings of my friends. It made it so that the bad feelings were pushed away and buried, never to be dealt with. I made it so the only feelings we should ever have are good ones, as unrealistic as that was. It was...tiring. I am so fucking tired of pretending that I have it all together."

"It *is* tiring," I tell her. "Believe me, I know. And those feelings never stay buried, they always slip back out. You can't hide from them. You have to face them head on."

"Yeah."

"Hey, listen, I've been there," I tell her, kissing the top of her head. "I have. And I know I'm not the one to spew advice. Because maybe I'm still dealing. I can't tell you the number of times I would try to console my mother after my sister's death and tell her, 'Hey it's okay, because I'm still here, and dad's still here.' It was stupid. Inconsiderate. Because she *knew* we were there. She was grateful for us, but that wasn't the point. She just wanted to feel what she was feeling because it was real, and it was honest, and Atarangi deserved that. And I didn't know how to deal with her grief. Or my own. The easy solution was to get her on pills, so she didn't have to feel the pain."

"Yeah, but it's your mom. You can't blame yourself for wanting that for her either. No one wants to see someone they love in pain."

"No. I don't blame myself. I would do anything to ease her suffering, and I guess I also hoped it would ease mine. If I told my mother we were okay, it meant we were, even if we weren't. But the result was, we never fully grieved. We sucked it up. Put on a brave face. Pretended we were strong and fine when we weren't. They kept her room the same because to take it down would mean they'd have to face some ugly feelings. Back then, I threw myself into boxing because beating shit up with my fists was the only way *I* could handle the feelings inside me. Different coping strategies, and I'm not sure they really worked. I mean, look at me. I'm not fine."

"And how does it make you feel, to admit that?"

"Good..." I close my eyes and let myself feel it. Really feel it. "I'm not fine."

"Louder."

"I'M NOT FINE!" I yell into the jungle.

"I AM ALSO NOT FINE!"

"I AM NOT OKAY! AT ALL!"

"I AM A HOT MESS! HEAR ME ROAR!"

I start laughing at our screaming match. "I'm pretty sure they heard us back at the barracks."

"Ugh," she says, exhaling heavily. "I don't want to go

back there. I feel like I made a fool of myself. And Lacey is just going to rub it in my face."

"She won't. Richard gave her a talking to."

She pulls back and squints up at me. "I don't believe that."

"Believe it. I may have stuck up for you as well, but I'd hope you'd think that's a given with me."

Her smile is amused. "I don't think anything is a given with you, Tai. You have been the grumpiest motherfucker up until recently."

"Maybe I just needed to get laid."

She rolls her eyes and winds up, punching me in the chest. "You're an ass."

"See, back to basics."

Tell her how you really feel.

She was brave with you, opening herself up for the first time, do the same with her.

Tell her you want her, not just for now, but for all of time after this.

I swallow the words down before I have a chance to say them.

Not yet.

A drop of water splashes on Daisy's forehead.

"Please tell me that wasn't bird poop." She winces. "I've had enough bad luck lately."

"It was water. And bird poop is good luck."

"For who, the bird?"

A drop now falls on my head.

I look up.

It's spitting with rain.

"I think the storm is here," I tell her.

"Already?"

As if on cue, the sky darkens, opens up, and dumps a deluge of rain on us.

"Ahhhh!" Daisy cries out.

We are soaked to the bone in seconds flat. The noise of the rain is deafening, every drop ricocheting off the leaves.

I grab her hand. "Come on. I'll take you back."

But she seems rooted in place. Not moving.

I give her a quizzical look.

"How are we going to get through this?" she asks, her voice quiet against the roar of the downpour, the rain running into her eyes, her mouth. "Not just this storm, but all the days ahead of us?"

"One sunrise at a time," I tell her. "One sunrise at a time, and with me by your side. Okay?"

I squeeze her hand.

She squeezes mine back.

"Okay."

THE STORM IS A FUCKING MONSTER, maybe even worse than the one that wrecked us.

It comes down on the Plumeria Atoll like it's out for revenge.

Perhaps it is.

Maybe it didn't like how lucky we got last time.

But it won't get us this time either.

When Daisy and I got back from the jungle, the storm was already blowing something fierce. The conditions on the island changed in a second, from hot and sunny, to windy and wet, the pressure in the air heavy, alive, and crackling.

Fred was already halfway across the lagoon with Lacey and Richard, though I knew they'd come back for us. So Daisy and I went around collecting what we could for the journey over. The storm would probably last a day, two at the most, depending on how big it is.

We worked quickly, silently. Daisy was no longer panicking, she was handling things really well, considering.

Then Fred came back. By then the lagoon's waves were whipped up and I knew it was going to be a bumpy ride. It didn't help when some of the water started splashing up into the boat, and then Fred mentioned the sharks.

Oh, you could see the sharks alright, dark shapes right beneath the surface, in a frenzy because of the currents and the weather.

I thought Daisy was going to freak out, but to my surprise, she was calm. She looked more curious about the sharks than anything. Perhaps she'd be a great marine biologist after all.

Finally, we made it to Fred's camp, and quickly got ourselves inside, where we are right now, in the mess hall.

Or at least, that's what Fred calls it.

It's really just a concrete building with a small, basic kitchen in the corner and a long metal table in the middle. For whatever reason there's a faded poster of The Avengers on one wall. All of us are sitting around the table in folding chairs, sipping coffee. Our wet clothes are piled in the corner to be dealt with later, and we're all in dry clothing, which is a small comfort, but still a comfort.

Outside, the rain and wind whistles and shakes, the concrete giving us extra protection from the elements. I only had a brief look at the camp before we hustled in here, but it seemed pretty standard with a small block for showers and toilets, five tiny freshly-painted raised bungalows, plus a research office. There's a small dock where the dinghy is tied up, and the view faces the outer reef, plus the calmer expanse of the east lagoon.

No one is talking.

Lacey is sitting there with her arms crossed in a huff, Richard has his glasses off and is rubbing the bridge of his nose, Daisy is taking dainty sips of her coffee and staring at everyone, and Fred looks especially forlorn.

"Should we start with the airing of grievances?" I ask.

Everyone turns to look at me, confused.

Well, Daisy smiles. She gets it.

"The airing of...grievances?" Richard asks, slipping his glasses back on. That poor fucker, he's been dealing with having half vision for the last week, plus his missing tooth. He probably needs a hug, a hug that Lacey ain't giving.

"It's from *Seinfeld*," I tell him. "During Festivus. Never mind. The point of it is, I think we have a lot of things we need to say to each other, and I think this is as good of a time as any to say it."

"Captive audience," Daisy comments.

"Something like that."

I look at Lacey, expecting her to have the most to say, but she just looks down at her nails.

"Richard?" I ask him.

He shrugs. "I don't really have any problems with any of you."

Pretty sure that's not true.

"Daisy?"

She shakes her head. "Everyone knows how I feel."

"Fred?"

"I'm worried about Wilson," he says with a sigh. "I had to leave him on the other island to get you guys. I should have gone back for him...just hope he stays put. Takes shelter."

I frown. "I'm sure he'll be fine, Fred."

He's a feral goat, I add silently.

"How about I go first," I say. "I care about each and every one of you. Yes, even you Fred."

"And Wilson?" he asks.

"Sure," I say slowly. "The most important thing, though, is that in order for us to get through this together, these next weeks or however long it takes, we have to learn to trust each other. And trust isn't just about trusting someone with your life, it's about being able to speak your mind, trusting that the other person isn't going to walk away from you. I think that's what we need right now. If we don't have trust, we don't have each other. Live together, die alone."

"Tai," Daisy warns me. "Stop ripping off quotes from TV shows to use in your speech."

I wave dismissively, sitting back in my chair. "Fine, fine. Just trying to help."

Richard clears his throat. "Okay. I do have something to say. This is the circle of trust, right Tai?"

I never used, and never would use, the phrase "circle of trust" but I nod anyway.

"Lacey, dear, my Lacey loo, Lacey lingerie," Richard says. She looks up at him and he gives her a wane smile. "Sometimes you can be a real bitch."

My jaw hits the floor.

With wide eyes I look at Daisy, who is gobsmacked, her eyes mirroring mine.

Lacey herself is stunned, gasping, blinking at him. "*What?*" she finally manages to say.

"Sorry, it had to be said. I love you sweetie, you know I do. But I let you get away with a lot of shit, and if I were a better husband, hell, a better friend, I would have let you know sooner that you need to be better."

Lacey is still blinking, trying to compose her thoughts. Her face is going pink. "I can't believe you just called me that," she says, her voice shrill. "Asshole!"

Richard nods. "Now, I know it's hard to hear from me because you're not used to it, and perhaps the term I used was a bit harsh."

You don't say.

"I'll accept the term asshole. But goddamn it, Lacey, you need to give us all a break," he says, rubbing between his eyes. "I've had nothing but headaches since I got here because my glasses are compromised, so excuse me if my language is unfiltered at the moment. Lacey, you're a good person with a big heart, but if you keep burying it with resentment, then that's all that's going to come out. I know we touched on this earlier, but Daisy wasn't here. Now Daisy is. I think you know what to do."

We're all watching Lacey. The storm is raging outside *and* inside.

"Richard," Lacey whispers, as if to say, *don't make me do this.*

Richard just gives her a placating smile. "I'm not making you do anything."

Lacey goes from pink to red. She looks away, down at her coffee mug.

We're all waiting.

Finally, she turns to Daisy, though still avoiding her eyes, and says, "Sorry."

It's not quite the apology Richard was hoping for.

"That's okay," Daisy says automatically. Bless her for being so forgiving, but I want to see Lacey work for it.

"No," Lacey says, after she's had a moment to think. She looks Daisy in the eyes. "It's not okay. I'm really sorry I haven't been the best sister. I'm just...I want to be a good sister, I just feel like I'm a burden to you."

"What?" Daisy exclaims. "A burden? Not at all. How could you think that?"

"Because I'm not as happy as you. Because I'm moody, and I take things seriously. I feel like a wet blanket, but I can't help the way I am."

"I'm glad you're that way," Daisy assures her. "You're the realist. It keeps me on my toes. It balances me. Ying and yang."

Lacey's eyes well up. "I was so jealous of you, you know. Because mom and dad let you do what you wanted, when all they did was put pressure on me to be the best. I just wanted your freedom, I wanted how easily you seemed to handle each situation."

Now Daisy's eyes are watering. "No, no, I was jealous of you. Mom and dad only cared about you and what you did, they didn't care about me at all. I felt neglected, you got all the attention."

"That's just not true," Lacey sobs. Now she's crying and Daisy is crying.

Then Lacey gets up and goes over to Daisy's chair and puts her arms around her, and they're both crying together.

Honestly, this was all I wanted. Atarangi and I didn't always get along and though the last thing I said to her before she died was "good luck," I wish I could go back to all those times we were fighting and erase them. You never really know how to appreciate your siblings until they're gone and it's too late.

Shit, man.

If I keep watching this sappy scene, soon I'll be crying.

But a strange sound catches my attention, somewhere beyond the roar of the wind and the incessant patter of rain.

Fred suddenly gets to his feet, looking ill.

He stumbles toward the door, opens it to the storm, and runs outside.

"What the hell?" I get up, my chair scraping loudly on the concrete floor, and run after him.

The storm is intense. I'm soaked again in seconds and rain pours down in my face, tasting of the ocean salt that's been whipped into the air. The palm fronds are waving violently, and the air is charcoal gray.

I turn and see Fred running down to the lagoon. He runs up onto the dock, almost slipping, then frantically tries to undo the knot to the dinghy as the dinghy keeps slamming into the wood.

What is he...?

Fred stops, cups his hand over his mouth and yells toward the lagoon, "Wilsooooooooooon!"

Wilson?

At first I think Fred is doing his best Tom Hanks impression, but then I see Wilson, the goat, in the lagoon. He's only a hundred yards away, but he's drowning, trying to move his legs, barely keeping his head above water.

He lets out a panicked bleat, a sound that breaks my heart.

"Oh my god!" Daisy cries out from beside me, Lacey and Richard running up behind her.

"I'm coming Wilson!" Fred cries out but the knot won't come undone. "I'm sorry I left you behind, I meant to come back for you!"

"Are those sharks?" Lacey squeaks.

I look back. Why yes, in the distance behind Wilson, is a shark or two. They don't look too big, but they'd quite happily, and easily, tear a goat apart.

Fuck.

I look back to Fred, whose face is red, crushed in panic as he tries helplessly to get the knot undone, crying out every time his fingers slip. I saw him tie it up extra tight earlier because of the storm. I can't tell if he's crying or it's the rain, all I know is that he's about to lose his best friend.

Not if I can do something about it.

I kick off my shoes and run right into the lagoon, splashing through the shallows, knowing very well that whatever fuss I'm kicking up in the sand is creating the perfect environment for a shark attack.

"What are you doing, Tai!" Daisy is screaming bloody murder from the shore. "Tai!"

I have to ignore her. I keep going, pushing through the water toward Wilson.

Wilson stares at me with his weird goat eyes, giving me a look that says he's giving up. He's too exhausted to keep trying.

His head starts to go under.

The sharks come closer.

I push off the bottom and start swimming now, using quick powerful strokes, not a single second to waste.

Then I'm diving under, briefly opening my eyes into the sandy, murky water.

I see Wilson.

I grab him under his front legs and haul him up to the surface.

He spits out water, making a sad little gurgling sound, but he's alive.

Thank god.

And those sharks are still there, still coming. I can see their shadows for a moment, before they either dive deeper or are obscured by the growing waves.

I can't think about that. About the fact that at any

moment, in this limited visibility, any of them could mistake my legs for a goat.

It's that feeling when you have a target on your back.

I'm prepared to feel their mouths closing over my calf, teeth slicing into me.

But I keep going, then suddenly it's easier for me to walk. With all my strength, I run the last few yards out of the lagoon, the goat in my arms, and then pretty much collapse to the ground, Wilson leaping out of my grasp and stumbling a few feet away.

"Wilson!" Fred yells, running over to the goat. He's bawling, wrapping his arms around the goat, crying with relief.

Daisy is doing the same to me.

"You asshole!" she hits me on the arm. "You stupid asshole, you could have been killed!"

Then she throws herself on me, crying, and holding me tight.

I pat her on the head as I catch my breath, stare up at Lacey and Richard.

"That was a brave thing you did there, captain," Richard says.

Lacey just nods, wiping her tears away, and looks over at Fred and Wilson.

"Let's never fight again," Fred is whispering to Wilson, who is bleating softly. "Never."

I close my eyes and sigh, wrapping an arm around Daisy.

My work here is done.

THE STORM TAKES two days to fully pass. The night that Wilson almost drowned was the worst. The wind even ripped the roof off one of the bungalows, and we found the dinghy in the east lagoon, despite Fred's crazy knot.

The next day the wind had calmed but the downpour was torrential. It turned the lagoons a muddy color, and wouldn't let up. On Fred's weather system, it looked like the storm just parked itself over the atoll and decided to let it all out. Give us all a bashing, just for the hell of it.

The third day, the sun came out and we emerged from our mess hall and bungalows, blinking at the light like newborns. The air was fresh, the sun was bright, and filled with birds. We survived again.

And yet with the storm, I knew that something else had changed.

Shifted.

I could feel it deep inside my bones.

I asked Daisy to come with me. We took the boat across the lagoon to the barracks, and then headed inland following the stream for a bit, then trekked across to our old campsite.

We arrive on the beach to a sight I expected.

Out there, on the reef...the Atarangi is gone.

I had suspected the second storm would do this, would dislodge her from the reef and take her back out to sea where she would sink, but it still pains me to see.

I fall to my knees in the sand, feeling like I've had the wind knocked out of me.

"Where did it go?" Daisy asks, putting her hand on my shoulder.

I try to swallow the lump in my throat. "The ocean took her away. Took her to a watery grave."

She squeezes my shoulder and then kneels in the sand beside me.

"Are you okay?" she asks softly.

I shake my head no, because I'm not. Because the boat is gone, like my sister is gone.

It's all so final.

Then I shake my head yes, because I never really got to say goodbye before, and this time I do.

I close my eyes and grab Daisy's hand.

"We had a tangihanga ceremony for Atarangi," I whisper to her. "Like a traditional memorial, a chance to mourn. But it wasn't enough. I never let myself mourn." I take in a deep, trembling breath. "I think I'm ready now."

She squeezes my hand. "Then let's have one now."

And so I start to pray.

19

DAISY

Daisy's Log: Day ?

HOW DO we get through this?
One sunrise at a time.

HUMANS CAN GET USED to anything. We're nothing if not adaptable. It's probably how we've survived on this planet for so long. With each wrench the world tries to throw at us, whether it be sabertooth tigers, or famine, or disease, or Facebook, we have found ways to adapt and learn and come out better for it.

We've adapted to our new (albeit temporary) life here.

It's been two weeks since we were told rescue would arrive.

In those two weeks a lot has happened.

And a lot hasn't.

I think the storm helped, dredging up all of our feelings to the surface and making us confront each other *and* our mortality once again. When we lived through that, then we were ready to come to terms with what was happening, and we were finally able to move on.

Together.

As a team.

Adapt or perish, as Richard said.

Okay, that was a little bit dramatic since things weren't that dire for us. We have a fresh water source, we have shelter, we have clothes, we have coffee. We have had enough food to go around, especially with Richard fishing with the line, and Tai taking up spearfishing. Meanwhile, Lacey goes off into the jungles of each little island, pillaging it for fruit and other items, like the leaves of the beach almond tree which she makes into a tonic of sorts. If anyone complains about a headache from being in the sun too long, she'll come right over to you and stick the leaf up your nose. Richard says it works, but no one else has let her test it out.

The best and worst of her botanist treasure chest is the kava root. The bush grows everywhere here, and when you grind up the roots and add hot water to make a drink, it turns into a mild narcotic. It tastes awful, like dirt and pepper, and it makes your tongue completely numb, but it gets you high. It's completely replaced alcohol for us, and many nights we sit around the campfire, telling stories and laughing until we can't feel our lips.

Live together, die alone. We're living together.

But, of course, we miss home. You can have all your basic needs met, but those aren't your only needs. We miss civilization. Being around people. Restaurants and bars.

Bookstores. Hot showers and hair appointments. We're all the scraggliest bunch of castaways you can imagine, considering we've been here three weeks in total, plus ten days on the boat, and I definitely need a haircut, fresh nails and a wax. I mean, I'm lucky my body hair is fair, but this shit is getting crazy. Not to mention I just finished having my period. That was not fun. All I'll say is thank god Tai isn't squeamish about blood, and also praise be to the Diva cup.

Most of all, we miss the certainty. Or at least the illusion of certainty. Many late-night kava talks have touched on how the future has always been a dangling carrot for most of us. We know what to plan around, what to look forward to, we think we know what's coming, but the truth is we don't. And when it becomes apparent that we never had control, that we never could truly count on the future, that's when people get scared. The unknowing fog of it all.

Right now, it's that fog that weighs over all of us, even if we make the best of it.

I think we're all just having to dig deep right now, lean on each other, and have a little faith.

Besides...things can always be worse.

Right now I'm on turtle watch, which is pretty much my version of heaven.

I'm on the little island where my suitcase washed up, you know, Naked Island, which also happens to be a place where the local population of the hawksbill sea turtles come to lay their eggs. I've been watching them do this at night, watching from a distance as to not disturb them, and trying to count how many eggs they lay. I won't be here for them to hatch (in two months), which is kind of sad, but I like to at least hang out here and make sure no predators try to dig the eggs up.

Either way, Fred assured me that my work is much

appreciated, since looking after the critically endangered species is one of the things that the Nature Conservancy is trying to do.

Satisfied that none of the nesting sites have been dug up, I head back around the island and proceed to swim across the shallow blue lagoon, back to the barracks. That's where I live now, with Tai. Lacey and Richard live in the research camp with Fred. It's funny, you'd think that I would have wanted to live there too, since the buildings are new and have proper mattresses and pillows (and a flush toilet!), but I'm getting used to living here, like a bit of a vagabond. We don't even sleep inside the building anymore, we just lay our sleeping bag out on the beach and sleep under the stars.

Plus, I'm here with Tai, and that makes everything better. This living situation is the best for all of us. We all need our space, or we'll get up in each other's faces, and on each other's nerves. This way, Richard and Lacey, and Fred, can geek out over their researcher stuff over there, and Tai and I can have peace over here.

And sex. Lots and lots of sex.

Tai is lying on his back on the beach, a book across his face, the spear he fastened out of wood at his side. He looks like one sexy-ass warrior man.

That is until I get close and notice the book covering his face.

"Secrets of a Mafia Princess?" I read the title.

Tai jolts awake, snatching the book off his face.

"I was using it to shield the sun," he says, squinting up at me.

"Then why are your sunglasses and hat beside you?"

"Uh," he says.

I flop down on the sand beside him and poke him in the side. "You read romance, you read romance," I tease.

"It's not a romance," he scowls, waving the book at me. "It's about crime."

"It's a dark mafia romance, Tai. In fact, it's the first in a series."

"A series? You mean, it continues?"

I nod.

"Do you have the other books here?"

I shake my head. "No. And it ends on a cliffhanger. Will she marry her betrothed childhood sweetheart, Alonso, or fall for the enemy who kidnapped her?"

"Enemy that kidnapped her, *obviously*," he says.

I grin happily at him. Sometimes when I look at him, I feel like all the world is sliding into the right place, puzzle pieces in my chest that are finally coming together. It's scary and it's exhilarating and consuming all at once. The weirdest part is, even though things can't possibly feel right, they do.

The truth is...I think I've fallen in love with him.

I think I love him.

Oh, you love him.

"What are you smiling at?" he asks.

"You," I tell him, poking him again. I know he's ticklish there, right down his sides.

"Stop that." He actually giggles. It's the cutest thing in the world.

Fuck, I really am in love with him, aren't I?

Since when did this happen?

When you started letting him in.

When you stopped being and started becoming.

"Hey, I got an email today," I tell him casually.

The other good thing about Fred's place is that he has wi-fi from the satellite. It works every other day it seems, everything has to load without HTML, you can't surf the web or do anything fun, but we've still been able to communicate in emails. I've been in touch with my parents ever since. Actually, I've never talked to them so much in my life. There's something about being in such an uneasy, foreign situation that makes you want to reach out to your loved ones. Makes you realize how much they matter to you. New perspective and all that.

"From your parents?"

I shake my head. "No. Actually, from a job I applied for just before I left for New Zealand. Feels like another life, I totally forgot about it."

He studies my face. "And?"

I shrug. "They want to do an interview."

"That's great," he says. He sounds happy for me. In a way, I wish he wasn't. Does that mean he wants me to go back to the States?

"Maybe. I mean, great to know that it's a possibility. But...I've had some time to think. I'm not going to go for the interview."

"Maybe not *now*, but when you get back..."

I shake my head again. "I don't..."

Want to go back?

Want to leave you?

"Don't what?" he asks.

"I don't want to go back," I tell him, giving him a quick smile. "I don't want those kinds of jobs anymore. I want something...I want to do something for my soul."

"You're not going to join a monastery, are you?"

I laugh. "No. Could you imagine? Though my parents would be very proud."

"What do you want to do? What does your soul tell you?"

"I think..." I say carefully, still mulling it over. "I think I want to go to school. I never went. I was going to, but then as you know, I got the job and that was it."

"School? Like uni?"

"College? Yeah."

"Where? What are you going to study?"

"Okay...don't laugh, but I think I want to do marine biology."

He frowns. "Why would I laugh? I think that's perfect. That's what you always wanted to do."

"I know, I know. It's just, I'm old."

"You're, what, twenty-eight? That's not old. You're never too old to go back to school."

"Look, now you're just thinking of *Billy Madison*."

"It's true. People do it all the time. A lot of people can't afford to go to university right away. They go when they can."

"Well, that's another thing. I have saved up money but school is so damn expensive. Plus, I only have my high school grades to go on. I sucked at math, barely passed, and that's so important for anything to do with science."

"Daisy," he says to me, sitting up. "You're smart. You're going to have no problems with this, I promise you."

"I *was* smart," I tell him. "I feel like I've dumbed down over the years."

"You're going to have to go for this, you know it. You'll kick yourself if you don't at least try."

I rub my lips together, suddenly too shy to say the next part.

"I was thinking...maybe I could go to school in New Zealand."

There. I said it.

It has been said.

Tai blinks at me. "New Zealand?"

Oh crap. Oh no. Oh, that was the wrong thing to say.

"I mean, I'm not saying I'll be near you. No pressure! I just thought...you know, somewhere. Maybe down south where Lacey and Richard are."

He frowns, shaking his head. Okay, I guess going to school to be near them is a bit of a stretch. "Well, that's fine. I can come to you."

"What?"

You can come to me?

"Daisy, are you serious about this?"

I nod, wanting him to go back to what he said before, that he could come to me. "I think so."

"You think so? Do you really want to move to New Zealand, to go to school?"

"Yes?"

He puts his hand at my cheek and searches my eyes deeply, looking for something inside me. I want him to see what I feel for him. "You'll stay with me?" he asks, brows furrowed.

"Stay with you?" I repeat, my heart starting to pound.

"Yes," he says.

"Are you asking or—"

"I'm asking, Daisy. I'm asking that if you move to New Zealand, that we can be together. And if you go to a school somewhere else, we can be together there, too."

My stomach flips. Butterflies have been unleashed.

"You'd want that?"

"Gingersnap," he says, pressing his forehead against mine. "I'll go wherever you go. All I know is that I'm going to be with you. I told you that. One sunrise at a time, with me by your side."

I thought those were pretty words. I didn't think he really meant it.

"What about your chartering company?"

"I'll make it work. You're never too far from the ocean when you live on an island." He kisses me softly on the lips. "You have no idea what I'd do for you."

My god.

I am melting inside.

Whatever glacier my heart used to be has fully dissolved and I am nothing but a puddle. A sappy puddle of love.

Ugh.

Is this the person I've become?

One madly in love? Yup.

"Well, you have no idea what I'd do for you," I tell him, kissing him back, my hand sliding down his rock-hard abs, toward his swim trunks. "And I mean, sexually. In case you didn't know."

"You're never not obvious," he says, lying on his back and watching me as I take his already hard cock out of his trunks and make a fist. I start running my hand up and down his soft, rigid shaft, watching him watch me, before his eyes roll back and his head flops down on the sand.

I can't remember the last time I've done a good old-fashioned handjob. It's a skill that's sorely overlooked.

"God, don't stop," Tai says through a groan. "Keep going."

My hand goes faster and faster and—

"Hey! Hey you guys!"

Oh my god.

I quickly let go of his cock, and look up to see the dinghy approaching us from across the lagoon.

Lacey is sitting at the front, waving her arms at us,

looking to be smiling or something. Richard and Fred are behind her, also looking joyous.

Tai sits up, quickly tucking his dick away with a frustrated groan. "What the hell is she so happy about?" he grumbles. "Cockblocker."

Lacey was supposed to come over here later, and we were going to have a spa day, where I'd light my candle and give her a pedicure (sand makes the best foot scrub), but I have a feeling that's not it. Unless the boys want pedicures too. There's no way I'm touching Fred's feet.

The boat is barely at the shore when Lacey is climbing over the bow, and jumping into the water, running through it toward us, grinning.

She looks insane.

"What's going on?" I ask her warily.

"We're getting rescued!" she yells, barreling right into me and pulling me into a hug. "We're getting rescued!"

I stare at Tai over my shoulder, confused, too afraid to believe her.

"Is this true?" Tai asks them.

"It's the truth, Captain," Richard says, grinning. He points to his missing tooth. "And not a moment too soon, I think I was getting used to this look."

"We're getting rescued!" Lacey continues to squeal, jumping up and down as she holds me. My brains are getting jostled, it's hard to know what's right.

I look to Fred for help.

He nods, standing in the water beside the boat. "We have two hours to pack and get ready. Plane is already on route from Nadi as we speak."

"This is happening so fast," I say. "What happened?"

Lacey stops bouncing. "I told you that it would happen."

"Well, actually I told you all it would happen," Fred says, adjusting his ball cap. "It's been two weeks."

"Yeah but...I thought that we'd get a bit of warning first..." Tai says.

"No warning. Everything's last minute. But it's great isn't it?"

"Are you coming back with us?" I ask Fred. I've grown to really like this man. And his goat.

He wiggles his mustache. "Nah. I'm staying. Can't leave Wilson behind. But they're bringing in a new researcher, so that's very exciting. His name is Owen. Supposed to be brilliant. As long as Owen doesn't smell weird, I'm good. I put in a request for better coffee too, so here's hoping." He makes a show of crossing his fingers.

We're getting rescued.

WE'RE GETTING RESCUED!

It hits me like a jackhammer.

This is actually happening.

We're actually leaving this place.

We're going home—wherever home may be.

"Oh my god," I whisper, the tears coming to my eyes as I'm overwhelmed with awe. "This is happening. We're being rescued."

"We're going to be okay," Lacey says to me tearfully.

She hugs me again, hard.

Then Richard hugs the both of us.

Then Tai hugs us three.

And finally, Fred wraps himself on the end.

"Group hug," Fred says. "You were the finest castaways I've ever known."

He sniffles.

Great, if Fred's crying, now I'm crying.

I'm pretty sure all of us could have stayed in that group hug for a while, sniffling tears of joy, had Richard not said, "How large is the aircraft, Fred? Do you think it's big enough for Daisy's luggage?"

Everyone breaks apart and starts laughing, even though Richard was earnest in his question.

"You've seen the size of the dirt runway," Fred points out. "Supply planes are large, but the passenger ones are itty bitty. Daisy, I'm afraid with so many passengers, your luggage might not make it."

Everyone looks at me, expecting me to freak out.

I only feel relief.

"Are you kidding me? I hope I never see those suitcases again. Not my clothes, not my souvenirs, not my bag. I'm starting fresh, buying just what I need. Only things I'm leaving this island with are you guys, my phone, and my wallet."

"I'm impressed," Tai says. "Took you getting stranded on a deserted island to stop overpacking."

"Hey, I'm a changed woman, what can I say?"

"Okay well, if that's the case, grab what you need to and I'll come back for you two," Fred says, pushing the dinghy back out. "Your sister wanted to make sure we could all tell you the good news together."

At that, Lacey and Richard get back in the boat with Fred, and off they go.

I turn to look at Tai, totally dumfounded, shaking my head. "I can't believe it."

He grins at me. "I can. It's happening. We're getting out of here." He grabs me, one hand going to the small of my back, the other going to the side of my face, holding me. "Daisy," he whispers, his lips just grazing mine.

My heart flip flops.

"Yes?"

He swallows hard, his lips moving, wanting to say something.

Please say something.

Say what else I want to hear.

"This is it," he finally says.

I give him a small smile, ignoring the pinch in my heart. "This is it."

"Come on, let's at least clean up if you're not taking your shit with you," he says.

He kisses me and then walks off to the barracks.

I sigh and pick up the book from the beach. This is definitely coming with me.

Two hours later, and we're all gathered at the dirt runway that runs behind Fred's camp, facing the outer reef.

Except for Fred, who stands stoically with Wilson by his side, we all have our luggage ready to go. In the end I decided my beat-up LV Speedy was still worth taking. Not because it's worth anything on the resale market anymore, but because it went through a lot and it still works. It's not as pretty as it once was, but it's become more useful. In some ways I feel like I have become the bag and the bag has become me.

In other words, it's about time I get off this island. If I'm talking this way about a bag, talking to goats is the next step. It's a slippery slope.

"There she is!" Fred yells, looking through binoculars.

It's hard to see anything in the blindingly blue sky, so I

wait until the binoculars are passed to me. I eagerly peer through them.

The plane is coming. A prop plane, which makes me just a little uneasy considering we have to cross a lot of water in that thing, but a plane nonetheless.

I can't believe this is happening.

We all look at each and burst out laughing.

It's real!

The plane starts to make its descent, getting closer and closer, and then its wheels are hitting the runway, kicking up red dust, and bouncing along past us, the pilot saluting us.

"Yaaaaaay!" I scream.

Tai whoops and hollers.

Lacey is jumping up and down, clapping.

Richard is doing some kind of dance?

It made it. It's here.

Tai puts his arm around me and squeezes me tight, kissing the top of my head.

"Time to fly, Gingersnap."

I look up at him. I can't stop smiling.

Eventually the plane turns around, and then taxis closer to us before the propeller is turned off.

The pilot's door opens and the pilot steps out, coming around the side of the plane.

"You must be the castaways," he says to us as he passes by, going to the passenger door. "I heard Fred has been taking very good care of you."

"Aw shucks, Maurice," Fred says. "They've been taking good care of me."

Maurice laughs and opens the back door.

We all wait eagerly, expecting Owen, the new researcher and Fred's new roommate.

To our surprise, Owen is a woman. A very stately, pretty woman in her 50s with long grey-blonde hair.

"Everyone, this is Dr. Owen Stapleton," the pilot says.

I steal a look at Fred.

He is absolutely smitten with her.

He suddenly stands up straighter, taking his hat off and smoothing back his hair, he's blinking hard. "Dr. Stapleton. I'm Fred. Dr. Fred Ferguson."

He holds out his hand, then takes it back and wipes it on his shorts, then holds it out again.

It's so cute and awkward it's painful.

"Nice to meet you, Fred," Owen says, shaking his hand firmly. She gives him a coy smile. "You can call me Owen. I've heard a lot about you."

"Oh is that so?" Fred says, wiggling his mustache impishly.

They're still shaking hands.

That is until Wilson goes right underneath them and lets out a deafening "BLLLLEEEARRGH!"

I swear Owen jumps a few feet.

She looks down at Wilson. "Oh hello. Who do we have here?"

"BLLLEAAAAAARRRGH!"

"That's Wilson," Fred says proudly.

Please don't translate what Wilson just said, please don't translate what Wilson just said.

Stay cool, Fred.

"Here," Fred says gently, resting his hand on her arm to guide her. "Why don't I show you around?"

We all watch as they walk off toward the dinghy.

"Uh, bye Fred!" Tai yells at him.

He just looks at us over his shoulder and motions for us to go on our way.

I roll my eyes. "Figures. The minute someone better comes along..."

"So, you folks look all packed and ready to go," the pilot says. "How about we throw your stuff in the back, get you all buckled in, and let's ditch this place."

We look back at Fred who is down by the water, laughing at something Owen said.

Wilson stands between us and the lagoon. He watches us as we start getting in the plane, gives us one last little bleat, then runs toward the researchers.

Bye, Wilson.

There are five seats on the plane, one beside the pilot, four in the back. Tai volunteers to sit in the front with the rest of us buckled in the back.

Then the pilot turns the prop on and the plane roars back to life.

Lacey reaches across and holds my hand, giving it a squeeze.

It's too loud to hear anyone talk, but I know what we're all feeling.

The plane gets to the end of the runway and then starts going, faster and faster and faster, going over bumps and rocks, shaking like hell, then the pilot pushes the throttle forward and we're lifting off.

We all crane our necks to look at the land as it drops away from us.

I manage to see Fred and Owen, standing by the lagoon and waving up at us.

I wave back.

Goodbye!

Then Wilson takes the opportunity to headbutt Owen from behind.

I laugh. They're going to be just fine.

We're all going to be just fine.

Higher and higher we go, until we can finally see what Plumeria looks like from above.

Well, I'll be.

Cock and balls.

Bye Dong Island, I think to myself.

Then I sit back in my seat and close my eyes.

"Oh. My. God," I say, leaning back in my chair and patting my stomach. "That was mind-blowingly good."

"Fucking right," Tai says, munching on his last onion ring, eyes closing in bliss.

The four of us are sitting around a table in a bar just off Main Street in Nadi, Fiji. The remains of our first real meal after getting off the island are scattered in front of us. When we poured in here, like thirsty desert wanderers finding an oasis, the first thing we did was talk the ear off the waitress (obviously we were all dying for someone else to talk to), then order everything on the menu.

Everything except fish. We're kind of over that.

I had chicken fingers with tons of different dips, fries, a big fresh salad, and two pina coladas. I'm on my third one right now.

Lacey had a giant cheeseburger with fries and a Mai Tai.

Richard is still finishing his personal pepperoni pizza, sipping comically from a blue drink in a gigantic fishbowl, garnished with paper umbrellas and pineapple and those little plastic monkeys.

Tai had a double bacon cheddar burger with onion rings. He's also drinking countless bottles of beer, going through them faster than the waitress can bring them.

We are stuffed.

Blissed out.

Drunk, with a borderline food coma.

"Room for dessert?" the waitress asks as she comes over. Her name is Layla and she knows our whole life story by now. "It's on the house. Castaway discount."

I shouldn't eat dessert. My stomach is already freaking out after I just stuffed it with fried food after over four weeks of living on fish and canned shit.

But still I say, "Yes please."

We all do.

"All right," she says. "I'll get the menu."

"You know what," Tai says. "Just bring us one of everything."

She raises her brow. That's probably not what she meant by the castaway discount, but she walks away to put in the order.

I grin happily at everyone and take another long sip of my drink, the sugar and alcohol going straight to my brain. It's hot here in Nadi, more humid than it was on Plumeria, but there's a fan overhead creating a warm breeze, and all the windows open to the street. Cars drive past, tourists do their shopping as they enjoy the day.

I can't believe we're out in the real world again. I feel like I've been waiting for this moment forever. It was worth the wait, even as exhaust fumes come into the restaurant, even though there's a baby screaming in the corner of the bar.

At least we're all in clean clothes.

The flight from the atoll to Nadi was less than two hours, but it felt like forever. The plane was so tiny, and there was some turbulence from time to time, enough that it felt like we were dropping and pins and needles kept swirling inside me. What a way to go, to survive being shipwrecked, then end up in a plane crash.

But the plane handled it just fine—if it was a passenger jet, we probably wouldn't have felt a thing—and eventually we were touching down at the airport.

The first thing we did, before we hit up the bar, was to check into a hotel. We could have opted for any of the resorts on the beaches nearby, but we decided to go for a modest one, right downtown in the middle of action. Even a hostel would feel like a luxury resort to us, and the last thing we want to see is a beach.

Then, after we checked in, we went shopping for new clothes in the hotel gift shop. I'm currently wearing a pink dress that says Nadi on it. Tai and Richard are wearing matching shirts as a joke, a horrendous tie-dye with dolphins on it, and Lacey has on a tank top that says "Live, Laugh, Love, Fiji," which makes me laugh every time I look at it, because she is the opposite of the people who usually buy that slogan.

Richard even managed to get a new pair of glasses. I don't think the prescription is strong enough, but at least both eyes are evenly matched. Tomorrow he has a dentist's appointment since it's cheaper here than in New Zealand to get dental work, and then the day after that we're flying back to New Zealand.

Or, at least they are.

I'm supposed to fly home to California. Because I missed my last flight, they gave me a credit for another one.

I just haven't booked it yet.

That's not where I want to go.

I look at Tai beside me, drinking his beer.

I want to go where he goes.

That's my home.

"So, Daisy," Lacey says. I look over at her. She's been studying me as she smashes the mint leaves into her glass with her metal straw. "What's next for you?"

"Lacey Loo," Richard chides her. "We just got rescued hours ago. No one has to make any plans, let alone Daisy."

I give Richard an appreciative smile and straighten up in my chair. "Actually, there's something I wanted to tell you guys."

"Oh?" Lacey says.

"Yeah," I lick my lips and glance at Tai. He's staring at me with approval. I clear my throat. "I, uh, have been thinking lately about life, as you do, and about the fight we had."

"Daisy," Lacey says softly, looking reprimanded.

"No, no, no," I tell her. "It's not like that. I mean, the things I admitted. That I wasn't happy? That I didn't know who I was? Well, it got me thinking, what *would* make me happy? It got me thinking about the kind of person I want to become. Someone to strive for. And I decided...I'm going back to school."

"School?" Lacey repeats.

I'm totally prepared for her to get a bit patronizing with this, but I refuse to get defensive.

"Yes, college. I want to study marine biology."

Silence.

Lacey looks at me, then looks at Richard.

"I know it seems silly," I say quickly. Then I correct myself. "Or, maybe it seems silly to you. But it doesn't seem silly to me. It really interests me, really excites me. I think I'd be good at it, and more importantly, I think

I'd be really passionate about it. It's what I used to dream of and after all that time on the island, I realize that dream never went away. It was just dormant for awhile."

"Wow," Richard says. He smiles. "That's big news, Daisy. That's great news."

"Yeah," Lacey says. "It is. I mean it. It's just surprising, in a good way."

I shrug and pop the cherry from the pina colada into my mouth. "I'm full of surprises."

"That you are," Tai says quietly. He's watching me pull the stem out of the cherry.

I grin at him and chomp the fruit in half. Pervert.

"It's not going to be easy," Lacey says after a moment. "But that's how you know it's worth doing."

"I think it's a great choice," Richard says. "The world can always use another scientist."

"Not sure my parents agree with that," I say with a laugh. "They're going to wonder what the hell happened to have both their daughters turn this way."

"They'll be proud," Tai assures me.

"*I'm* proud of you," Lacey says. She reaches across the table and gives my hand an affectionate pat. It's awkward, but I appreciate she's trying.

"I haven't done anything yet," I remind her.

"But you've set your intentions. I'm proud of you for *wanting* that," she clarifies. "For wanting more."

"As am I," Richard says, raising his fishbowl, the umbrella nearly poking his lens out. Wouldn't that have been ironic? "Here's to Daisy."

I blush and raise my pina colada. "Here's to us. We made it."

"We made it," Tai says, raising his beer.

We all clink our glasses together. I look Tai deep in the eye as we drink.

"Not going to lie," I tell them all. "I thought we were going to die. Just because we were all ready to kill each other on more than a few occasions."

"I slept with a knife under my pillow," Richard jokes.

The waitress comes by at that exact moment with our desserts, carefully eyeing Richard as she places the treats on the table. It's hard to tell when he's joking.

"I have banana cream pie, macadamia nut cheesecake, a passionfruit tart, grasshopper pie, homemade mango and lychee sorbet, plus vakalavalava, a cassava cake that's popular here. Enjoy." Layla gives Richard one last weird look and walks away.

"I'm not sure I can eat anymore," Lacey says, staring at it all with overwhelmed eyes.

"I don't think so either," I tell her, picking up a fork and spearing the cheesecake. "But I've never backed down from a challenge."

The moment it hits my mouth though, melting on my tongue, my stomach calls out for me to stop. There is such a thing as overdoing it.

"So, where do you think you're going to go to school?" Lacey says, pulling the sorbet toward her and poking it with her spoon.

I glance again at Tai, who is lost in a daze as he starts sampling all the dishes.

"Actually, I want to study in New Zealand. I haven't obviously been able to Google around yet, but I bet at least a few universities have the program. Then I'll see if I can get in."

Now Lacey is *really* surprised. The spoon pauses halfway to her mouth. "Really? Why New Zealand?"

"Because..." I trail off. Do I really have to say?

I look at Tai. He's smiling politely as if asking, "Yes, why?"

Guess I do.

"Because I want to be with Tai," I tell them, feeling myself flush. God, I'm such a dork. Why is admitting this out loud so hard for me?

"Huh," Lacey muses, sitting back, tapping her spoon against her lips. "I suppose that shouldn't surprise me at all."

"Definitely isn't a surprise to me," Richard says, gesturing to us with his drink. "Just look at the two of you. It's quite apparent you're in love with each other. Even the goat knew that."

The room feels like it comes to a screeching halt.

At least my heart feels that way.

Love?

Did Richard really just say that? I mean, I know how I feel but there's no way in hell that Tai feels the same way, and now that bomb just dropped and everything is so awkward and my face is burning and—

"Damn right I'm in love with her," Tai says, before having a sip of his beer.

Oh.

My god.

My mouth drops open.

Words fail to come out.

Heart feels like it's grown too large for my chest, about to consume me whole.

He...*what*?

I swallow, staring at him.

He gives me a sly little grin. "What? You didn't know that?"

My eyes bug out.

Is he kidding me right now?

I shake my head. "You...you love me?"

"Uh oh," Lacey says, elbowing Richard as she gets up. "Richard, let's step outside for some fresh air."

"Nah, stay," Tai says to them, motioning for her to sit. "I don't care if the whole world knows it." He turns in his seat to me, leans over, and cups my bewildered face in his warm, large hands. "Daisy Lewis, I am utterly, totally, madly in love with you."

Oh my god.

I'm still in shock.

This is beyond anything I could have imagined. I feel like I'm not even here right now, and my body seems to pop and fizz with the kind of joy I've never felt before.

"You love me?" I ask again, my voice cracking.

"I do," he says, leaning in to kiss me softly on the lips.

This man. This beautiful man.

He *loves* me.

Tears suddenly spring to my eyes and spill down my cheeks, making our kiss salty and sweet.

He pulls away, resting his forehead against mine, breathing hard, like all of this has his heart rate up. It sure has mine going.

"I'm sorry you first had to hear it in front of your sister and brother-in-law," he says wryly. "I was planning on telling you tonight. Something a little more romantic."

"Sorry," Richard mutters.

"Don't be," I whisper to him, staring at Tai, feeling absolutely giddy. "It doesn't matter how I hear it, so as long as it's true."

"It's true, Gingersnap," he says. "I knew you'd get under my skin the moment I saw you."

"Did I ever," I comment.

Lacey clears her throat loudly.

I pull back from Tai just enough to give her a look. "What?"

She jerks her chin at Tai. Raises her brows. "Shouldn't you...you know?"

"Don't pressure her," Tai tells her. "I didn't say it to hear it in return. I said it—

"Because I said it," Richard says, sucking on his drink. He swallows. "But when I said it, I meant the both of you. You'd have to be a complete imbecile to not see that she loves you too."

I laugh, putting my hand at the back of Tai's neck. "He's right, you know. You can be a complete imbecile."

"Is that all he's right about?" Tai asks, so sweet, so hopeful.

I burst into the biggest smile. "No. He's right in that I love you. I love you and you're an idiot for thinking otherwise."

Tai's face cracks open, more fucking beautiful than ever. The joy reaches his eyes.

"You mean that?" he asks.

"I really do," I tell him. The words seem to flow out of me now. "I love you Tai Wakefield."

He shakes his head subtly, as if in awe, his dark eyes searching mine. Looking for the truth.

Then he finds it.

And it's real.

He kisses me again. A kiss that pulls me under, a kiss that lifts me up.

Eventually, I become fully aware that we're making out in the bar *and* making everyone uncomfortable, so it's no surprise that Lacey and Richard tell us they'll see us later.

After everyone settles up with the bill, Tai grabs my hand and takes me straight back to the hotel.

We barely make it inside the hotel room before we're attacking each other like crazed animals, hands and mouths everywhere. I just really want that ugly tie-dye shirt off him, so I'm yanking it impatiently over his head and tossing it to the floor.

"That's more like it," I tell him, running my hands over his chest, down his abs, savoring his taut, warm skin, my pale hands against his bronze skin. "How about we take this in the shower?"

His eyes light up.

A shower.

A fucking proper shower.

We're a tangle of lips and tongue as we make our way to the bathroom, Tai pulling my dress and bikini over my head. His hands slide down to my underwear, but I went commando after I arrived in Fiji, kicking my last pair of undies to the curb.

"You're full of surprises," he says, reaching around and taking a firm hold of my ass with both his hands, bunching them up as he leans down to kiss me.

God, I love kissing this man.

If this continues, I won't even make it into the shower.

Spurred by that thought, I open the shower door and turn the water on. Watching it pour from the rain head attachment makes me all sorts of giddy. I put my hand through the stream, testing it.

"It's hot!" I cry out happily. "Hot water!"

"Not the only thing raising my temperature," Tai says, stepping in the shower with me, completely naked. As usual, his erection could poke a girl's eye out.

I grin at him and pump a few squirts of coconut-scented

body wash out of the bottle, before lathering up my hands and sliding them down the thick length of his cock.

"You don't waste any time," he moans, closing his eyes.

"But I'm going to take my time with you." I grin.

I start pumping my fist up and down his cock, until his breath gets sharper, then I start bringing the soapy suds all over his body, cleaning him from head to toe.

"This is torture," he says through a stilted groan, his head back, the water running down the strong planes of his handsome face. "When is it my turn?"

I take his hand and squirt more body wash in his palm. "Now," I tell him, standing under the stream.

It. Feels. So. Good.

He looks at me, his gaze burning with raw desire, then crouches down low. He puts his hands at my ankles and then slowly brings his palms up along my calves, the back of my knees, the inside of my thighs. His touch is light, slick, slippery.

I'm shuddering, anticipating his fingers.

When they find me, already wet, they stroke soft and slow.

I never knew how much I needed this.

With one hand continuing to slide over my sensitive parts, the other slides up over my belly, up to my breasts. He palms me, feeling the weight in his hand, then hooks his thumb around my nipple.

I gasp, squeezing around his fingers as they gently push inside.

He continues to work me with both hands, my nipple a hard pebble against his thumb, ecstasy spreading outward until it feels like my spine is a lighted Roman candle.

"Fuck," I cry out, my eyes pinching shut.

He covers my open mouth with his, his tongue slipping

inside, teasing mine, pulling me into a deep, searing kiss.

In seconds, I am seeing stars.

"Fuck, Tai," I manage to say. "Oh, god."

He grunts in return, working me until I am weightless, my legs shaking, my body quaking with unfiltered bliss. I feel like I'm made of stars and sunsets and sunrises and everything bright in the universe.

"Feel better?" he whispers against my mouth, smiling.

I stare at him in a daze, my eyes heavy. "Yes," I croak.

"Good. Time for your hair," he says, putting his hands on my shoulders and turning me around. He squirts shampoo into his hand and starts lathering up my hair, his strong fingers digging deep.

Have you ever come, *hard*, and then had your head massaged?

Dear lord, I'm in freaking heaven here.

Then, while the conditioner sits, I do the same to him.

Like a sexual spa day.

Finally, when we're all clean and dry, we make our way over to the bed.

It's king-sized with soft covers, and the moment Tai pushes me back onto the bed, I know how easy it would be to fall asleep here.

But the sight of him naked as he climbs on the bed, his big body prowling over me, pushes the idea of sleep to the back of my mind.

I am in love with this man.

And he is in love with me.

Every cell in my body feels so damn alive.

He plants his elbows on either side of me, holding my face in his hands. My legs spread for him, his heavy cock resting on my stomach.

"I love you," he tells me, voice hoarse. He's looking so

deep into my eyes that I feel him inside me, like he knows every inch of my soul. "And I'm sorry I told you the way I did."

"Please, Tai. Don't be." I give him a reassuring smile. "It was the greatest thing I ever heard; nothing can ruin that for me."

"I wanted…" he trails off, licks his lips. "I wanted to tell you earlier, but I was so afraid you wouldn't feel the same way. I wanted to be sure. I thought I could just keep it inside until I knew how you felt. And then I realized, in a way it didn't matter how you felt, because I knew how I did. And the fact that I'm in love with you…it means I'm not a broken man. It means I'm living life again. I'm ready for a life with you."

Oh no. More emotional tears are threatening my eyes.

I swallow, wrapped up in his sincerity.

He goes on, running his thumb over my lips. "You know that Soundgarden song, *Rusty Cage*?"

I nod. Not sure where this is going.

"That's what I've been living with all these years. For far too long. I've had this rusty cage in my chest, and I got so used to it, I never even bothered to see if it could open. But you opened it, Daisy. You not only opened it, you ripped the cage right out of my chest." He swallows thickly. "I feel like a free man now. I owe it all to you. Wonderful, beautiful, unforgettable you."

I sniff, reaching up and wiping away a tear. "You have to stop making me cry, Tai."

He places a kiss at my neck, running his hand down to his cock and positioning it between my legs.

"Only if I can keep making you come."

I don't even have to answer that.

He pushes inside me, to the hilt, the breath expelled

from my lungs, and then he's rocking into me, slowly, carefully, a lazy kind of rhythm.

I dig my nails into his back, holding him as close to me as possible, not wanting to have any distance between us. He returns in kind by pistoning his hips against mine, his cock driving inside me in short thrusts, keeping us as connected as possible.

The orgasm takes us both by surprise. He cries out softly, his brow furrowed in concentration, then release, pumping inside me. I am weightless once again, calling out his name, holding him tight.

His pumping slows. Sweat drips off his forehead and onto me.

He rolls over onto the bed and then takes me by the shoulders, pulling me on to him.

I lay my head on his chest as it rises and falls, both of us catching our breath, our hands entwined.

For a moment I think I've fallen asleep and when I open my eyes, I'm shocked to see where I am. Not on the island. In a hotel room, in Fiji, safe in his arms.

"Daisy," he whispers.

"I'm here."

"It sounds completely selfish, but I wish you didn't have to go home," he says to me. "I hate not knowing when I'll see you again."

My heart squeezes with his words. "Don't worry. I won't be gone for long. I haven't even booked the flight. I just need to go and cancel my lease and pack up my things." I pause. "I don't want to do it either."

"I was thinking," he whispers to me, his fingers playing with my hair. "Maybe I'd come back with you to San Francisco."

I blink. Raise my head and rest my chin on his chest, staring at him. "Are you serious?"

"When am I not?"

"When you're making fun of me?" I joke.

He frowns. "Oh, I take making fun of you *very* seriously."

I pinch his nipple and he yelps. "I mean it."

"I mean it too," he says, wincing.

"Who's going to run your business?"

"My manager can handle it. He's been running it all this time I've been gone, and it's the end of the season now anyway."

I'm having a hard time believing this. "You would actually do that?"

He nods. "Won't even go home, Gingersnap. I've started to realize what home feels like is wherever you are." He smiles at me, his eyes crinkling. "Tomorrow I'll call the airlines, change my flight."

"Ohhh, maybe we can get a Skycouch!" I say excitedly. Put that other couple to shame.

"Whatever you want," he says. "As long as we're together."

I lay my head down on his chest, listening to his heart beat steadily, grinning against his skin.

The future still seems a little hazy, but at least I know to not be afraid of it. To rise up to the challenges ahead, no matter how difficult, to let myself smile through the good, and cry through the bad.

I just know I won't be alone in it.

We'll face the future together, whatever it holds for us, one sunrise at a time.

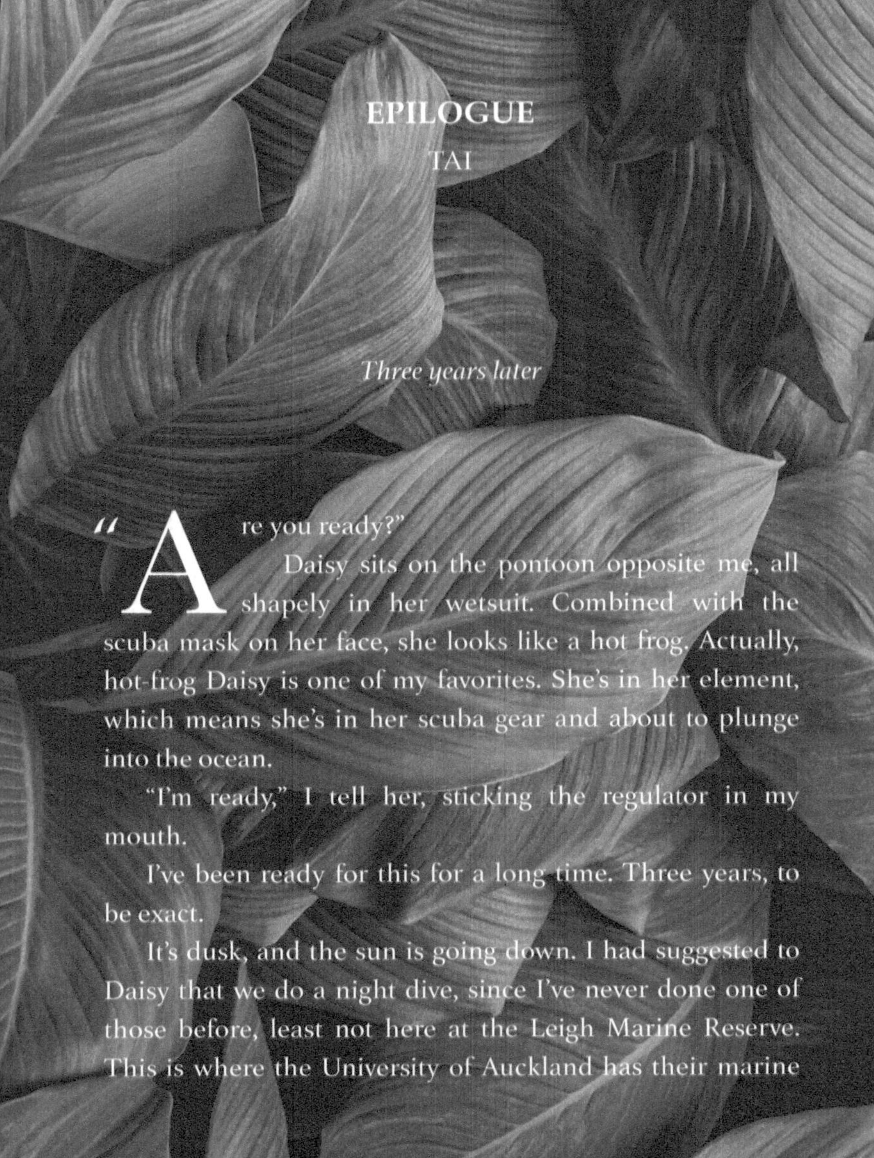

EPILOGUE
TAI

Three years later

"Are you ready?"

Daisy sits on the pontoon opposite me, all shapely in her wetsuit. Combined with the scuba mask on her face, she looks like a hot frog. Actually, hot-frog Daisy is one of my favorites. She's in her element, which means she's in her scuba gear and about to plunge into the ocean.

"I'm ready," I tell her, sticking the regulator in my mouth.

I've been ready for this for a long time. Three years, to be exact.

It's dusk, and the sun is going down. I had suggested to Daisy that we do a night dive, since I've never done one of those before, least not here at the Leigh Marine Reserve. This is where the University of Auckland has their marine campus, overlooking Goat Island (a place that Wilson would enjoy). Daisy is in her second year of marine sciences at the university and is absolutely thriving in the program.

It's a Friday night. Usually the two of us are curled up on the couch at the beach house we're renting on Bream Bay, our dogs snoozing at our feet. It's about half-way between Russell and Leigh, where the campus is. Since the program she got into was north of Auckland, we figured the easiest thing to do was to rent a place together between the yacht charter and her school, so that I could still work and she could attend her studies.

When she graduates, then we'll move into my place back in Russell. Or perhaps we'll go elsewhere. We've got a big enough nest egg now to have a lot of options. Even though I had to sell a few boats to pay for Daisy's tuition, the boat business is booming. After our shipwreck made the news, Deep Blue Yacht Charters became a household name. I had assumed that the event would have soured people on sailing, but I guess any publicity is good publicity.

Daisy says it's because I've been on TV a lot, talking about it, something to do with my movie star good looks, blah blah blah. Regardless, there's even some sailing reality show that our local Channel 2 wants to do with us. Daisy is completely comfortable with the spotlight, but I'm not. We'll have to see.

Either way, we've decided to let our future be as fluid as possible, planning the bare minimum and going with the flow. Any bumps or setbacks in our way, and we know we'll get around them together.

I guess you could say it's one of the good things that came out of the whole shipwrecked ordeal. Actually, after all was said and done, only good things did come out of it.

Yes, losing my ship hurt. I'm not going to lie. I loved that boat, spent a lot of years taking care of it. But she didn't go down without a fight, and in the end she protected us when it mattered. I can take pride in having had that ship, and I have hundreds of memories to draw upon.

A lot of those memories were some of the last I would have with her.

A lot of them involved Daisy.

I remember her trying to make eggs during a particularly rough morning, the waves slamming into the boat just as she was flipping them, and they landed right on her head.

Then there was the way she gasped when she first saw the night sky.

How she'd talk, talk, talk during those long night shifts, waiting for the dawn, and how I pretended to hate it. But I didn't.

The way she'd try and do her yoga when she thought I wasn't looking.

But I was looking. I was always looking at her. It was impossible not to.

In the end however, even with Atarangi gone, it made Daisy and I grow closer.

It caused my heart to open up and find space in there for her, just as she found the space for me.

It brought us together like nothing else could, and for that I am forever grateful.

It made Daisy and her sister grow closer, too. They still fight, of course, but there's now trust between them when they fight.

As for the newlyweds, I'm sure the shipwreck prepared that couple like years of pre-emptive counseling. They're solid as a rock now, and I have to say, both of them have lightened up considerably since then. They like to trek all over the South Island and camp, and Richard recently bought a motorbike. I've not actually seen him on it yet, but if he passed the test, then I guess he's okay to ride.

They're also going to be parents soon. Lacey is six months pregnant with a boy. They're absolutely over the moon with joy, and Daisy and I have already been appointed godparents. The both of us aren't too keen on the idea of kids ourselves, especially now that we have a couple of rescue dogs, and a cat, but we both plan on spoiling the baby immensely. Anyway, the kid is going to want a tough uncle to look up to. At least that's what Daisy says. She says Dick Boner Junior shouldn't have to follow the footsteps of his father.

The shipwreck also brought all our families closer together. When I got back to New Zealand, after spending three weeks with Daisy in San Francisco, I made a point of spending more time with my parents. Not that I didn't before, I was always visiting since I lived so close. But I wanted to get to know them on an even deeper level. I also just wanted to relish the time I have with them, knowing how easy it is to have all that taken away.

Meanwhile, both Daisy and Lacey have formed a closer relationship with their parents. They've spent a Christmas out in Oregon, and her parents have also managed to come to New Zealand again. The girls don't believe it sometimes, but their parents are very proud of them.

I know it's cliché, that good things come out of the bad, that what doesn't kill us makes us stronger, that the light at the end of the tunnel can be brighter than the light before. But they are cliché for a reason, because they're true. If you can't find rhyme or reason in this crazy, unpredictable world, at least you can find solace in that.

Daisy looks behind her at the setting sun, then turns around, and gives me the thumbs up.

I raise my hand and tug at the writing slate attached at my BCD, or buoyancy compensator.

She does the same.

Then falls back into the water.

I copy her, flipping backward, fins over my head.

I hit the water with a splash and then right myself.

I see Daisy on the other side of the six-foot Zodiac and swim through the bubbles over to her.

She gives me a thumbs up again.

I do the same.

Then I follow her lead.

It would be easy to say that Daisy turns into a mermaid underwater, with her voluptuous body, and that flowing red hair, but I'd say she's more like a shark. She's quick, confident, and knows exactly where she wants to go. She's done countless dives at this spot, just off Goat Island, because so many of her classes are here, and she knows the underwater landscape like the back of her hand.

The water here is clear, and in the dying light, a gemstone green.

I watch as she goes and spies on an octopus moving along the sand, she points excitedly at the rays swooping over the reef.

It's beautiful, it's magical.

It's time.

While she's following the rays, entranced by them, I unclip my writing slate and start writing on it with the attached pencil.

Will You Marry Me?

Yes, it's simple, and maybe a bit corny.

But this feels right for us, here, under the waves.

It's been a few years that I've wanted to do this, but I wanted to get all our ducks in order first. Wanted to make sure that this was what the both of us wanted.

I can't imagine my life without Daisy. She makes everything that much better.

I hold out the slate, waiting for her to turn around and see me.

Finally, she does.

She's too far away to read it properly, so she swims closer.

Stops.

Bubbles erupt from her mouthpiece and her eyes go wide.

I point at the slate for emphasis, just in case she doesn't understand it.

She stares for a few moments more, then hastily unclips her slate and writes something with what seems to be a lot of exclamation marks.

Turns it around.

Yes!!!!!!

I grin, the mouthpiece falling out.

She removes hers and does an underwater cheer.

Swims over, wraps her arms around me, then kisses me on the lips.

Mine.

She's mine.

And we should probably go to the surface.

I still have to give her the ring.

We kick up and burst up through the water. The sky is now dark, the moon and stars are out, and the water is starting to sparkle with bioluminescence.

"Are you serious?" she asks me, grabbing my arm.

"Of course I am," I tell her, bringing her closer to me and kissing her again. "Will you marry me, Gingersnap?"

I reach into a pouch and bring out a ring. It's attached to a chain, so I don't lose it.

She gasps as she sees it. "Tai. This is *gorgeous*."

"It's the koru," I tell her, the spiral in the middle of the rose gold ring, with the sparkling diamond in the center. "The curl of a new fern. Symbol of new beginnings."

"And it's rose gold."

"Like that damn luggage you loved so much."

She snorts. "Yes."

"Is that a yes about the luggage, or that you'll marry me?"

"Yes," she cries. "Yes, yes, yes I'll marry you!"

"So agreeable," I muse.

She laughs. "I guess so. Fuck. My god. I can't believe I'm going to get married!"

"I'll be there, too."

She giggles. "I'm serious. I just...I'm so happy. So happy." She looks around her. "Though as beautiful as this all is, I don't think I feel like being underwater anymore. I can't concentrate."

"I didn't think so," I tell her. "Come on, let's go back to shore."

Once on the boat, we go straight back to the campus dock and we quickly get changed out of our wetsuits and gear. Then I take Daisy by the hand and lead her down the beach and around the corner.

There, just as I'd hoped, is a picnic laid out on the sand, a blanket covered in different appetizers and lots of wine, all framed by flickering candles.

"You did this?" Daisy yelps, hand to her chest.

"Well, your classmates helped me," I tell her, eyeing the people running away in the shadows.

"Congratulations Daisy!" one of them yells, while the rest hoot and holler.

"Oh my god, Tai," she says, smiling with tears in her eyes. "I never knew you were so romantic."

"Well, I have to keep you on your toes, don't I?"

Then I drop to my knees and propose all over again, relishing the feel as I slip that ring on her finger.

I take a moment to admire it on her dainty hand, then I yank her down to my level, so she's sitting on the blanket.

"Now, we feast," I tell her.

I picked out quite the spread, and diving usually makes Daisy ravenous anyways. But this time, she barely eats. She's too busy planning the wedding already.

"We'll have to invite Fred and Owen," Daisy says. Then she frowns. "Though I don't think New Zealand would let Wilson in."

I laugh. As it happened, Fred and Owen, the research scientists of Plumeria Atoll, fell in love. They lived on the atoll for a good year before Fred decided to make an honest woman out of Owen, then they packed up and moved to Fiji. They now live on the beach.

With Wilson.

We have yet to visit, but it's definitely part of our plans. Or at least, it's one of the options for the future. Maybe we'll sail there.

"Don't even think about it," Daisy says to me, recognizing the twinkle in my eye. I've suggested a few times that we should get on the boat (we now have a fifty-foot catamaran) and go on another ocean passage, but heading up to Fiji again would be pushing it.

"You don't think it would be a fun honeymoon?"

"Tai," she warns. "Don't make me tickle you."
Of course she does.
We fall back into the sand, laughing.
We stay up until sunrise.

THE END

WHAT TO READ AFTER LOVEWRECKED

If you're wanting to check out any of my other contemporary romances, I have too many to list, but here are some of my favorites:

Like best friends to lovers?
    - BAD AT LOVE (a quirky friends-to-lovers romance)
    - THE PACT (two best friends agree to marry each other by the time they're thirty)

Nordic Royals series (all standalone!)
    - THE SWEDISH PRINCE

(The Prince of Sweden falls for an American girl - spin on Roman Holiday)

- THE WILD HEIR

(The bad boy Prince of Norway has to marry a good girl princess in a marriage of convenience)

- A NORDIC KING

(The widowed King of Denmark falls for his much younger nanny)

And if you like age gaps and forbidden romance, try:

- BEFORE I EVER MET YOU (young single mom falls for her father's best friend)

- HEAT WAVE (a woman falls in love with her dead sister's ex in this sensual forbidden romance)

ACKNOWLEDGMENTS

What a time to be alive, huh? Well, I don't know about you, but I've had a hell of a time coping with what's going on in the world right now (and if you're reading this from the future, I hope this fear and worry is just a distant memory).

I honestly didn't know if I could write. I had another book I was supposed to finish (The One That Got Away) but it was too complicated for my world-weary brain, too angsty for my grief-stricken heart. I'm an empath and a method writer, and I just couldn't feel for the world and write that book at the same time. My concentration levels were shot, and it just wasn't working.

So I put it aside and decided to write something easier, happier. Something that would take my mind off this pandemic. Something that would give me the warm fuzzy feelings I needed, while feeling totally relatable at the same time.

Tai and Daisy's story was born. I was in New Zealand (again – I went to university there, I have family there, and if any of you want a more in-depth romance set there, I recommend Where Sea Meets Sky!!).

I digress, I was in New Zealand again. I was on that boat (I pretty much grew up on a sailboat, so that's my happy place). I was on Plumeria Atoll (AKA Dong Island, AKA The Island of Dr. Boner). I was wrapped up in a whole other world, where things were different but familiar (hello toilet paper shortage & dreaming about going to restaurants). It was a soft and sexy escape (although as my editor pointed out, only I would put a harrowing shipwreck scene in a rom com haha).

All this to say, it wasn't easy to write this book. It's still hard during a pandemic to concentrate when there is so much going on. But it did get done, and I cherish my time spent on Lovewrecked. It proved that I could still do my job, and have a good time doing so, while hopefully providing an escape for others.

Of course, I am not okay right now and I'm pretty sure many people are in the same boat. I just want to say that it's okay to feel your feelings. It's okay to be scared, frustrated, angry, sad right now. It just means you're human. And if you feel like pulling a page from Daisy's log, go outside right now and scream "I AM NOT OKAY!" It feels good to admit it (though you may scare your neighbors...or maybe they'll join you).

This acknowledgements is really just a thank you to you all. You're doing amazing. At a time like this, it's worth remembering that, and I really, truly hope Lovewrecked brought a smile to your face, for at least a few hours.

And remember, we all need to take this one sunrise at a time.

ABOUT THE AUTHOR

Karina Halle is a screenwriter, a former music & travel journalist, and the New York Times, Wall Street Journal, and USA Today bestselling author of River of Shadows, The Royals Next Door, and Black Sunshine, as well as 80 other wild and romantic reads, ranging from light & sexy rom coms to horror/paranormal romance and dark fantasy. Needless to say, whatever genre you're into, she has probably written a romance for it.

When she's not traveling, she and her husband split their time between a possibly haunted, 120-year-old house in Victoria, BC, their sailboat the Norfinn, and their condo in Los Angeles. For more information, visit www. authorkarinahalle.com

Find her on Facebook, Instagram, Pinterest, BookBub, Amazon, and Tik Tok.

ALSO BY KARINA HALLE

And With Madness Comes the Light (EIT #6.5)

Come Alive (EIT #7)

Ashes to Ashes (EIT #8)

Dust to Dust (EIT #9)

Ghosted (EIT #9.5)

Came Back Haunted (EIT #10)

The Devil's Metal (The Devil's Duology #1)

The Devil's Reprise (The Devil's Duology #2)

Veiled (Ada Palomino #1)

Song For the Dead (Ada Palomino #2)

Love, in English/Love, in Spanish

Where Sea Meets Sky

Racing the Sun

The Pact

The Offer

The Play

Winter Wishes

The Lie

The Debt

Smut

Heat Wave

Before I Ever Met You

After All

Rocked Up

Wild Card

Maverick

Hot Shot

Bad at Love

The Swedish Prince

The Wild Heir

A Nordic King

The Royal Rogue

Nothing Personal

My Life in Shambles

The Royal Rogue

The Forbidden Man

The One That Got Away

Lovewrecked

One Hot Italian Summer

All the Love in the World (Anthology)

The Royals Next Door

The Royals Upstairs

Sins and Needles (The Artists Trilogy #1)

On Every Street (An Artists Trilogy Novella #0.5)

Shooting Scars (The Artists Trilogy #2)

Bold Tricks (The Artists Trilogy #3)

Dirty Angels (Dirty Angels #1)

Dirty Deeds (Dirty Angels #2)

Dirty Promises (Dirty Angels #3)

Black Hearts (Sins Duet #1)